Refuge

AFTER THE COLLAPSE

Refuge

AFTER THE COLLAPSE

Scott B. Williams

Book Two of *The Pulse* Series

Ulysses
Press

Published in the United States by
ULYSSES PRESS
P.O. Box 3440
Berkeley, CA 94703
www.ulyssespress.com

ISBN 978-1-61243-295-3
Library of Congress Control Number 2013957314

Printed in Canada by Marquis Book Printing

10 9 8 7 6 5 4 3 2 1

Acquisitions Editor: Keith Riegert
Project Editor: Alice Riegert
Managing Editor: Claire Chun
Editor: Sunah Cherwin
Proofreader: Renee Rutledge
Production: Lindsay Tamura
Cover design: Keith Riegert
Cover photos: city © Bruce Rolff/shutterstock.com; ocean
    © chrstphr/shutterstock.com; building fire © fotostokers/
    shutterstock.com

For Nancy, in appreciation for all that you do.

ONE

Larry Drager woke to large drops of rain splattering across his face and neck, interrupting a pleasant dream in which he was still a freelance delivery skipper sailing other people's yachts between the islands in the trade winds of the Caribbean. But though he woke in familiar surroundings in his comfortable berth in the thirty-six-foot catamaran he'd built by hand on a beach in Puerto Rico, there was no gentle swell rocking the hulls beneath him and no sea breeze to stir the humid air. Larry rolled to one side and reached up to close the hatch over his bunk. In this windless swamp, miles from the coast, leaving it open did little anyway, other than invite inside more of the mosquitos that had been a constant nuisance since sundown the evening before.

He wiped the rainwater away from his face and beard with a towel and slid out of his bunk to stand in the narrow cabin of the starboard hull. The rain was now drumming steadily on the decks above his head, so he opened the old Nalgene water bottle marked with warning X's that he kept near his bunk and used it to relieve himself, closing the lid tightly when he was done and putting it back out of sight to be emptied later when he went on deck. The launching of the boat had been so rushed that installing a proper marine head was among the first items deleted from the to-do list. At sea a simple bucket sufficed and made more sense for this kind of craft anyway.

It was only a couple of steps from the foot of his bunk to the galley area under the main hatch, and Larry yawned and stretched as he put the ball of his foot on the manual sink pump and worked the pedal up and down a few strokes to fill the kettle for his morning coffee. While he was waiting for it to boil, he pulled on his shorts and looked out through the acrylic port lights on both sides. The rain was slow, but steady, and clearly the gray of dawn would not give way to sunshine anytime soon. He lifted the companionway hatch just enough to vent the steam from the boiling water and spooned coffee grounds into a French press on the narrow counter space.

Until the rain hit his face, Larry had slept well enough despite the mosquitos, especially after sipping a couple of shots of rum before going to bed. He always slept better on any boat than he did ashore, and even here, uneasy as he was anchored so far inland, there was no place he'd rather be than on board his vessel. But he couldn't help being nervous at the thought of having to thread his way through miles of twists and turns to follow the river back downstream to the Gulf of Mexico. Larry was a blue water sailor, and the *Casey Nicole* was a sea boat, not some houseboat built to float on pontoons in muddy water. While this deep oxbow lake, surrounded by hardwood forests and out of the current of the river channel, might be an ideal refuge in a hurricane, Larry had little use for such places in any other circumstance. In the cloaking gray of steady rain, the riverside trees closed in even more. Larry felt trapped, and he knew that that feeling was not simply an illusion. It was dangerous as hell to be here. Even if his mast were not down and his sails stowed in the lockers below, they would be useless in such confined waters. But a locked-down drawbridge blocked his exit back to the Gulf. With his rig up, or even with it down, getting back to open water was subject to any number of unknown obstacles, especially considering how fast the situation was deteriorating.

This was only the second night the catamaran had been anchored here, and he'd been alone since the morning before, when both members of his crew had taken off upriver after mounting the vessel's only auxiliary engine to the transom of an old aluminum Johnboat they'd found half-sunk and abandoned in the swamp. Without that outboard, the *Casey Nicole* was virtually stranded. Larry consoled himself with the idea that in the worst-case scenario he could probably pole the big cat downstream to open water. But even with a draft of only two feet it would be a frustrating ordeal of running aground and winching off submerged sandbars and snags concealed by muddy water, and would take days at best. And attempting that would be difficult enough, even with full use of both hands and arms. Larry knew he was lucky to still have them both at all. A machine blow that was meant for his head had slashed clear to the bone of his right forearm, and though it would eventually heal, there still wasn't much he could do with what had once been his stronger hand. The pain had gotten better but his frustration had increased. Larry Drager wasn't used to limitations and he wasn't used to depending on others; but dependent he was, and there was little he could do but wait for his crew to come back.

He had high hopes that his brother, Artie, and his best friend, Scully, would be successful in their quest, which was the whole reason for his being here in the first place. If they were not, nothing else mattered much anyway. He knew his brother would not leave until he found his daughter, and Larry wasn't going anywhere without all of them.

Artie had taken a week off from his busy career as a doctor to visit Larry on the islands for a short vacation, something he rarely did. It was his misfortune that during that short time a series of solar flares unprecedented in modern history had sent an electromagnetic pulse to Earth that apparently destroyed the electrical and communications grid. Artie found himself cut off from any means of talking to his daughter or getting back to New Orleans by air, as inoperable electronic and computer circuitry effectively grounded any flights to the mainland or elsewhere. So on this very boat, that Larry and his friend Scully had been building by hand on a beach in Culebra, they'd sailed 1,500 miles to New Orleans unaided by GPS, lighted navigation markers, or communications of any kind.

But they'd arrived too late. Larry's niece had already fled the chaos that had gripped the blacked-out city, and though that meant she and her friends were likely still alive, not finding her in New Orleans had put a considerable kink in their plans to pick her up and quickly sail away again.

But at least they knew where she was going, or intending to go, anyway. The note Casey had left in her father's car in the parking lot at the airport had led them here. Somewhere upstream, where the water was too shallow for the big catamaran, was a secluded cabin. If she and her two friends had made it there, then Artie and Scully had a good chance of finding them. But there was no way of knowing how long it would take. The cabin was on a smaller tributary off the main river. They couldn't tell from the map if it was navigable all the way by motorboat or not. Even if it were, there would probably be shoals and fallen trees and other obstacles to slow them down. But Larry was confident that if anyone could do it, Scully would find a way, and Artie would die trying before giving up on finding Casey.

As he sipped his coffee, Larry unfolded the big chart that encompassed the entire Caribbean basin and Gulf of Mexico and retraced the route they'd sailed to get here. In the happy event of Artie and Scully returning with Casey and her friends, returning to his home waters in the vicinity of Puerto Rico and the Virgin Islands was out of the question. Even if the voyage back were not a bash against the prevailing winds, those well-populated islands could not offer a secure refuge or the resources they needed. Wherever there were sizable populations of people, those who were still alive would be desperate and becoming more so every day. It had been weeks since the solar flares. Without transportation to move supplies and communications to find out where, if anywhere, things were still normal, those stranded by the collapse of the grid were running out of options. A seaworthy boat powered by the wind and big enough for several people to live aboard gave Larry and those he loved a better chance than most, but there was still the question of where to go once they were free of the clutches of this river and back on the high seas. They needed an island refuge, ideally one that was totally uninhabited, but with a safe, all-weather anchorage and sources of fresh water as well as food from both the sea and the land.

Looking at the chart, Larry again found himself wishing they were somewhere on the west side of the North and Central American landmass instead of the east. If they were anywhere in the Pacific, they would have far more options, from the reef-bound atolls of the South Seas that few boats of normal draft could access, to the wilderness islands of the Inside Passage in coastal British Columbia and Alaska. But the Pacific was not an option. Transiting the Panama Canal after the collapse was out of the question, and the catamaran was not the kind of vessel suited to sail around Cape Horn. They would have to find some place on the Atlantic side, and Larry knew of some possibilities far to the west of the touristy islands where he normally worked. He measured a route along the seedier shores of the Caribbean from the Mosquito Coast region of Honduras and Nicaragua south to the cocaine-smuggling hideouts of Panama and Columbia. Larry knew there were some good opportunities to stay out of sight in those places, at least for the short term, which in this situation was the most important consideration. He just hoped he wouldn't have to wait here much longer. Larry was meant to be in motion, and the waiting was driving him crazy.

He finished his last cup of coffee and put the chart away. The rain had slowed to a drizzle so he pushed the companionway hatch the rest of the way open and climbed the steps to the spacious cockpit deck that spanned the gap between the two hulls. He stretched and scanned his gray and green surroundings, looking for any sign the sun might break through, but that didn't seem likely to happen soon. The hammering of a woodpecker echoed from somewhere in the expanse of hardwoods surrounding the river, and from where he stood he watched two squirrels chasing each other from tree to tree, their leaps sending cascades of falling rainwater from the leafy branches. Fish were striking the water with loud splashes, and Larry reached for his binoculars to scan the muddy banks for alligators; anything to pass the time. Seeing none, he returned to the galley below to put on water for oatmeal. After he had eaten, he passed the morning alternating between studying charts, reading, piddling around the boat, and making lists of small projects that could be completed once they were underway again.

Bored with the waiting, Larry had crawled back into his bunk for an early afternoon nap when a faint, unexpected sound reached his ears from somewhere downriver. He strained to hear it better. After he listened for another couple of minutes, there was no mistaking it. He rushed to the deck to hear it better. The sound was the steady throb of a slow-turning diesel engine—the kind of engine used to push a displacement-hulled boat. He had to wait several more minutes to determine if the sound was getting closer, as the many loops and bends downstream would put any approaching boat on a parallel course as often as not. But the more he listened the more he was sure that a boat was indeed coming up the river. There was really nowhere else it could be going anyway, unless it turned back and went the other way before reaching the entrance to the dead lake.

The engine sound was steady as it turned at a constant rpm. If the boat it was pushing kept moving, Larry knew he would soon have company. Whoever it was could not possibly miss the big primer-gray catamaran anchored in plain sight just out of the channel of the river. There was no way to hide it, even if he hauled in the anchor and moved further from the river into the oxbow. The dead lake was simply not big enough to provide an anchorage out of sight of someone coming up the river by boat.

Larry was thinking fast. Maybe whoever it was would not present a threat, but he couldn't make that assumption. With that kind of engine it was not a typical recreational fishing boat; maybe some kind of older commercial fishing boat, a small shrimper or oyster boat. They had to have a reason to bring a boat like that this far upriver. Boats like that were usually built of wood or steel and equipped with diesel engines so ancient and simple the pulse would have had no effect on their ability to run. Were they simply coming upriver seeking a safe hideaway, or maybe going to a hunting camp or cabin somewhere farther upstream? Maybe that was it, but Larry found himself wishing he still had his Mossberg 12-gauge pump on board. Naturally, he'd insisted that Scully and Artie take it; with the journey that lay ahead of them it seemed they were more likely to need a shotgun than he. As a result, Larry was left with nothing for defense but a flare gun and a couple of machetes.

He glanced at the sea kayak still lashed across the forward decks and briefly considered the idea of launching it, paddling just far enough among the cypress knees and flooded trunks to stay hidden. It was an option, but not really a very good one, even if he hadn't an injury that would make any paddling painful and difficult. If he left the catamaran apparently unattended, even honest survivors coming by might be tempted to board it and look for supplies they could use, and they might even be tempted to take the whole boat if they assumed it abandoned. Larry decided he couldn't take that chance. It would be better to be seen on board. Maybe the strangers would wave and keep going, or simply stop for a short visit. The sound of the diesel was getting closer anyway, so there was no more time to consider other options.

He stepped below to the nav station in the port hull and loaded the plastic 12-gauge flare pistol. It wasn't designed to be a weapon, but at point-blank range a burning flare could be a powerful deterrent. He slipped it into the baggy side pocket of his cargo shorts and then placed one of the machetes close at hand but out of sight under a cockpit seat cushion. As he did so, Larry touched the stitches Artie had sewn to close the wound in his forearm and really hoped he would *never* get into another machete fight.

Holding the binoculars with both hands, Larry stood on the main deck and focused his attention downriver, searching anxiously for whatever was coming around the bend. He didn't have long to wait. Standing out in stark contrast to the green backdrop of forest and the muddy brown of the water, a blue-and-white painted wooden trawler, around thirty-five feet in length, finally made the last turn and steamed into view running the river mid-channel.

Whoever was at the helm must have spotted the big catamaran immediately, as the engine speed was suddenly reduced to near idle and the boat quickly slowed to a drifting speed while the crew tried to assess what they were seeing. Larry stood unwavering as he watched through his Steiners. The vessel was indeed a coastal fisherman of some sort. It didn't carry the tall outriggers of a shrimper, but there were trawling nets and other gear, and the rub rails were festooned with old automobile tires serving as fenders. As he watched, two men stepped out of the pilothouse, one aiming binoculars of his own back at Larry, and the other carrying a scoped hunting rifle at the ready position with both hands, angled barrel-up across his chest. At the same time, whoever was steering allowed the boat to fall off to port and into a big circle, keeping its distance as the man with binoculars sized him up. Larry waved but neither of the men waved back. As the boat turned away from him he saw someone else come up on deck from the main cabin. This one was armed as well, carrying what looked like a shotgun similar to his own Mossberg, which he was missing so desperately now. This man and the one carrying the rifle moved forward as the boat came back around full circle, and when they were in position on the foredeck to cover any offensive action from the anchored catamaran, the helmsmen revved the engine back to half-throttle and steered directly toward him.

Larry lowered the binoculars and waited, standing his ground on deck to project confidence, but also being careful to make no moves or gestures that would appear threatening. He still had one hand on the flare pistol in his pocket, but in the face of their weapons he knew it would be dumb to brandish it, much less attempt to scare them off with it. It was hard to tell if these men were merely being cautious or if they were up to no good. But one thing was for certain; he was about to find out. All he could do was wait and see.

Though about the same length as the *Casey Nicole,* the old wooden fishing boat was a heavy displacement vessel that probably outweighed the ultra-light catamaran by several tons. As it drew nearer, Larry nervously moved to the side nearest the approaching boat to fend it off, as it was clear now that the fishing captain planned to bring his vessel alongside. He had shifted to neutral and idled down again, but the boat still carried its way and was approaching too fast for comfort.

"Hey! Back it down! You'll smash my hull in!" Larry shouted with his hands outstretched in a "STOP" gesture to the captain, whose face he could now see behind the pilothouse windshield.

The man at the helm ignored him, allowing the bigger boat to continue its glide directly toward the catamaran as Larry scrambled to place a fender into position to cushion the blow. He knew the fisherman didn't care about his own topside paint. The tire fenders were for docking alongside concrete wharves and the scarred and battered hull planking of the heavy boat was stout enough that they were not really needed anyway.

At the last minute the captain put his helm hard over so that his hull came alongside the catamaran rather than ramming it bow first, but even so the impact was enough to knock Larry off his feet. The *Casey Nicole* was pushed several yards, until her strained anchor line brought both boats to a stop. Larry heard the sound of splintering wood and fiberglass. He was furious as he scrambled to get back up and see what had broken. Before he had a chance to even look, the two men on the foredeck of the fishing boat had boarded the *Casey Nicole*.

"What the hell do you think you're doing?" Larry screamed.

The one carrying the shotgun stepped closer. Larry found himself staring into the black abyss of a cavernous barrel pointed right at his face from three feet away. Before he could say another word, the man suddenly diverted his aim skyward and pulled the trigger, unleashing a thunderous blast that temporarily shattered both Larry's nerves and his ears. He couldn't hear what the gunman shouted next over the ringing in his ears, but the meaning was clear as he brought the muzzle of his weapon back in line with his face. Larry dropped to the deck as fast as he could, still focused on the shotgun. As a result, he was completely caught off guard by the other man's kick, which landed on the side of his head and sent him sprawling.

TWO

Casey Drager woke with a scream. It took her a few seconds to realize that she had been having a nightmare, and that Derek, the deranged hunter who had taken her to his hideaway deep in the swamp, was not on top of her, holding her down and demanding to know why she'd betrayed him. Casey took several deep breaths as her dad put his arms around her. Then the others she had awakened joined him in telling her that everything was all right, and she was safe now. Slowly, she remembered where she was and what had happened. She remembered what she had done to Derek, and that he could *never* bother her again outside of her nightmares.

Casey trembled as she hugged her dad, looking past his shoulder at the dark, rain-sprinkled waters of the Pearl River flowing past the sandbar where they'd all been reunited the day before. After all she had been through since leaving New Orleans, it was almost incomprehensible that her father, Artie Drager, a doctor at the V.A. Hospital in Mobile, Alabama, had managed to find her in such a remote place. Scully, the wild-haired Rastafarian she had met only once, almost a year before, while visiting her uncle in the Virgin Islands, was here as well. And as if that weren't enough, her best friend and college roommate, Jessica, and Grant, her older grad student friend who had urged them both to get out of New Orleans with him, were both here too. A little over a day ago, Casey had doubted she would ever see any of these people she loved again.

But it was true and they were really here. She and Grant and Jessica had listened in fascination as her dad and Scully told them of their voyage all the way to New Orleans from the Caribbean with her Uncle Larry. She remembered the catamaran project that had been under construction on the beach during the summer vacation she and Jessica spent with him. It had looked a long way from even floating at the time, but he *had* completed and launched it and it had carried the three of them all the way to the lower reaches of this very river.

"I'm sorry, Dad. I didn't mean to wake everyone up. I just thought…"

"It's okay, Casey. You just had a bad dream. You're safe now though. I'm never letting you out of my sight again until things are back to normal, and probably not even then!"

Casey didn't answer. She just hugged her dad tighter, making sure she wasn't dreaming this too. The night before she had told them all most of what had happened since that day Derek had grabbed her and tied her up, stashing her in his canoe like so much baggage and taking her away to a place deep in the swamp from which he thought she could never escape. She had not mentioned the gory details of what she'd done to Derek to ensure he would not follow her, but she knew that Jessica and Grant knew. They had found the secret camp after she'd escaped, and she knew they could not have missed the body lying face down by the fire pit, the skull split open by a bloody axe she'd tossed to the ground when the deed was done and her captor was no longer a threat.

Casey wished that part had simply been a bad dream, that it had never happened; but she knew it had, and she knew that at the time she hadn't had much choice. If she hadn't acted then, she wouldn't be here now with the ones she loved. She regretted that she'd worried them all with her scream in the dark, but now that everyone was awake, they were up for the day. Scully pointed to the lightening sky to the east and said that it would be daylight soon. Raining or not, they were all anxious to get moving now that everything had changed once again with their reunion on the riverbank. The conclusion of her father's quest and the end of their ordeal on the river was an incredible relief, but the future was still very much uncertain and the greater repercussions of the event that had set all this in motion were still unknown and unknowable.

"I still think we should all stick together," she heard Jessica say as Grant once more brought up the subject of trying to reach his parents' cabin, far upstream on a tributary of the main river. This had been the subject of intense debate the evening before as they sat around a small campfire and discussed what lay in store. The cabin was the reason she and Jessica had left New Orleans with Grant in the first place. After the power went out and it became obvious that food and other necessities would soon be impossible to obtain in the city, Grant had talked the two of them into leaving with him on bicycles. It had seemed like a preposterously difficult thing to do at the time: pedaling some ninety miles to cross the Causeway over Lake Pontchartrain, and then the state line into rural Mississippi. Now Casey realized that in comparison to what they'd actually been through, that ride was nothing, and would have been easy if only they had been able to complete it as planned.

"But it will only be a couple of days; three at the absolute most," Grant said, trying to reassure Jessica that the separation would be brief. "It will make a tremendous difference to our future. We just don't know how long this situation is going to last."

"It *can't* last forever," Jessica said. "We've got *some* food, and like Casey's dad says, there's more on Larry's boat. I just think it's too risky to stay in these woods any longer. I want us to all get on that boat and get as far away from here as possible."

"I do too; *believe me!* There's nothing I'd rather do, but the fact remains, we've got to eat, and there's going to be six of us on board for who knows how long. I'm just saying that we're facing a lot of uncertainty. The canned goods and other stuff in that cabin could make a big difference a couple weeks or a month from now."

Casey wasn't sure which course they should follow. On the one hand, she could see the advantage of getting their hands on any supplies that might be available. Her ordeal with Derek, living mainly off of game he killed in his hunting forays near the hidden camp, had certainly made an impression. While hunting was natural for someone as experienced and well equipped for it as he was, she couldn't imagine living that way over the long term. Using game, fish, and wild edible plants as a supplement was one thing, but she knew that Grant was right; they needed more canned and dried provisions that would keep while they traveled.

Jessica's worries were valid too. If Grant took the John-boat with the outboard upriver in an attempt to reach his parents' cabin, *anything* could happen. Their recent experiences had already proved that. A boat with a working motor would make him a target for desperate people seeing him go by. She knew there were a lot of stranded people that would love to get their hands on such a conveyance. *Any* form of mechanized transport was priceless now. Armed or not, Grant could be ambushed before he knew what had happened. In their discussions the previous evening, it had been decided that if he went, Scully should go with him. One of them could operate the boat while the other literally rode "shotgun" in the bow to keep a lookout for danger. Scully was the logical choice, because there was no way her dad was going to let her or Jessica out of his sight for a minute, and besides, even more than Grant, Scully was at home in the bush. While they were gone, she and Jessica could continue downstream in one of the canoes with her dad to the place where her Uncle Larry was waiting with the catamaran. Grant and Scully would tow the other canoe behind the Johnboat to serve as an extra cargo barge for the food, tools, and other equipment in the cabin.

She knew her dad was torn on the idea of splitting up as well, but he finally joined in favor of Grant and Scully making the attempt, while Jessica remained adamantly opposed to it. Casey wondered how much of Jessica's reluctance had to do with the inevitable attachment she must have developed to Grant after all those days alone with him. She wondered how Grant felt about that as well, and if the two of them had bonded to the point that her own long-term crush on the older grad student was now hopeless. But whether that was the case or not, Casey couldn't begin to process romantic feelings right now anyway. What she'd been through was simply too much, and just being alive was enough for her for now. Being reunited with both her friends and her father just made her appreciation for life that much sweeter, despite the image that kept replaying in her mind of the brutal way she'd taken another life to save hers, like a video on an endless loop. She knew she was going to have to be strong, though, and put her feelings of remorse aside. Life, as well as death, was different now, in the aftermath of the pulse. Reality had changed for everyone, not just for her. All that any of them could do was simply try to survive until things got better.

"I think that if Grant and Scully are willing to take the risk, we need to let them try, Jessica," her dad said. "By the estimates Larry plotted on the map before Scully and I set out, we calculated we had more than enough fuel for the outboard, especially since the return trip is downstream. If they get there by tonight or sometime tomorrow, they can load up everything they find of use and easily be back at the catamaran to rendezvous with the rest of us the day after. One or two extra days is not going to make that much difference in the long run."

"It's not the extra day I'm worried about," Jessica cried, upset at being outvoted. "Anything could happen to them up there. We don't even know if there's anything left in that cabin. Other people have probably found it by now and taken all the stuff."

"Maybe," Grant said, taking her in his arms as her tears ran onto his shoulder, "but maybe not. It's pretty far off the beaten path by road. We won't know for sure if we don't go there. You've got to understand that this is a risk worth taking, Jessica. The supplies in that cabin could mean the difference between life or death in the long run."

"Not'ing gonna happen, girl," Scully chimed in. "I an' I going wid he an' dat Mossberg ready wid I. Travel in de bush is my specialty an' we going quickly an' come bok safe. Not to worry 'bout a t'ing. Soon we all sailin' back to de island, find some place in de sun where everyt'ing gonna be hoppy again."

"Scully's right, Jessica. With the two of us to watch each other's back, we'll be fine, and we'll be armed."

"We've got plenty of weapons to choose from, thanks to that Derek's obsession with guns and Casey's presence of mind to bring them all with her, so you guys need to take one of his rifles, too, in case you need something with more range than a shotgun."

"I'll take that short lever-action then, if you don't mind, Artie." Grant said. "I've shot those before and it'll be handy to use in the boat if we need it."

Hearing this, Casey was glad the Winchester was going to be out of her sight for a while. It had been Derek's favorite and he was always walking around with it slung over his shoulder every waking minute that she'd been with him. She hoped they wouldn't need it or the shotgun, but she was glad they were going to be well armed. Casey didn't know Scully well, but from what little time she'd spent with him during that vacation on the islands and from what her Uncle Larry had told her about him, she felt good about Grant having him along. She was going to worry about them both until they were all together again, maybe tomorrow; there was no way around that, but at least they were as prepared as possible under the circumstances. Casey turned to Jessica and put her arm around her shoulder to reassure her:

"They're going to be fine, Jessica. You know Grant can take care of himself, and Scully's one tough customer, from what Uncle Larry says. Chances are, they won't see a soul on the whole trip anyway. After seeing what you've seen of the river, you know how remote it is out here."

"I just don't want anything to happen to him, Casey. You know, if it hadn't been for Grant, we would still be in New Orleans. We'd probably even be dead by now."

"I know, Jessica, I know. It's going to work out, though. We've come this far, and soon we'll all be heading out on the boat to someplace better. Look at it this way: if they get that food from the cabin, you won't have to eat fish and other dead things."

"I don't care about that anymore. I already know I can't be a vegetarian right now. I'd rather eat a live rabbit than see something happen to Grant."

"I know, I feel the same way, but even if we want to, it's going to be hard to catch enough animals and fish to live on; like Grant said, there are six of us now. Scully and Larry will know how to get most of the food we need from the sea when we get to someplace safe, but it may be a long voyage to get there. I don't like the risk either, but this really is our best chance, I think. Come on; let's just help them get ready. The sooner they leave, the sooner they can get there and then get back to us."

Grant and Scully were both anxious to be underway as quickly as possible. The five of them shared a hurried breakfast of coffee and rice made from the supplies taken from

Derek's camp, and then goodbye hugs were exchanged all around before they shoved the flat-bottomed aluminum boat and the canoe that had been Derek's into the river. Scully made the towline fast and started the engine. Casey fought back tears as she watched the two of them motor away in the rain, and, holding hands with Jessica and her dad, stood watching until the boat disappeared around the first wide bend upriver.

"We might as well get going, too," her dad said. "I'm not sure how long it will take in the canoe, but I'm guessing it'll be sometime after noon before we get down to where your Uncle Larry is waiting."

"It'll be great to see him again," Casey said. "I didn't expect to see him again for years, at least." Her recent vacation to the islands had been the first time she'd seen her free-spirited uncle since she was in high school. Uncle Larry seldom came back to the mainland, and even on the islands, his job as a yacht delivery skipper made him a moving target, and always hard to find.

"You're going to be amazed when you see that boat, Casey. I'm still amazed and I'd been living on it for weeks when I left to find you. I just can't believe he built it by hand. What I really can't wait for you to see though, is what he named it."

Casey wondered what could be so special about the name of her uncle's boat. Her dad had mentioned it like it was a big deal at least twice now, and her curiosity was piqued. Regardless of the name, she was looking forward to being aboard any boat bigger and more comfortable than a canoe. After this experience, she didn't care if she *ever* saw another canoe again. A big boat with indoor bunks and a real galley would be an incredible luxury. As they set out downstream, she paddled hard from the bow of the canoe, anxious to make rapid progress and get there as soon as possible. With her dad paddling and steering from the stern and Jessica adding to their efforts from amid-ships, they were moving at nearly maximum hull speed for the slender craft.

After leaving the sandbar where they'd been reunited, they were once again traveling through swampy, low for-estlands where the river flowed practically at the bases of the trees on either margin of the channel. There was no sign of human activity for miles as they paddled through the dismal gray morning, the rain finally giving way to mist and overcast skies. After taking a twenty-minute break on a muddy bank studded with cypress knees, they paddled on until mid-afternoon found them in an area that her dad recognized as being close to their destination.

"It can't be much farther," he said. "I remember passing the entrance to that lake, because it looks a lot like the one that Larry picked to anchor the boat in," he said, pointing to the mouth of an oxbow that extended far into the for-est to the west of the river channel. "I remember thinking that if we'd only known about it, we could have brought the catamaran that much farther upriver, but I think Larry was nervous enough as it was. He was feeling more and more closed in the further we got from the Gulf."

"He's a sailor through and through, Dad. It would take something like this to ever get him inland, even for a minute."

"Yeah, the sea's in his blood, all right. I don't know where he got that gene and why I didn't, but he certainly knows what he's doing out there. I just can't tell you how incredibly lucky we are to have him and his boat in this situation. After what I've seen, I know he's right when he says that a boat is the only really safe place to be."

"That's exactly why I didn't want Grant going the other way!" Jessica said, still unhappy about the decision made earlier that morning.

"He's going to be fine, Jessica. You've got to stop worrying so much. You'll see. They'll be back with us tomorrow with a boatload of stuff. It'll be worth it."

"She's right, Jessica. Scully will look out for both of them. I'd feel safe going anywhere with him. You'll see…." Artie's reply was cut short by a sudden, echoing sound that seemed to come from the direction they were heading. It was faint and far away, yet close enough that there could be no mistaking what it was.

"That was a gunshot, wasn't it?" Jessica asked,

"Yeah, I think so," Casey said.

"There's no doubt about that," her dad agreed.

"We must be pretty close to the boat by now, aren't we? I hope it doesn't have anything to do with Larry. Could it just be him shooting something, Dad? Maybe he got bored and went hunting."

"No. He doesn't have a gun on the boat. That Mossberg shotgun Scully took this morning was his vessel defense weapon. He's had it on board since we left Culebra, and that was the only firearm any of us had. That shot must have been from someone else."

"Then we'd better paddle faster!" Casey said, "Uncle Larry may be in trouble."

"Hold on now, Casey. Sounds like that can be deceptive in the woods, and carry farther than you'd think. It's hard to know if it was even anywhere near Larry and the boat. We *do* need to hurry as much as possible, but let's also proceed with caution and try not to make too much noise. We don't want to run into any surprises, but we need to be ready if we do. Here, you need to take this."

Casey turned around on her seat to see her dad put down his paddle and reach into the duffle bag in the bottom of the canoe to retrieve the pistol that Grant had returned to him yesterday. He had left it in his parked car at the New Orleans airport, and Grant had found it when he'd gone there to leave Casey's note explaining their plans to leave the city and go to the remote cabin. It was only a .22 Long Rifle automatic, but Casey had learned to shoot with it years before and knew she could use it with accuracy and control. He passed it to her by way of Jessica so she would have it ready at hand if something happened, but she was glad to also see her dad taking out the Saiga AK-47 she had taken from Derek's camp. Her dead abductor's other hunting rifles were also in the bag, but if they needed to shoot from a moving canoe, it would be better to have the firepower of the AK's 30-round magazine to make up for the inevitable misses.

"Okay, we can go on now, but try not to make any splashes with the paddles. If somebody's around, we don't want to let them know we're coming and give them time to set up an ambush."

"This is *exactly* the reason I didn't want Grant and Scully to take that boat upriver," Jessica said. "We should have all stuck together."

"It's going to be okay, Jessica. It was only one shot. It was probably just someone else out here hunting. Everybody in a place like this has got to get food somehow. Whoever it is, they are probably no threat to us. We just need to be cautious, that's all."

Casey hoped he was right. The last thing she wanted was another confrontation out in these woods. All she really wanted was peace and safety; two simple things that she'd taken for granted all her life but that seemed like nearly unattainable dreams today. To wish for more was beyond comprehension now.

THREE

Grant glanced over his shoulder from the bow of the John-boat as Scully steered it into the first bend upriver from where Jessica, Casey, and Artie stood watching them go. He didn't like the idea of splitting up the group any more than Jessica did, but he had to let reason get the better of emotion. There was nothing easy about this life in the aftermath of the pulse, and with no information on the scope of the damage, and no word from anyone who came from any place that was not affected, it would be foolish to assume things would get better anytime soon. While it might be true that other survivors had found and ransacked the small cabin his parents had built years ago for weekends and vacations, the location was remote enough that there was a good chance they had not. Grant knew that some of the local rural people in the area were aware of the cabin, but he also knew that most people living out there full time were already fairly well equipped and self-sufficient as a lifestyle choice. Those people would respect the property of others and likely leave the cabin alone, at least to a point. Those who wouldn't do so were the desperate and ill-equipped who were making an exodus from the desperation of cities like New Orleans, where there was little chance of survival in the midst of so many. Many of them would not make it out of the suburbs, as Grant and his friends had already seen, but those who did would sweep the countryside like a swarm of locusts, looking for anything they could find to sustain life. It was certain that some of them would eventually find their way to the cabin, but if he and Scully could just get there first and get the supplies and tools he knew were stored there, he didn't care what happened after that to the land or the building. Staying there to defend it would be suicide, and they now had a far better option anyway. Grant was happy indeed at this turn of events, marked by the arrival of Casey's dad and Scully on the river. The prospect of sailing away from the mainland on a seaworthy boat gave him more hope than anything that had happened since he had left New Orleans on bicycles with Casey and Jessica.

In those first days after the power grid collapsed, he had thought of the cabin as the best refuge until order was restored and supplies and aid started arriving from other regions. That was when he still maintained hope that the blackout was a local or regional event and that the damage could be repaired in a few weeks, or at most, months. Now he knew for certain that it was more widespread, to at least as far away as the eastern Caribbean, so he knew the cabin in the woods was almost certainly an unsustainable option. Staying put *anywhere* was probably a bad idea, especially anywhere that others could get to on foot. At least with the sailboat they could anchor at remote islands reachable only by other boats. That would eliminate the threat from the majority of the population right from the start. And the best thing about it was that he would be with Casey and Jessica through it all, wherever the journey might take them and however long the situation lasted. The two of them were all he really had here anyway, with his parents living in a remote part of Bolivia that made communication with them difficult and infrequent even in normal times. Grant was certain they were better off than most folks, even if the effects of the blackout indeed reached that part of South America. He had no other relatives or close friends still living in the New Orleans area, so if not for Casey and Jessica he would have been dealing with all of this alone.

Grant had barely known Casey before and had just met her roommate, Jessica, after the blackout occurred. With his close friends either at other universities or starting their careers in other cities, Grant had mostly kept to himself while working his way through a graduate degree in anthropology at Tulane University. He had first run into Casey while assisting one of his professors on a field trip for an undergrad class. After that she had occasionally stopped to chat when they passed in a hallway or on campus. He found her attractive, but at the time had failed to realize how interested in him she really was. As he often did with girls, he missed an opportunity to get to know her further by never taking the initiative to simply ask her out for a date, which he now realized she would have certainly said yes to. Had it been Jessica stopping to chat, he would have been even shyer. Jessica was one of those girls he considered out of his league—so gorgeous he would have barely made eye contact with her—and he wouldn't have dared to assume she'd be interested in him. They wouldn't have had anything in common anyway, as she certainly didn't appear to be the outdoorsy type, and as a theater major she was too busy with rehearsals and performances to go camping or on field trips. While Jessica could get the attention of most any guy she wanted and was used to getting her way, Grant saw that as a strike against her in a time of crisis. At first, she had seemed clueless to the real nature of the danger they were in, and he thought she would have a much harder time dealing with it and adapting than Casey would. And he was right up to a point, at least in the beginning. But after spending days alone in the wild with her as they searched for Casey, his opinion of her had changed along with the changes in her own attitude. Jessica had turned out to be tougher than she looked, and her readiness and ability to adapt to changing circumstances both surprised and impressed him.

It also surprised him that she didn't want him out of her sight. By the time they left New Orleans on the bikes, he already knew Casey wanted to be more than just friends. It was becoming obvious that she had a crush on him even if he hadn't realized it before. Now it was clear that Jessica did, too. Grant wasn't sure how any of this would play out, but the last thing he wanted to do was come between the two friends or hurt one or both of them. With everything else they all had to deal with, that kind of drama was the last thing any of them needed. As he often did when faced with choices, Grant trusted that he would be presented with some kind of sign to tell him what to do. He trusted that whatever was to happen, it would work itself out. But one thing he was already sure of was that he wanted to make this trip to the cabin as fast as possible and get back to the company of both Casey and Jessica. He had been worried about them from the moment he and Scully left them behind, even though he felt they were safe with Casey's dad.

He saw that the canoe was riding fine at the end of its towline in the wake of the outboard, and that Scully was a natural at reading the channels of an unfamiliar river and avoiding shoals and obstructions. Grant had decided he liked Scully the moment he met him. It was clear that the Rastafarian islander was unperturbed by the hardships and dangers of this new reality they all found themselves in. A man with his confidence and skills could be nothing other than a valuable asset to the group, and Grant was glad he was along for this trip upriver. While he would have been willing to make this run to the cabin alone if necessary, it felt good to have someone watching his back, and to know that his companion was competent at handling both boats and guns. Scully had the Mossberg shotgun on the stern seat beside him and Grant was cradling the lever-action carbine in his lap as he scanned the dark forests at the water's edge for any signs of danger. Each bend of the river could reveal a surprise, so he kept his attention focused, knowing there might be little time to act if something was amiss.

The battered old Johnboat that Casey's Uncle Larry had patched up after they found it abandoned in the swamp was no speedboat, by any stretch of the imagination, but compared to the canoe he had been paddling for more than a week it sure seemed fast. To paddle upriver from that far down would have been so slow the trip to the cabin would have taken well over a week, but the motor pushed them against the current with ease. In less than four hours they were out of the big swamps of the lower Pearl River and had entered the Bogue Chitto River, the smaller tributary stream upon which the cabin was located. It would have been difficult to find if Grant had not been familiar with the confluence, but he had paddled this way just days before with Jessica, as they tried in vain to catch up to Casey and her abductor.

Grant knew this part of the Bogue Chitto was three or four long days away from the cabin at the normal pace of a canoe going downstream, and he had only been this far down it one other time during a weeklong canoe-camping trip that ended near the coast. These lower reaches were unfamiliar to him, but easier for Scully to navigate because the channel was still wide and deep, much like the Pearl. The banks here were mostly overhung with bushes and other foliage fighting for sunlight at the edges of the dark forests along both banks. When they finally came to a small sandbar with a gently sloping beach that would make landing the boat easy, Grant motioned for Scully to pull over.

"I need to stretch my legs and take a pee," he explained.

Scully nodded and reduced the engine speed to idle, allowing the boat to drift to the bank. Upon landing they walked around the sandbar for a few minutes, looking for signs that other people had been there since the last rain. But there was nothing but raccoon and alligator tracks, including the trail of a big gator that had left slide marks with its tail where it had apparently crawled into the water earlier that same day.

"Nevah knew so much bush in dis place," Scully said. "Before I comin' here, I t'ink everyt'ing in dis country is like Miami and New York."

"So you thought America was just one big city, huh? I think a lot of people from other countries think that until they come here. When I was in Guyana all the villagers there had that impression. All they asked about was the cities. But what struck me about the jungle there was how much it was like these swamps and woods around here in the Deep South."

"A mon could live hoppy in dis bush, you know," Scully said, looking at the tracks and watching as a largemouth bass struck at something on the surface of the river near the far bank.

"Yeah, there's plenty of game and fish, but I don't know how long it will stay that way. It looks like nothing but wilderness right here along the river, but you get just a short distance away on high ground and there are roads, farms, and small towns. The people that live in these rural areas will be hunting nonstop when they run out of what they have on hand."

As if to prove his point, the silence of the forest was shattered by two gunshots in rapid succession, far in the distance, but still close enough to distinguish as coming from a large-caliber rifle.

"Mehbe somebody shoot somet'ing to eat jus' now, mon."

"Probably. Could have been a deer. These woods are full of deer, even though there have always been plenty of outlaws who hunted them out of season even before all this happened."

"A mon's got to feed his family when dem hungry. Not to worry 'bout what de law seh."

"Yeah, that's true, and more than ever now. But now that there's no law at all, it may not be as good as it seems. We're really on our own now."

"Not to worry, Grant. Let's go. We going to dat cabin and get bok to de boat tomorrow. Where Larry sailin' nevah havin' law to begin. We goin' to de sea an' livin' like dem pirate in de old days. De wind, de sun, de sea…a good boat, good friends, lotta fish an' some island to hide on, mehbe plant de ganja seed. Who can ask for somet'ing more, mon?"

Another hour of motoring after leaving the sandbar put them into a part of the Bogue Chitto that looked completely different than the swampy lowlands they had left downstream. Here, the forests were predominately pine, and the channel was bounded by alternating areas of steep clay banks and bars of mixed sand and gravel. The water ran swift and clear over shallow shoals, and fallen trees and stumps were everywhere, forcing Scully to slow down and carefully pick his way among them to follow the deepest channel. In some places, they even had to get out of the boat and wade, towing it and the canoe upstream behind them, with the motor shut down and tilted up. The outboard was vulnerable to damage with so many obstructions and they couldn't risk bending or breaking the prop; without it, getting much farther upstream would be hopeless. As a result of all this stopping and starting, the afternoon hours slipped away and Grant realized they were going to have to camp for the night. The trip was going to take the better part of two days instead of the one long one he'd hoped for. They found a place on a high sandbar before it got too dark to see, and though there were no paths or other signs that the spot connected to a nearby road or farm, they kept their camp dark, putting out their cooking fire as soon as the rice was done.

"So tell me, mon, how you knowin' de two most beautiful girls in de college an' how you talkin' dem into going to de bush wid you?"

Grant laughed. "I don't think it was me so much as it was the promise of a roof over their heads in a place where everybody wasn't going crazy. I told them there was a generator at the cabin, and that we would have lights, a fan, and plenty to eat and drink. I think that's what they were interested in.

"Anyway, I met Casey last semester when she came along on an anthropology dig I was helping my professor with. We kind of kept running into each other around campus and stuff, but I never asked her out. I didn't think she liked me that way. I had seen her roommate around, but we had never been introduced. I sure wouldn't have gone after her. She was one of those girls that always had guys hanging around, you know what I mean?"

"So she had a boyfriend before, den?"

"Oh sure. Good-looking guy, pre-med student, nice car, parents with money…. I doubt it was serious, and she probably would have dumped him anyway, but guys like that always get the hot girls on campus."

"But if a mon havin' a girl like Jessica, where he at now? Why she wid you an' not wid he?"

"Because he was stupid, that's why. I invited him to come to the cabin, too, but he wouldn't hear of it. He didn't believe the blackout was serious. They had a big fight. He stayed in New Orleans and she came with me and Casey."

"An' now, both de girl dem likin' you! I can see it in Casey eye when she lookin' at you, mon. An' I can hear it in de way Jessica, she don't want you goin' up de river wid I. So what you gonna do, mon? Two beautiful girl, an' dem got not'ing to do now, no place to goin' bok to. All de world fresh an' new now dat Jah, he seh enough of dis technology an' desecration of he creation an' put out de light for good. Mehbe you gonna soon be married, mon, an' start a family down in de island!"

Grant laughed at this. "I don't know about all that, Scully. I was just trying to help out a friend, and her friend, too, of course. I needed them as much as they needed me, though. I would have hated to try and make that trip out here alone. Casey's one tough and smart woman, I'll tell you that. But Jessica surprised me, too. I thought she would break down at first, but man, she's really hung in there when things were at their worst. They're both survivors, and I'm glad they both came with me. I'm really glad Casey's got her dad and her uncle and that she's with them now. I know how close she was to her dad. She told me what happened to her mom when she was just twelve. I feel for Jessica though, the not knowing. Her parents live in Los Angeles, and there's just no telling how long it'll be before she finds out anything. She must be worried sick, and I'm sure they are, too. Right now, all she has is Casey and me. So, I guess it's natural she would want to cling to us both."

Grant fell asleep in the sand next to the canoe thinking about what Scully had said and wondering what life really was going to be like wherever they ended up on the boat. He didn't know what, if anything, would develop between him and either of the girls, but he did know that it was likely he would have a lot of time with both of them to find out.

They left at daylight the next morning to continue their struggle with shallow water and obstructions, making slow but steady progress against the current, even swifter in these upper reaches of the Bogue Chitto. One place where the water was particularly fast was a series of drops that funneled past clay shoals and created an area of small standing waves. It was a bit of a stretch to call it white water, but it was the closest thing to rapids he knew of on the river. As they worked their way through it, he remembered that this place was not far below the bridge crossing where Casey had been abducted. He and Jessica had run it shortly after heading downstream in pursuit.

Grant still blamed himself for leaving Casey alone in the first place. They should have all stuck together, but instead he had foolishly left her to guard the bicycles they no longer needed while he and Jessica set out to look for a canoe just a short distance away at a weekend camp house where Grant knew some were stored. Upon learning of roadblocks along the state line, effectively blocking them from using the road to cross into Mississippi where his family's cabin was located, Grant had decided that a canoe was the only way to slip by the authorities unnoticed. From the bridge where they'd left the bicycles, it was only a few miles of upstream paddling, and while inconvenient and slower, certainly safer.

The canoes had been there, stored in a rack beside the camp just as he had remembered, and he hadn't felt bad about "borrowing" one, knowing the absentee owner wouldn't likely have transportation to get to this remote place anyway. He had selected the one best suited to carry the three of them, and he and Jessica had dragged it down a steep bank and launched it when they were surprised to see a lone canoeist traveling the other way, heading down-stream. The lone paddler had returned their wave, but they had not spoken. He was long gone by the time they reached the bridge and found Casey missing.

Grant remembered the stab of fear he'd felt when he deciphered the footprints in the sand that told the story of what had happened. He'd never felt so helpless in his life as he did when he and Jessica had taken to the river to try and catch up with that mysterious paddler who he then knew had somehow taken Casey with him, evidently hidden under the pile of gear they'd seen protruding well above his boat's gunwales. It had been so disheartening to know how much of a head start he'd had before they realized what had happened. Trying desperately to catch up, they'd had no way of knowing if he was still traveling downstream ahead of them, or if he had left the river with her, hiding the canoe in the forest somewhere along the way. At the time Grant thought the odds of ever seeing her again were slim to none, but they had to try. They were both determined to search for her for as long as it took. That they found her at all was more luck than anything else, and as it turned out, Casey had escaped all on her own.

Grant cautioned Scully to slow down and keep to the far side of the channel as they neared the camp where he had taken the canoe. Even though the canoe they were towing was the one that had belonged to Derek, and not the one from the camp, he was still concerned someone might be there now and would be suspicious of anyone traveling the river. Grant had the lever-action rifle in his hands and at the ready, but as they passed under the bluff there was no sign of life, and the small cabin appeared as abandoned as it had on that day he and Jessica had been there, the remaining boats still in the shed where he'd left them.

They approached the bridge upstream with equal caution, but there, too, there was no one to be seen. He knew the motor would alert anyone in the area of their approach, and it was possible that if someone were around they were hiding and watching, but if so, they were afraid to show themselves. Grant wondered if the bicycles they had stashed in the dense canebrake near the bridge were still there, but it didn't really matter. Bicycles were useless to them now, and he had no intention of traveling by road anytime in the foreseeable future.

Just upstream of the bridge, Grant stared as they motored past the sandbar where Casey had been taken after a swim in the river. He wondered if the rains had washed away all the signs of her struggle by now, and figured they surely must have. And though he knew she was now safe with her father and aboard her uncle's boat, he also knew the ordeal she had just been through would affect her for a long time to come, even if life as they had all known it before was immediately restored. What she'd done in order to escape would scar anyone, but Grant was just glad she'd been strong enough to do it.

Passing that place meant they were only about five miles from his parent's cabin. The outboard motor was still running smoothly, but they had used more gas than Scully and Larry had estimated it would take. Grant assured him this would not be a problem, as there was gasoline for the generator stored at the cabin. With that added to what was left in the boat, they would have enough to motor all the way back down to the lower Pearl. Grant was relieved to be so close and to see that they still had at least four hours of daylight, judging by the angle of the sun. It would be great if they could go through everything in the cabin and get it sorted and loaded in the boat and canoe before dark. Then, if they left at first light in the morning, they could easily rejoin the others on the catamaran by late afternoon, as running downstream would be far faster, even with all the shoals and logs. Going with the current, they could simply tilt the motor up and muscle their way past most obstacles with the paddles.

Navigating against the current in this upper section of the Bogue Chitto was a real challenge in the Johnboat, however, and Grant had to keep a constant lookout for obstructions and shallows from the bow, instructing Scully by hand signals which way to steer. Several more times they had to get out and wade, dragging the boat and canoe over logs barely covered by an inch or two of clear-running water. Grant was intimately familiar with this section, and as they passed a prominent clay bluff that loomed some forty feet over the river on the right bank, he motioned for Scully to slow down.

"The cabin is just two more bends in the river up from this point," he said.

Scully shut down the outboard and allowed the boat to drift until he could grab an overhanging branch to hold their position in the current. "Mehbe we need paddle now, not to make de noise in case somebody in dat place."

"That's what I'm thinking, too, Scully, only this boat would be too hard to paddle against the current. Why don't you wait here while I hop in the canoe and go take a look? From here, I know I can paddle there in about fifteen minutes. I hate to waste the time, but I don't want us to run into a surprise either."

"Dat's a good plan, mon. You take de rifle an' keep a sharp eye. I an' I waitin' here and when you come bok we takin' de boat."

"And if I don't come back?"

"Den I comin' wid de Mossberg!" Scully grinned, holding up the shotgun.

After pulling the canoe alongside, Grant climbed in and knelt in the middle, bracing against the center thwart and beginning his upstream paddle with long, purposeful strokes. The aluminum canoe was inefficient and slow, but, still, he was able to make decent headway, and at the first bend he cheated the current by playing the eddies near the bank. He hoped this entire exercise was merely an unnecessary precaution, but he realized it *was* possible that some-one had taken up residence in the cabin, and, if so, would be reluctant to give up the bounty they had found there, free for the taking.

When he'd rounded the second bend, Grant landed the canoe on the small sandbar at the base of the steep bank below the cabin. From that vantage point, he could see no sign of anyone, so he made his way up to the top and circled around through the woods to the side of the small clearing in which the cabin was built. From this angle, all he could see was one side of the board and batten cypress structure. There was a small window in the middle, but a closed curtain on the inside made it impossible to determine if the cabin was occupied or not. Grant worked his way further along the edge of the clearing until he could see the front door, which was closed, just as it should have been. Holding the rifle ready in both hands, he stepped out of the woods and crossed the small yard to the door. He was about to reach for the key he knew had been hidden in a crack in the planking to one side when he saw that he wouldn't have to. The door casing around the dead bolt lock was cracked and split, and though it appeared shut, Grant now realized that the door was merely pulled to and not latched. He pulled the hammer back on the rifle and pointed it at the door as he kicked it the rest of the way open with one foot. The door swung wide and Grant knew immediately that someone had moved in and set up housekeeping in the cabin. Parked right in the middle of the open living area, with a small puddle of oil staining the varnished floor beneath it, was an old, beat-up, and rusty Harley Davidson motorcycle. Grant took a deep breath to suppress his adrenaline rush as he realized that whoever had ridden it in there was not in the cabin at the moment. A quick look around, though, was enough to assure him that whoever it was, they were using the supplies he had come to get. Grant quietly pulled the door to as he exited and quickly made his way back down to the canoe.

FOUR

Paddling as quietly as possible and conversing only in low whispers, Artie, Casey, and Jessica listened carefully but heard no follow-up shots after the single, distant blast that had shattered the silence and caused them to take the precaution of readying weapons. Artie relaxed a bit after nearly an hour went by, figuring that it was probably just a hunter, and that whatever quarry he or she had been shooting at was successfully downed with one shot. Experienced hunters would take care to do that, if at all possible, because conserving ammunition was critical in a time when getting more was so difficult. There would be some, like the survivalist nutcase who had abducted his daughter, who would have had large stockpiles on hand, just hoping some breakdown of law and order like this would happen, but most regular country folk who hunted in the legal seasons would likely only have a few boxes of their favorite caliber. Looking at the large duffle bag in the bottom of canoe, Artie was glad Casey had maintained the presence of mind to gather up her dead kidnapper's weapons and ammo. With this newly acquired stash, he assumed they were now better armed than most, and if they were careful, what they had should last a long time. From the two encounters they'd already had in the Caribbean on the way here, he knew that even on the boat they were not safe without weapons. A fully functional sailboat was in fact a prime target for desperate folks anywhere on the waterfront, many of whom might now look to piracy as a viable occupation.

"How much further is it?" Jessica whispered as she rested her paddles across the gunwales of the canoe for a moment.

"I'm not sure, but we've got to be getting fairly close," Artie answered.

"What is that?" Casey asked, lifting her own paddle out of the water and cocking her head to one side to better hear whatever sound she was referring to.

Artie stopped paddling as well, letting the canoe drift soundlessly as they all listened and finally heard what Casey had heard.

"Is it some kind of truck or something?" Jessica asked.

"It's definitely a motor!" Casey whispered.

Artie tried to think where he'd heard a similar sound. It *was* a motor, but the rhythm wasn't right for a truck engine. It was turning slowly, with a methodical chugging that didn't vary with accelerations and gear changes as a truck or automobile engine would have. The distance and the echo effect of the surrounding forest made it harder to discern, but then it made perfect sense. "It's a boat! I think that's a diesel engine. It must be some kind of bigger boat than a Johnboat with an outboard."

"Is it coming this way?" Jessica asked.

"Shh! Let's listen for a minute," he held his hand up, motioning them both to silence as they drifted in the almost-still water. The engine sound was steady and unchanging in speed, but it did seem that he could hear it more clearly now. If it was indeed a boat, then it must be coming up the river in their direction, although Artie knew from studying the charts with Larry that there were a couple of alternate channels connecting the two major east and west branches of the Pearl River. This basin that was known as the Honey Island Swamp was some five miles wide and sixty miles long. But though there were countless routes a canoe could thread through, only two or three of the channels were deep and wide enough for any kind of big boat.

"We'd better keep paddling," he said to the girls. "I would like to find some place we can get off the main river if the boat *is* coming this way. There's no sense in being caught out in the open when we have options."

"I agree," Casey said, shifting her grip on the paddle and dipping the blade to begin stroking again. "Better to see whoever it is first than to be seen by them."

Jessica said nothing, but joined in the effort with equal enthusiasm. Considering what they had been through, none of them wanted to chance an encounter with strangers from the vulnerable position of a canoe in the middle of the river. After paddling another ten minutes, they spotted a narrow slough opening into the river from the west bank and Artie signaled for everyone to stop paddling. "Let's pull over there and listen for a couple of minutes."

The entrance to the slough was just five or six feet wide. Overhung with leafy branches, its banks dense with palmettos, it was barely noticeable from mid-river and would make a perfect place to hide and wait. Artie steered the canoe toward it and then back-paddled to put it in the opening stern first. Then he held them in position by sticking his paddle blade deep into the muck of the bottom and they remained quiet while they listened to the boat engine.

"It *is* coming closer!" Jessica whispered.

"Yes, you're right. Okay, let's back all the way in here. We need to get the canoe out of sight; there's no way to know who they are and what they're up to, and I don't feel like taking any chances at this point."

Casey and Jessica nodded and helped Artie as they pushed the canoe backwards, their paddle blades sinking deep into the muddy bottom with each stroke. Beyond the entrance, the slough curved away in a slight bend, allowing them to tie the canoe to some bushes on the bank in a way that it could not be seen by anyone passing by on the river. Once they'd done that, Artie whispered that he wanted to get a look at this approaching boat, and Casey and Jessica said they did, too. Leaving the canoe, they crept into a position of concealment among the palmettos on the bank and waited.

As the sound of the approaching engine grew louder, Artie was really glad they had found a place to hide the canoe in time. He was getting sick of this feeling of fear every time there was a potential encounter with other people, but he knew from repeated recent experiences that the mistrust and suspicion was justified. And after what Casey and Jessica had already been through, he wasn't about to put them into any situation of unnecessary risk. They crouched in the jungle-like palmetto thicket and tried to ignore the mosquitos that buzzed around their faces while they waited. It was bizarre to hear an engine of any kind after so many days without noise from traffic in the distance, aircraft overhead, or any other machinery. In the profound silence since the grid went down, Artie had realized for the first time just how loud the modern, industrialized world really was. The boat that was coming their way didn't sound thoroughly modern at all though, but rather like a relic from a bygone era. The throbbing sound of the slow-turning diesel brought to mind the image in the old Bogart movie of the *African Queen* steaming up the Congo. The mosquitos, the greenery of the palmettos and the heat and humidity no doubt added to that impression.

Fifteen minutes passed like an hour. As they waited the sound grew louder and the boat drew closer. When at last it came into view, it looked much as Artie had already pictured it: dilapidated, old and made of wood, hand-painted a fading and peeling blue and white with what was probably latex house paint. It was also big compared to the typical boats one would expect on a river like this; Artie guessed at least thirty feet. There was an oversized cabin house with a rounded front and large windows on all sides, so that the helmsman could see to navigate while remaining inside in inclement weather.

At first, the glare of sunlight reflecting on the panes made it impossible for Artie to see anyone inside the wheelhouse, but as the boat drew abreast of their hiding place he could see one man steering and another leaning back against what was probably a chart table or counter. Both men were shirt-less and smoking cigarettes and Artie noticed that the one who was not steering had a weapon slung over his shoulder. He couldn't tell in the shadows if it was a shotgun or a rifle and there was no way of knowing if there were others on board or not, as the main cabin was quite large.

Artie was frozen in place as he watched, not daring to move, and without glancing to look, he was sure the girls were just as cautiously still watching from their positions on either side of him. The fact that one of the men was car-rying a weapon didn't mean much one way or the other. He expected that anyone in their right mind traveling the waterways or roads would be armed if at all possible, considering the circumstances. The boat was obviously a commercial fishing vessel, and must have been the own-ers' means of earning a living before the pulse event. Artie figured if they knew enough about fishing or shrimping to do it full time before things fell apart, they could probably catch more than enough food to survive and barter for other goods now, especially considering they were lucky enough to have a boat with a still-running engine. But he wondered what they were doing here and where they might be going. He knew from what he had seen upstream that such a boat could not travel much farther in that direction. But there were the cutoffs and channels that could lead to someplace he didn't know about. Wherever they were going, they appeared confident in their navigation and seemed unconcerned about running aground or getting lost. The boat steamed by until he got a view of the stern, and that's when Artie felt his heart almost stop. It wasn't the name *Miss Lucy* painted in bold blue letters across the white stern that shocked him; instead it was what he could see lashed to the rail on the starboard stern quarter. There could be no doubt as to what it was: Larry's long and slender two-seater kayak, its white hull and distinctive yellow decks making it unmistakable. Artie knew it well, as it had been part of the scene on the deck of the catamaran for their entire voyage. With Scully in the bow seat he had paddled that very kayak into the dangerous fringes of New Orleans, slipping unseen along a hidden canal to get to the car he'd left parked at the airport before all this madness began.

If that *was* Larry's kayak, and Artie knew that it was, then these men must have somehow gotten it from Larry. There could be no other explanation.

Artie tightened his grip on the Saiga. A part of him wanted to fire a warning shot and order them to stop, but the fishing boat was already about to round the next bend upstream and would be out of sight in just another minute. And the men *were* armed. He couldn't risk a firefight with Casey and Jessica right there beside him. Even though they would have the element of surprise, there were just too many unknowns. *Maybe Larry made a trade with these fishermen for something they had that he wanted; but what, fuel? Surely they must have some gas on board, even though their boat was diesel powered. They might have a generator or something they would need it for. But would Larry give up something as useful as the kayak for a few gallons of fuel?* Artie didn't think so, but maybe if it was a lot of something...like maybe a lot of food as well as gasoline. But it still worried him, and as the fishing boat chugged upriver out of sight, Artie knew what they had to do.

"Come on, we need to hurry," he whispered to Casey and Jessica, "We need to paddle as fast as we can and get to the catamaran."

"Do you think those men saw Uncle Larry?" Casey asked.

"Yes, that was his kayak tied to the rail. I don't know why he would have let them have it, and I want to make sure he's okay."

"Do you think they stole it or something?" Jessica asked.

"I don't know. All I'm sure of is that it *was* the same kayak." Artie told them that it had crossed his mind to fire a warning shot to try to force the captain of the boat to stop so he could question him about it, but then he'd reconsidered because it seemed too risky. They were armed and would likely as not return fire.

"Oh my God, they're going upriver the same way Grant and Scully went!" Jessica said, more worried than ever now.

"You don't have to worry about that, Jessica. That boat is way too big to go much farther upriver and certainly can't get even as far as the sandbar where we camped last night. They'll probably turn off on one of the side channels we passed this morning. They probably have a hunting camp somewhere in the swamp. We know it's not on the main river, or we would have passed it this morning. They will probably be long gone before Grant and Scully come downstream tomorrow. What we need to do is get to Larry and the catamaran as quickly as possible."

When they got back in the canoe, Artie grabbed his paddle and began digging it into the water in long, forceful strokes. He wasn't as worried about keeping quiet now. The diesel engine of the riverboat had shattered the silence anyway, and he figured that if those men had recently visited Larry where the catamaran had been anchored, it wasn't likely that anyone else was in the vicinity between here and there. He remembered the distant gunshot they had heard earlier, and his worry for his brother increased. Maybe it wasn't just some random hunter, as he'd told the girls. And seeing Larry's kayak on that boat definitely ramped up his concern.

Twenty more minutes of nonstop paddling brought them to the entrance of the oxbow lake in which the catamaran was anchored, and as they paddled into view from just upriver, the long, upswept gray hulls of the unusual vessel looked completely out of place against this deep-woods background, even with the rig down and stowed across the decks. Larry was nowhere in sight, but Artie assumed he was down below.

"Larry! Hey Larry, it's me, Artie!" he shouted as they closed the distance to inside of a hundred feet. There was no answer and his brother did not step up to the deck as expected.

"Oh my…wow, I can't believe this!" Casey said, staring as she stopped paddling and then looked over her shoulder from the bow at her dad and Jessica. "Why did he do that?"

"I told you that you had a surprise coming!" Artie grinned as he watched Casey take in the name of her uncle's catamaran. The hastily painted lettering that read *Casey Nicole* was clearly visible on the stern of the port hull, which was the closest side from the direction they approached and couldn't be missed. Artie had known all along that the name was going to elicit a reaction like that from his daughter. He just wished Larry had been on deck to see her face the moment she saw it.

"Awesome!" Jessica said. "He named her after you!"

"I…. I just can't believe it." Casey whispered, dipping her paddle again, clearly wanting to get closer.

The canoe skimmed across the calm water, and Artie called his brother's name again, still getting no answer. *Could he be asleep down below? Surely the shouting would have awakened him by now.* Then, as their angle of view changed and they drifted adjacent to the stern of the other hull, Artie felt a rush of adrenaline at what he saw: a four-foot-long area of the starboard hull, near the stern, was smashed in and broken. Artie saw exposed plywood and the torn fiber-glass sheathing that had covered it under the gray primer. Something had hit the boat with a tremendous impact. He yelled out his brother's name again as loud as he could and still got no answer. Frantic now, he dug in with the paddle and with frenzied strokes steered the canoe until it was alongside the hull, just forward of the damaged area. Then he stood and grabbed the wooden toe rail on the deck and held the canoe alongside.

"Tie us off and stay here, Casey! Larry! Larry, are you okay?" Artie banged on the hull with his free hand as he shouted. "Larry! Where are you?" After checking that Casey had secured the canoe, he pulled himself up to the deck with both hands and clambered aboard. He was about to step onto the bridge deck that spanned the gap between the hulls when he saw the condition of the cockpit. The com-panionway hatches had been ripped off of their attaching hinges and stuff from inside the cabins was strewn every-where. A sickening sense of fear for his brother overcame him as he realized that the *Casey Nicole* had been ransacked, and clearly by whoever had also smashed in the side of the starboard hull. Such damage could only be done by an impact with a bigger boat, and Artie didn't have to wonder who had done this; he *knew*. He and the girls had watched the perpetrators of this attack steam right by less than half an hour before.

"Pass me that rifle and stay in the canoe," he said to the girls as he pointed to the Saiga he'd left in front of the stern seat. Jessica handed it up to him.

"Where is Uncle Larry, Dad?"

"I don't know, just don't come up here until I tell you it's okay."

Sidestepping the clutter on deck, Artie made his way across the cockpit of the catamaran, steeling himself as he approached the port companionway, where Larry's bunk was. Larry wouldn't let anyone do this to his boat without a fight. Would he find his brother below, badly wounded or already dead? He didn't want to consider the worst, but he had to know. Calling out his name again, Artie peered down into the cabin. The galley was a wreck of pots and pans on the cabin sole, along with cushions from the bunk forward of it. Boxes and bags that had contained their food stores, and had been neatly organized in the lockers below the bunks and cabinets, were strewn everywhere. But there was no one in the cabin. When Artie was sure of that he crossed the cockpit to the starboard hull and entered the nav station.

The electronic instruments, including the Garmin color chartplotter and the Icom VHF radio that had been useless anyway since the pulse were missing entirely, ripped out of the wooden cabinet faces that had housed them, the broken wiring dangling loose in the holes left behind. Just as in the port hull, the interior of the starboard hull was a wreckage of broken and empty containers. Practically everything of value had been taken by the marauding fishermen, but where was Larry? He was not in this hull either, and there was nowhere else on board he could be. Artie was frantic now as he climbed the companionway steps to go back on deck. He had just exited the cabin when he was stopped in his tracks by a scream from Casey: *"Dad!"*

Artie knew by her tone that she was not in danger. It was worse than that. Dropping the rifle, he rushed back to the stern deck to find that Casey was pointing to something on the bank beyond the bows of the catamaran. The boat had swung around slightly on its anchor, revealing an area of muddy shoreline they had not seen when they first approached. Lying among the twisted cypress roots, half in and half out of the water, was a still figure that Artie knew immediately from the thick blond hair and deeply tanned arms was his younger brother.

FIVE

It had been more than three weeks since the solar flares, and Joey Broussard had finally accepted the fact that the lights weren't going to come back on anytime soon. As he walked along the deserted gravel road in the Mississippi woods with his buddy, Zach, the afternoon sun and the humidity made him long for an ice-cold beer. As he daydreamed about the beer he could almost taste it, but he had stopped wondering how long it would be before he could actually down one again. It was just torture to do so. Living without cold beer sucked. Being out here in the middle of nowhere sucked. Not being able to listen to his music sucked. And most of all, knowing his girlfriend had left him when he needed her the most *really* sucked.

It wasn't like he was in love with her or anything; Joey knew their relationship wouldn't have survived more than a semester or two whether the blackout occurred or not. Jessica was hot and all, but he was sure there were plenty of hot girls in his future through the rest of his time at Tulane and beyond. In fact, he was quite sure there would be plenty as young and fine as she was long after he finished medical school and started knocking down the big bucks as a surgeon of whatever sort he decided upon later. At least that's what he was supposedly shooting for. In reality, Joey's main focus was on having a good time, and as long as he kept his undergrad grades reasonably respectable, the cash infusions from his dad that enabled his lifestyle continued to flow. He was only in his sophomore year and there was plenty of time later to get serious. He would worry about the future when the future arrived.

Most of the time he'd been spending with Jessica *definitely* qualified as good times. Like him, she was a night owl who liked to party. During the wee hours, after her late-night play rehearsals, they had run all over the city together and somehow found their way back to his crib in time for more fun before their morning classes. She was still living with her roommate Casey, but lately before the blackout she'd spent at least three or four nights a week with him. He hadn't wanted her to move in full time, that would be way too much of a commitment for him, but it would have been nice if she'd stuck it out by his side when everything turned to shit in New Orleans.

And now she was supposed to be here, but wasn't. Finding her so he could talk some sense into her was the main reason he and Zach had made the dangerous journey to this backwoods cabin in the first place. That and the fact that they didn't really have a better option for someplace to go that was safe from all the madness they had left behind. But when they got here, Jessica and her friends were nowhere to be found, and there was no sign they'd been here either. He didn't even know if she or her friends were still alive, but he did know that she had left him and left New Orleans with the intention of coming here. Like a fool, she had followed Casey and that asshole friend of hers, Grant, that she apparently trusted more than she did him. Why did she think a prick like that had all the answers? Why couldn't she have just waited in the city with him a little bit longer?

The cabin *was* secluded and all, and *was* well stocked, just as Grant had said it was, but little good it had done any of them, since they hadn't arrived to use it. Joey had known all along that it was dumb to try and ride that far on bicycles. He had tried to tell her, but she wouldn't listen. He could live with the knowledge that he had tried his best to talk her out of it, and that left him with a clear conscience, but he was still pissed, even though he knew it damned sure wasn't his fault. If she *were* dead, as he feared she might be, it was because of her own hardheaded actions.

When Joey and Zach had finally arrived at the cabin, it was clear that no one else had been there in the two weeks since the blackout. The door was still locked and the considerable amount of canned goods and other staple foods packed in the pantry was untouched. There was a Honda 5KW generator with several gallons of gasoline in two jerry cans, a propane grill with a large, still-full bottle of cooking gas, as well as a two-burner camp stove with a half dozen one-pound disposable propane bottles. The well had a manual backup pump that allowed access to the cold and pure water deep below ground, and besides that, the Bogue Chitto River ran clear and swift just forty feet beneath the base of the clay bluff upon which the little cabin was situated. The cabin was indeed a first-rate getaway, but Joey and Zach missed the city, and both of them were ready for this disruption of their routine to be over.

But as bad as this was, out in the middle of nowhere and cut off from the outside world, staying back there in New Orleans was far worse. Joey had tried it at first, stubbornly refusing to give up on his belief that the blackout was simply a temporary glitch of the utility grid that would be corrected quickly. Joey came from money, and unlike many of his pre-med classmates at Tulane, he wasn't living in a crappy apartment or sharing some run-down rental house with a roommate or two. No, Joey's house was in the Garden District of New Orleans, on a street where the neighbors were mostly already successful doctors or other high-earning upper-middle-class professionals. His dad had bought the property as an investment that Joey could live in while he completed his education, but Joey found it to be extremely conducive to extra-curricular activities as well. It was not something he wanted to give up, the electricity and other utilities out or not. Joey had hung on as long as he could, determined to protect his house and his stuff from the looting and burning that became rampant in the aftermath, when people discovered grocery stores were empty, cars didn't run, cell phones didn't work, and the police were just as bewildered and helpless as everybody else.

After Jessica said she was leaving with Grant and the subsequent altercation, Joey had locked himself in the house, trying to ignore the sting of her slap across his face. When he'd pushed her new friend through the porch railing outside his door, instead of taking his side, as he expected a loyal girlfriend to do, she'd turned on him like a rabid dog, defending this virtual stranger that her roommate, Casey, was so enamored of. Joey had let her have a piece of his mind after it happened, but no matter what he said, she insisted she was through with him and rode away on the bicycle with Grant without looking back. But Joey knew women and knew how to get his way with them. They could say whatever they wanted when they were really pissed, but in his experience they almost always softened up after a few days and came back. At the time, he'd figured she would be back by the next day at the latest, just as soon as she realized how stupid it was to try and ride out of the city by way of the Causeway on a bicycle. He would wait her out and wait out this bullshit panic that had nearly everyone in the city in its grip. He had finally managed to find a couple of cases of hot beer, which he paid some swindler a hundred dollars for, and when that ran out, there was always whiskey and tequila.

Throughout the afternoon after Jessica left, he'd noticed the increasing frequency of sporadic gunfire nearby and the smell of smoke from burning houses that made breathing difficult, even with his doors and windows closed and locked. The few law enforcement officers who were still attempting to do their duty, at least in affluent neighborhoods such as his, were clearly becoming overwhelmed. Throughout the day, he heard the commotion and knew it was simply a matter of time before the looters got to his own door. Joey was at a loss as to how to stop them once they did. If the New Orleans Police Department, with all their weapons and training, couldn't control the rioting, what could he do, alone and unarmed, hiding in his upscale enclave in the midst of a city gone mad? But one thing he knew for sure, if he did leave the house vacant at a time like this, it would be stripped and probably burned in no time flat. He was determined to do all he could to prevent that from happening, reasoning that most of the looters were looking for easy targets and would probably avoid occupied houses since there were so many already empty.

Those first few days after the world had turned upside down had seemed like a nightmare that was impossible to wake up from. He had thought it was bad enough the second day, when he realized he couldn't buy cold beer from a store *anywhere* within walking distance, and options beyond that were out of the question. Joey had spent his childhood in Baton Rouge, so he was no stranger to blackouts that lasted for days after the occasional Gulf hurricane, but *cars*? Who would have thought anything could shut down all the cars and trucks on the road? Or destroy cell phones and computers and just about everything else electronic, for that matter? Joey had witnessed the strange, glowing colored lights that lit up the sky that night before everything changed. But at the time, the spectacle was nothing more than an unexplained but still awesome fireworks display that he and Jessica watched through his bedroom window. Both of them were pretty well wasted from a party they'd been to earlier, and this light show seemed like the perfect finale to another evening well spent before they passed out in each other's arms. It wasn't until the next morning when he discovered he couldn't use his phone or start his car to get to his first class that Joey knew something was wrong. And it was only hours later, after stumbling around the city on foot among other bewildered residents, that he understood the significance of the lights from the night before. But even so, at the time he had stubbornly refused to believe that it would not all be back to normal in a day or two. He clung to that belief the day after that, and he was still trying to hang on to it, as he stayed locked in his house alone, the night after Jessica had pedaled away with Grant.

It was sometime late the following afternoon when he heard something at his door, and at first he thought maybe she had come to her senses and decided to come back to him. But the knock at the door quickly became a fierce pounding that he knew was the effort of a much bigger person than Jessica. He leapt up from the sofa in a panic, certain the rampaging mob had finally arrived to ransack his house. In desperation, he opened the living room closet and fumbled through his golf bag, first grabbing his five iron and then putting it back for the three, feeling its solid heft as he prepared to wield it as a bludgeon against the first one to come through the door. He was shaking with adrenaline as he raised the club behind his shoulder, poised to strike with all the force he could muster. The pounding got harder until he was certain the door would be broken down, but then a voice from the other side brought an instant wave of relief. It was only Zach, his best friend, and the last person Joey expected to see that day. Zach had been away to play a weekend gig with his band at a club near LSU, and, though he was supposed to return on Sunday night, he never did. Joey had been certain that he had stayed longer for some reason and gotten stranded there when the pulse hit in the early hours of Tuesday morning. But there was no mistaking that voice; Zach had somehow made it back.

He lowered the golf club and reached for the dead bolt. When he opened the door, he saw that his buddy was alone. He also looked like he'd been on the losing side of a recent barroom brawl. His left eye was bruised and swollen; dried blood from his nostrils was encrusted on his upper lip, and his black Pearl Drums T-shirt was so ripped and torn it could barely be considered a garment. But Joey was happy to see him. He hated being alone, and if Jessica wasn't coming back, having Zach as company was the next best thing.

At least he would have someone to talk to. Joey let him in, but not without a barrage of questions about where he had been, what had happened to his face and how he had managed to get back to the Garden District of New Orleans through all the chaos outside.

Zach had pushed his way past him and pulled the door shut behind him, turning to lock it as he did. "Joey, we've got to get out of this city, man. We'll be dead if we don't."

"Where have you been, dude? I figured you had to be stuck in Baton Rouge with no way to get here. Who did that to your face?" Joey handed him a warm Bud Light in a can from the half-empty case on the floor by the sofa, opening one for himself as well.

"Some punks on the Interstate," Zach said, indicting his face. "Yeah, there was this girl named Lindsay at the club who kept hanging with me on all my breaks. She was really into our original stuff and said she dug drummers. I ended up at her place after the show and she was so cool I stayed Sunday and Monday night, too. I got up Tuesday morning and left before daylight to try and get back here for my eight o'clock class. I was on the bridge about five miles west of the airport when all this shit happened. I was probably doin' eighty-five and I just about flipped my Pathfinder when the engine died and the power steering stopped working. A bunch of other people did wreck, some of them pretty bad. It was some crazy shit. I've never seen anything like it; everything on the road came to a halt. Like everybody else,

I got out and opened the hood and stared at the engine, but I didn't have a clue what could be wrong. Nobody else did, either. I stood around talking to a bunch of other drivers close by and we were just all wondering what the hell could have happened. On top of all the cars being fucked up, nobody had a cell phone that worked either. I mean, not just that there was no signal, but the phones were *dead*! But I know you know all about that. It's the same everywhere, as far as I know."

"Yeah, it seems like it. I didn't believe it at first, but I'm starting to think this is more than just New Orleans."

"It's gotta be, or the power companies or someone would have been here by now. But anyway, I waited around for what must have been three hours. Nothing changed and it was getting really hot by late morning, so I decided the hell with that. I thought I was pretty lucky because I had this piece of crap old bike of Lindsay's in the back. She had it in her apartment after finding it in a thrift store, and said she wanted to ride it but it needed new tires and it wouldn't shift right. I was into her enough that I knew I wanted to see her again, so I told her I would fix it up for her and bring it back the next weekend. It did need work but I figured it was rideable enough to get me at least to the first exit off the Interstate, so I could get off that damned bridge, get something cold to drink, and try to find a phone that would work. The bike was way too small for me, but it sure beat walking, which was all that the other people stuck out there could do. I was clipping along fine and could see the exit just ahead when I ran into those assholes.

"There were four of them, probably all still in high school or more likely dropouts. They saw me coming, and instead of moving out of the way like all the other people I passed, they blocked my path at the last minute and caused me to swerve into the guardrail and fall. Before I could get back up, one of them punched me right in the nose and another one grabbed the bike and hopped on it. I tried to stop him but then I got knocked down again with the punch that gave me this shiner," Zach said, indicating his bruised left eye. By the time I got up, the bike was gone and the other three were running off behind the one riding it. And what really sucks is that no one would help me. There were several people around from all the stalled cars, but they just stood there and watched it happen."

As Joey listened to his friend's story a flood of emotions from the events earlier that day overcame him. He smashed the golf club he was still holding into the useless TV sitting on a table against the nearest wall, much to Zach's astonishment.

"I *told* her something like that would happen!" Joey screamed. "She wouldn't listen to me though; wouldn't listen to reason at all! Just took off with Casey and that asshole on those bikes, just asking for something like that to happen!"

"What are you talking about, man?"

"Jessica! She left on a damned bike just yesterday morning! Left with Casey and some dipshit she knew from the Anthropology Department who talked them both into trying to ride bikes out of the city to some cabin in the woods he's got up in Mississippi. I told her it was crazy, that they would never make it. I tried to get her to stay here, but she wouldn't listen."

"Well, you got a better idea? I got on Lindsay's bike because I was just trying to get off that damned bridge. I would have made it, too, if not for those punks."

"If they took your bike, what chance do you think Jessica and Casey had to make it ninety miles on bikes with just one skinny dude with them?"

"Ninety miles! That's a hell of a long way!"

"I know. I tried to get her to just wait here. I thought we should all stick together. They wanted me to go with them, but I thought it was too dangerous. And besides, I didn't want to leave my house to the looters."

"It's too dangerous to stay here though," Zach said. "You're not going to stop the looters anyway. How many do you really think you can hold off with that fucking golf club?"

"Yeah, I know, but what else can we do? How did you get here anyway, after they took the bike?"

"I walked, how else?"

"So what were you thinking? What do you plan to do next?"

"I don't know, it's not like I've got a plan or anything. I just wanted to get back to my apartment first. I need to go through my stuff; see what I'll need. I stopped by to see if you were here first because it's on my way and I figured it would be better to stick together if you were."

"I don't know, man. I still don't like the idea of leaving the house. I've been hearing shooting ever since before Jessica and that jerk left."

"That's all the more reason *to* leave, Joey. You can't hold out here. We need to get some stuff together and figure out a way to get the hell out of this city. If I'd known it was this bad, I never would have come back in the first place. But it'll be worth it to get to my apartment. I'm pretty sure my roommate, Brandon, did not make it back here after this pulse thing happened. He had gone to Fort Walton Beach with some friends and they weren't planning on coming back until Tuesday night, anyway. And if he didn't, he's got some things at the apartment he won't be needing but we will."

"What?" Joey asked, laughing. "An old antique diesel truck that will still run?"

"No, his rifle, for one. He's into deer hunting, if I didn't mention it before. And he keeps his rifle under his bed. It's some kind of high-powered big game rifle with a scope on it. I don't know if he's got bullets for it or not, but I'm pretty sure he does. I don't know shit about guns, to be honest."

"I do," Joey said. "It's been a long time, but I went deer hunting a bunch of times when I was in high school. Used to go every season after Thanksgiving with my uncle. If you think that rifle's there, we'd better get going and try to get it. Any gun is better than nothing, it doesn't matter what kind it is. What else has he got that we can use?"

"A ride out of here."

"A ride! Are you serious? I thought you said he *didn't* have an old diesel truck!"

"He doesn't. He's got something better. He just found it on Craigslist a few weeks ago—cheap!"

"So what is it?"

"A motorcycle. Not just any motorcycle—a Harley Davidson Sportster!"

"So, what's so special about that? How is all that shiny chrome going to help us? I'll bet it won't run."

"Sure it will. Here's the thing about Harleys; they're like 1940s technology. Those things are so primitive all they need to run is some gas and oil. It's a 1993 XL1200 Custom, which means it's got old-fashioned points and plugs and a carburetor! And believe me, it's not shiny. It looks like shit, so it's exactly what we need."

"Huh! I didn't think about that. Maybe it will run then. Why the fuck did he want a Sportster though? I thought that was the smallest bike Harley made? Can we both fit on it?"

"It might not be comfortable and we might look gay as hell, but would you rather walk? I don't know where we'll go, but if it'll get us out of here, that's all that matters."

"If it'll run at least ninety miles, I know where we'll go," Joey said, or at least I will after we stop by Jessica and Casey's apartment. I heard them talking about leaving a map to that cabin so Casey's dad could find them if he made it back from wherever he had gone on vacation."

◉ ◉ ◉

They had indeed found the rifle and the old Sportster that belonged to Zach's roommate. The bike was rusty, with broken turn signals, missing mirrors and a torn seat held together with duct tape, but the engine had started right up, and they had left the city on it the next morning. The ride north had been harrowing, with several close encounters with people on foot attempting to stop them and steal the bike. Joey held them at bay by brandishing the rifle from the back while Zach drove.

Once they reached the cabin and discovered that Jessica and her friends had not made it there first, they settled in and made themselves at home. The days came and went but Jessica and the others still did not arrive. Joey began to wonder if they ever would. There was plenty of food, and everything else that was essential for survival, in the cabin, but sitting around all day doing nothing was boring. Joey took to spending his days hunting, to break up the monotony and to have fresh meat for the fire pit grill out back behind the cabin. Most days Zach tagged along with him, but instead of sitting and waiting patiently for a deer to come along, they usually walked along the long gravel road leading through the woods to the cabin, hoping to see one. It was on one of those afternoons when they'd given up on yet another fruitless hunt that Joey stopped in his tracks in the middle of the road. They had wandered farther from the cabin than usual, on the road that roughly paralleled the river to the south.

"Listen! Do you hear that, Zach?"

Zach did, and the sound spurred them to get back to the cabin as fast as they could. They had both recognized it as an outboard engine, and that could only mean one thing. Someone was coming up the river in the direction of the cabin. When the sound suddenly stopped, Joey wondered if the boat had already arrived. It took him and Zach another twenty minutes to cover the rest of the distance, as they slowed to a stealthy approach and left the roadway for the final two hundred yards.

Leading the way through the concealment of the forest, Joey had just reached the edge of the clearing in which the cabin stood when he saw someone walking down the bank to the river. Whoever it was, the person was about to slide a canoe that was resting on the small sandbar below back into the water and step into it. Joey immediately raised his rifle to get a better look at the lone figure through the telescopic sight. A tremble of rage came over him as he saw who it was and his finger automatically moved to the trigger as the crosshairs of the scope centered on Grant Dyer's head. Remembering the humiliation of that morning in New

Orleans, it would have been all too easy to squeeze off a round, but he resisted the urge. Grant would know Jessica's whereabouts, and Joey wasn't about to let him paddle out of sight without asking him. He moved his aim a couple of feet to the right and fired, sending the bullet into the water just inches from the canoe and causing Grant to make a panicked dive to the muddy sandbar as the rifle blast rang out through the forest.

SIX

Casey Drager had been so happy just moments before, when they rounded a bend in the canoe and at last caught sight of the big catamaran her uncle had built with his own hands. It would have been enough just knowing they had made it to the boat that would be their ride out of this awful swamp, but to top it off, she had been shocked to see her own name painted on the side of her uncle's pride and joy. She had expected him to momentarily come on deck and flash her a big grin when he saw her reaction to the name. Then she would have clambered aboard and given him a huge hug, not just because he named his boat after her, but because she had really missed him, because his lifestyle made it so difficult to spend time with him. That happiness had turned to icy fear a few seconds later as she and her dad and Jessica paddled closer and saw the smashed-in hull. Her dad's worry that the men in the fishing boat had been up to no good had proved true. Seeing Uncle Larry's kayak lashed to their deck had given them cause for concern, but now there could be no doubt.

After looking in vain in both cabins, Artie had practically fallen into the canoe from the deck of the catamaran when Casey pointed to what she noticed at the water's edge when the boat drifted away from the bank, swinging on its anchor. There was no doubt that the limp figure lying among the cypress roots at the water's edge was any other than her uncle; the only question remaining was whether or not he was still alive. The three of them paddled over in stunned silence, letting the canoe drift the last few feet while all eyes were fixed on Larry's motionless body. From this distance they could all see that his hands were tied behind his back and his feet were also bound together with what looked like a nylon mooring line from the boat.

Before the canoe touched the bank, her dad was already splashing through the knee-deep water to reach his brother's side, quickly tilting his head back to open his airway and then dropping an ear to his chest to listen for a heartbeat. Casey felt short of breath herself and felt her own heart racing while she waited for the verdict. She knew it would only take seconds; after all, her dad was a physician. But her fear was transformed to a flood of deep relief when he looked up with a tentative smile and announced: "He's alive! Help me untie him."

She and Jessica were beside him in the mud immediately, working on the knots in the heavy rope around his ankles and legs while her dad washed Larry's face with lake water dipped up in his hand and rolled him over far enough to get at the bindings on his wrists.

"He's taken a pretty good impact to the top of the head, Casey. It looks like they hit him with something hard and knocked him unconscious."

"Why did the bastards have to tie him up like this, too? Wasn't beating him up enough? What's wrong with people?"

"They're savages, that's what. It's a wonder they left him alive at all, but it looks like they left him like this so he would suffer first and then die, the low-life sons of bitches! But thank God he's alive, Casey! We could have been too late. It's not going to be easy, but we're going to have to get him into the canoe and then somehow get him back on board the boat without making things worse."

After her dad completed a quick examination, shifting Larry's limp body around and poking and prodding to check for signs of fractures or internal injury, he announced it was okay to move him. It took all three of them to lift him into the canoe; but with she and Jessica each taking a leg and her dad lifting from under his arms, they managed to gently set him down in the bottom between the seats and thwarts. With Larry taking up so much space, there was only room for her and Jessica in the boat. The two of them paddled while her dad swam, hanging on the stern, kicking with his legs to help out until they maneuvered back alongside the catamaran.

"How are we ever going to get him up there?" Jessica wondered. The distance from the waterline to the decks, even in the lower stern sections, was nearly four feet.

"We can't do it with brute strength alone, that's for sure. We sure don't want to risk dropping him and hurting him more. But I think the solution is on board, if they didn't take it."

Casey and Jessica waited in the canoe with Larry while her dad pulled himself out of the water onto the stern nets and boarded the boat to search the storage lockers. She could see that Larry was breathing steadily, but he was still unconscious.

"I found it! Now we can get him up here."

Casey and Jessica both looked up and saw the familiar Lifesling rescue device that Uncle Larry had shown them when they'd gone to visit him on the islands during their summer break the year before. As part of their safety drill before they set sail, he had explained how it worked and that it was the only way to safely retrieve someone who had fallen overboard, especially if they were injured and the seas were rough. A combination flotation device and harness, the Lifesling could be connected to a halyard, and with the big two-speed winch mounted in the center of the cockpit, anyone on board could lift an unconscious person from the water and move them safely back on deck. *But what good would it do them with the mast down and no halyard to attach it to*, she wondered?

Her dad had an idea. Even though the mast wasn't standing, Larry had blocked it up using two-by-fours to store it horizontally so that it ran down the centerline of the boat, parallel to the hulls. The blocking held it some three feet above the main crossbeams, so, he said, by using the mainsheet tackle attached to a strop around it, they should still be able to lift Larry high enough to get him over the aft beam and into the cockpit. It was tricky getting the Lifesling in position around Larry's chest without tipping the canoe, but with her dad lying flat on deck and reaching down to help, the three of them managed to do it. Then they lined the canoe around the hull and Casey and Jessica each took a line from it, one on the starboard stern deck and one on the port, so that they could hold the canoe steady while her dad went to the winch in the center of the main cockpit to begin cranking the handle, lifting Larry's dead weight inch by inch until his torso was high enough that they could pull him onto the deck. Casey and Jessica guided him down gently while her dad eased the tension, and finally Larry was resting firmly on the deck.

With Larry stretched on his back out on the smooth surface, her dad gave him a more thorough examination to check for further injuries. The most noticeable was a bruise on the side of his right cheek that was swollen and dark, and the lump on the top of his head where he had been hit by whatever hard object had rendered him unconscious.

"Of course it's impossible to say for sure without X-rays, but I'm satisfied he doesn't have any internal injuries or fractures. There doesn't seem to be any evidence of nerve damage or paralysis, but it's possible he could have a severe concussion, and could remain unconscious for a while."

"He seems to be breathing okay," Jessica said. "And he's not coughing up blood or anything like that."

"That's right. That's always a good sign, Jessica. I think we're just going to have to wait, but we've got to keep a close eye on him to make sure his airway stays open and keep a check on his pulse. Why don't you do that while Casey and I look around the boat to see what else is missing? We need to figure out what we're going to do next."

Casey followed her dad into the main cockpit area and they began opening the gear lockers on deck. The men from the fishing boat had been through every part of the boat, that was obvious, but it also appeared they'd been in a hurry and had not taken everything. What they did take, though, was enough to change the whole picture. Instead of a well-stocked, ocean-ready sailing vessel, Casey realized the catamaran now looked like a vessel that had been looted for valuables after a hurricane. Gone were all the ship's navigation instruments and electronics, as well as the extra gasoline tanks and fuel lines for the outboard motor that was now on the Johnboat Grant and Scully had taken upriver. Her dad said there had also been two extra anchors in one of the lockers, but those were missing, too, leaving only the main bow anchor that was still holding the boat to the muddy bottom of the oxbow lake. The looters had also taken Larry's expensive binoculars, the spearfishing gear, spare batteries and flashlights, as well as the kayak, its paddles, and practically all the food stores that had been aboard.

"They didn't leave us much, Casey, but at least they didn't take the sails or any of the rigging, as near as I can tell."

"Could we even sail, though, with that damage they did to the side of the hull?"

"I don't know. Larry will have to answer that, and he will know how to fix it when he comes to. The boat is not taking on water, that I can see, so I don't think it would be a problem just floating down the river, but I'm sure it's got to be fixed before we put to sea. We'd better hope Grant and Scully bring some extra gasoline from that cabin though. I don't know how we'll get down the river without it. And we'd better hope the food he said was there was still there. But at least we have a little, thanks to you for having the presence of mind to gather up everything that guy had in the camp before you left."

"It was the logical thing to do."

"Most people couldn't have survived what you went through, Casey. You're a brave young woman. I'm really proud of you."

While Jessica kept a close watch on Larry, Casey and her dad sorted through the mess in the cabins, reorganizing the galley so that they could cook a hot meal from those food items she'd brought. It was nearly dark by the time they had eaten and she was washing up the dishes down below when she was startled by an excited cry from Jessica: "I think he's coming to!"

Casey was on deck in an instant. When she looked at Larry she saw that he had moved one knee to a bent position, and was rolling his head back and forth. Her dad was already at his side, and Casey knelt there with him, reaching down to touch the side of her uncle's head that was not swollen and bruised. As soon as she did, Larry half-opened his eyes, squinting against the light of a battery-powered LED lamp her dad was holding on him.

"Uncle Larry! It's me, Casey! It's okay; you're going to be okay. I'm here with you, and Dad and Jessica are, too!"

Larry's pupils moved slowly beneath his half-closed lids, searching back and forth between the three faces hovering over him. He was clearly disoriented and confused, and she wasn't sure if he understood what she had said or recognized any of them. She took one of his hands in hers as her dad gently lifted his head.

"Larry, it looks like you took a pretty hard lick to the head. Just try to relax and don't move too much. We're here with you now and everything's going to be all right. Casey, why don't you or Jessica try and find a cup or something in the galley and get him some water? There should be water in the tank, just use the foot pump under the sink."

Jessica left to get the water. Before she returned with it, Larry was fully awake, but clearly dazed and disoriented.

"Where's Scully? What are you doing here, Doc? What's Casey doing here?"

"Scully will be back soon, Larry. We came here to find Casey, remember? And find her we did! Isn't that amazing? Casey's right here, see her? And I know you haven't forgotten her gorgeous friend, Jessica! Their friend Grant, who helped them get out of New Orleans, will be here, too, when he and Scully get back."

Casey saw the confusion in her Uncle Larry's eyes. It was as if he wasn't sure of what his brother was telling him, or maybe the blow to the head had caused him to forget her and Jessica. But he remembered Scully and he remembered her dad. He had always called her dad "Doc" since before she was born, according to him. Her dad was the older of the two brothers, and had always been the "normal" one who had cared about his grades, gone on to graduate from university, and later completed medical school to become a doctor. Uncle Larry had been a free spirit his entire adult life, running off to the Caribbean to crew on boats after a Spring Break trip to Florida during his first and only year of college. He had quickly learned to sail and became a delivery skipper, moving other people's boats all over the world, but also managing to take long voyages on his own boats in between jobs, due to the low cost of living on a boat with no mortgage, no wife and no children.

"We've gotta get out of here, Doc. Tell Scully to help you. He'll know what to do."

"Larry, Scully's not here yet. He'll be back tomorrow or the day after. When he comes, hopefully he and Grant will have more gas and food. Those men who did this to you took all our supplies."

"They were in a trawler. There were four of them, I think, and they were armed. There was nothing I could do." Larry pulled himself up to a half-lying, half-sitting position, resting on one elbow. He touched the bruise on the side of his face with his other hand, wincing in pain as he did so.

"I know, Larry. We saw them when we were on our way here. We heard a boat coming and we hid the canoe and watched them go by. They were heading upriver. I know it was the same boat, because they had your kayak on the deck. If I had known they had done this to you, I would have stopped them. But they're long gone now."

"No, they're coming back. They said they were. I thought one of them was going to shoot me. He fired a 12-gauge right over my head, and then one of them kicked me in the face. There was nothing I could do but lie there while they were going through all our stuff. I heard them talking and arguing about what to do. One of them wanted to shoot me right then. But the captain or whoever he was said no. They were arguing about what to do with the boat, too. They decided to leave it here while they went to some hideout they've got in the swamp, but they're coming back soon, Doc. They're coming back, and they plan to take the boat with them when they go back downriver to the coast. That's why we've got to get out of here. We've got to get going right now."

"We can't, Larry. Scully and Grant aren't here yet and they have the motor. They won't be back until, at the earliest, late tomorrow, or maybe the day after."

"What are you talking about, Doc? What do you mean they won't be back until tomorrow? Why aren't they with you? You found Casey and Jessica? Why didn't you all come back together?"

"I wanted us to," Jessica said, "but Grant wanted to try and go to that cabin of his and get his stuff."

"And it's a good thing they did, too," Casey said. "Without the supplies they're bringing, we would have nothing now that the boat has been ransacked."

"But we can't wait until tomorrow. When those men come back, they're coming to get this boat, and if they find us here, they'll kill us all. Do you even have my shotgun, or does Scully still have it?"

"Scully has it, Larry. But we've got something even better. It's a long story, but you'll see. First, we've got to make sure you're okay. I'm pretty sure you've got a concussion. Are you feeling dizzy or nauseated? Do you even know what they hit you with?"

"I don't remember anything about that, Doc. I was just lying on the deck, listening to them talk while they tore through the boat taking all our stuff. I figured they were going to shoot me anyway when they were done. The last thing I remember was hearing them having a disagreement about that, and one of them saying the alligators would take care of me. They must have hit me upside the head after that."

"Yep, and I guess that's what they had in mind. They left you for dead, tied hands and feet and lying in the mud over there on the bank. I guess the gators *would* have gotten you eventually if we hadn't come along."

"It must be my lucky day, then," Larry smiled, still grimacing in pain as he did so.

Casey bent down and gave him a gentle hug and a kiss on the forehead, and Jessica did the same. "I'm sorry they hurt you, Uncle Larry, but I'm so glad you're alive!"

"It seems like pain has been my middle name ever since the lights went out," Larry said, looking at the slowly healing wound in his forearm where a machete had slashed it to the bone.

"Dad told me about that. You've had a rough time but maybe all that's over now. Soon we will be sailing! This boat is *amazing*, Uncle Larry!"

"It was a lot nicer before those bastards came aboard." Larry suddenly remembered the impact from the fishing boat and strained to see the damage from where he was lying. "How bad *is* it, Doc?"

"It's not good, but I know you can fix it, Larry."

"If they didn't take my damned epoxy, too."

"I'll look and see."

"Don't worry about that right now. It can be fixed. The main thing we need to worry about is getting out of here before they come back. If we lose this boat, we lose our only hope of survival."

"But we just told you, Grant and Scully are not back yet. We can't leave without them!" Jessica said.

"Of course not. Larry wouldn't think of that."

"Actually, I *would*, Doc. Scully would understand, and he would want us to get out of here before those men come back. We could rendezvous later."

"How, Larry? How would Grant and Scully ever find us?"

"We could hang around somewhere just off the coast. Scully would know to look for me there. He would know we would have had to go downriver. There's no other way we *could* go in this boat."

"But they've ransacked the boat, Larry. They took all the food, the navigation instruments, and who knows what else, and we don't even have the outboard, even if they hadn't taken the rest of the gas. How would we even leave if we wanted to?"

"We're not," Jessica said. "I'm *not* leaving without Grant!"

Jessica's crush on Grant was clearly at least as strong as her own had ever been, Casey now realized. She began to wonder just how close they'd actually gotten during the many days they'd spent alone together while searching for her. She figured she would find out how Grant felt soon enough, once they were all together again on the boat. She didn't want to leave without Grant either, or without Scully, for that matter. She wasn't surprised her Uncle Larry had suggested it, though, at least as a temporary dodge to get the boat to safety. She understood how important it was that they not lose the boat; if they did, they would lose *everything*. But it occurred to her that there was another way:

"Why do we have to run from them?" she asked. "Why should we just let four bad men determine what we do? There are four of us, too, even without Grant and Scully."

Larry just laughed at this. "Casey, you have no idea what you're saying. These men will *kill* us if they come back here and we're still on this boat. Yeah, there are four of us, but I've got a bad arm, not to mention a headache. Your dad used to be a pretty good shot when we went bird hunting with your grandpa, but as he just said, Scully has my shotgun, and I'm sorry, but even if he didn't, I just don't think you realize what kind of men we're dealing with."

"You're wrong on the last part, little brother," her dad said, and filled him in on just what she and Jessica had been through since leaving New Orleans. Uncle Larry was dumbfounded upon hearing the full story, especially the details of her ordeal with Derek and what she had to do to escape. But his face lit up when he learned of the weaponry she had liberated from her dead abductor's camp.

"We can set up an ambush," Casey said. "You know we'll hear them coming with that loud old motor a long time before they get here. They'll be expecting to come back to an empty catamaran, thinking you are already dead. We have all these woods surrounding the boat to hide in and they'll never dream what they're about to run into. With the AK-47 and Derek's other hunting rifle, we'll have the advantage of both firepower and range, as well as the element of surprise. They'll never even know what hit them!"

"Damn, Casey! I know you did what you had to do to escape that Derek guy, but when did you become so eager for a fight? It doesn't bother you to murder these guys in cold blood?"

"It's not murder, Uncle Larry. The way they beat you and left you for the alligators would have been murder—if we hadn't come along when we did. Taking all our supplies and then planning to come back to take the whole boat is as bad as murder, and would effectively seal our fate if they got away with it. I'm not *wanting* a fight at all, just being realistic about what it takes to survive the way things are now."

"You've got a point, I'll give you that, but even so, if we go through with this, it's not going to be without risks. Ambush or not, there's a lot of potential for something to go wrong. You all need to understand that going into it."

"Well, little brother, if we don't do it, we're liable to have to fight them anyway, and on less advantageous terms. You know yourself that without that motor, it will be hell getting this boat back down the river, and they'll surely catch up to us."

"Yeah, I was thinking that. We don't know how long we'll have to wait for Scully and Grant to get here. Even if they were here now and we had the motor, I'm not sure we'd make the coast before those guys get back here and find the boat missing. Without open water and wind to fill the sails, we don't stand a chance."

Casey and her dad helped Uncle Larry to his feet. She noticed that both of the brothers looked much older and more weary than she'd ever seen them. Her dad looked up the river in the direction from which they'd come and swore. "If only I had known. I practically had them in my sights when they went by. I could have wasted them all before they even knew what hit them."

"Well, I guess you'll get a second chance at that, Doc. Now, if we're going to do this, we need to make a plan quickly. By the time we hear the boat coming, it'll be too late, so we'd better all know what we're going to do and be prepared to do it immediately."

SEVEN

Sitting in the Johnboat, the bow tied loosely to an overhanging branch to keep it from being swept back downriver in the current, Scully waited while contemplating the surprising diversity of life surrounding him in this riverine forest. It simply amazed him that there was so much bush in this country that he had always pictured as an endless landscape of rich capitalist development and urban sprawl. Until he saw it for himself, no one could have convinced him that a person could travel here for days by boat and see only trees. It was as if the Americans had overlooked this low-lying, swampy forest, or maybe they simply hadn't gotten around to leveling it yet; Scully didn't know. It was also surprising to him that there were no villages of poor people living in simple huts along the river's banks, as there certainly would have been in any such place in the island nations where he had spent his life. Larry and Artie had said there would be many desperate refugees fleeing to places like this from the cities, but if there were, they had not made it here yet. Maybe most of them were dead already. Scully would not be surprised. From what he had seen when they sailed to

New Orleans, these people had no idea what to do when their electricity stopped working and their cars stopped going. All that money they worshiped and spent their lives pursuing could do nothing for them now. Instead of returning to the land where simple people could eke out a living from the earth and water, they robbed and killed each other in their desperation to continue living an unsustainable lifestyle they were not willing to give up. Scully just shook his head at the thought, especially as he sat there in the boat surrounded by so much life.

Waiting there on this small, obscure river, Scully could enjoy a few moments of peace and tranquility, turning his mind away from the carnage he'd seen and the brushes with violence he'd already survived in the sea journey to get here. The search that brought them to this country was over, and soon he would be back on the open seas he loved, sailing the trade winds among the sun-drenched islands of the endless summer latitudes. He knew that between himself and Larry, they could find safe refuge someplace better, but it was reassuring to him as he sat in the Johnboat and waited that if need be, he could live in this bush just fine.

He was staring into the semi-clear waters, watching a large fish of a type he had never seen and wishing he had a spear with which to impale it, when the stillness was shattered by the thunderous report of a rifle. The sound had certainly come from upriver, in the direction Grant had paddled, and judging by the volume he was sure that it was close enough to be about the same distance Grant said they were from the cabin before he'd set off alone in the canoe to reconnoiter. Scully couldn't be sure, but the report was so loud that he thought it could have been from a high-powered rifle rather than the pistol-caliber carbine Grant was carrying. He knew sounds could be deceptive in a forest, though, so there was no way to tell. The one thing he *was* sure of was that Grant had to be close to whoever fired that weapon, if he did not do it himself.

Scully listened as the normal sounds of the river gradually resumed, first with a few tentative birdcalls and then the background buzz and chirp of insects. A second shot never came, either from the original shooter or in the form of return fire from a different weapon. Grant should have had enough time to reach the cabin and start heading back, but there was no sign of him, and now the sound of the gunshot raised all kinds of possibilities. Had he shot at someone who was looting the cabin, or had he been ambushed by someone already living there? Had he fired the carbine as a warning to someone or perhaps simply shot at a deer or other game animal? Scully trusted that whatever the answer was, Grant had not carelessly discharged a round for no reason. Though he had only met him the afternoon before, he was a good judge of character and could tell Grant was not like those people who were dying in the cities. This was a young man who had been smart enough to get Casey and Jessica out of New Orleans, despite great difficulty and risk to himself. And while he hadn't spent his life living off the land, as Scully had spent much of his, he seemed unafraid and comfortable traveling in the bush and on the river.

Scully considered his options when Grant did not show up shortly after the sound of the gunshot. Not knowing for sure who fired it or why, he didn't want to simply start the outboard and motor upstream to the cabin. The sound of the motor would not only alert others to his presence, but would impair his own ability to hear signs of danger as he approached. He knew he couldn't stealthily paddle such an ungainly boat upstream either, so he decided the best approach would be to walk. Grant had told him the cabin was on the left bank from the perspective of one traveling upstream, so Scully untied the bow painter and used the paddle to ferry the boat across the river, where he secured it to a sturdy tree growing at the water's edge.

The bank on this side of the Bogue Chitto was steep, its slopes mostly composed of red clay that was slippery and wet from seep springs dripping from somewhere in the vegetation above. Scully grabbed his machete, cradled the Mossberg shotgun in his left arm, and began climbing. Since he never wore shoes, his bare feet were toughened to surfaces much rougher than this soft clay and mud, so getting up the bank was easier with his toes digging in for extra grip. Grant had warned him that there were venomous snakes in these river bottom forests, so he took care to look before each placement of a hand or foot. Because of the steepness of the bank and the impenetrable undergrowth near the water, it was impossible to follow the river by walking along the bank unless he used the machete, but that would make far too much noise. It would be quicker to shortcut directly across the wide looping bends the stream took, anyway, though Scully was aware that in doing so, he might miss seeing Grant if even now he was paddling back downstream to where he was supposed to be waiting. If that were the case, he was sure Grant would wait for him, but first he wanted to find that cabin and see what was going on there.

Weaving under and around briar patches and thickets, Scully moved quietly through the woods in a direction he guessed would intersect the next bend of the river. Despite his frequent stops to look and listen, and the care he took to avoid making noise, he quickly reached the riverbank again just where he expected it to be and followed it as closely as the underbrush permitted where it began a long, sweeping loop in the other direction. Knowing he was getting close, Scully held the shotgun at the balance point in his left hand, ready to drop the machete and bring it to his shoulder in an instant if needed. When the long bend at last began to straighten out, he could see an opening ahead of him in the forest and knew it must be the place where the cabin stood.

He still had not heard another manmade sound since the single rifle shot, so he had no idea what to expect. As he approached the edge of the clearing he could see the wood-planked building. Rather than walk right to it, he worked his way closer to the river to look for Grant's canoe. When he reached a vantage point that allowed him to see the riverbank he discovered there was no canoe in sight, but he could see footprints in the mud and the telltale drag mark of a canoe hull. Scully took that as a good sign, because it likely meant that Grant had made it here and had already headed back downstream. If so, he needed to quickly make his way back to the boat as well. But before he did, he wanted to have a look at the cabin himself. He stepped out into the clearing and made his way down to the water's edge first to inspect the tracks. As soon as he was close it was apparent that there was more to the story than he'd thought. Grant's hiking boot prints were clearly visible in the mud, but there was another set of footprints as well, made by an athletic shoe of a similar size. Scully looked down the deserted river for any other sign but saw nothing. He then turned to the cabin to see if he might find some clue there, but as soon as he started up the hill he was stopped in his tracks by a shout:

"Drop that gun and freeze right there, asshole!" the voice from the cabin commanded.

Scully did as he was told, knowing he had screwed up and dropped his guard. He had been too focused on Grant's whereabouts to completely assess the situation. He should have made sure the cabin was empty before stepping out of the woods, but it was too late for that now that he found himself standing in the open, the barrel of a rifle pointed at him from a window in the back of the cabin.

"Get down on the ground! Away from that shotgun and keep your hands where I can see them!" the person pointing the gun at him continued.

Scully thought this man must be a cop of some kind, the way he was talking, but after he did what he was told and got down on the ground, the person holding the rifle on him stepped outside. He was as young as Grant, if not even younger. He had wavy brown hair, but no beard or mustache, and was dressed in a T-shirt and jeans. Scully figured he might have learned to bark orders like that from watching action movies, but he had a rifle and it was pointed his way, so the dialogue mattered little. He could see that the weapon was equipped with a telescopic sight, and immediately concluded it was the high-powered rifle he'd heard earlier.

"Who are you, and what are you doing here?"

Scully looked up as the young man stepped closer. He didn't look like a person accustomed to killing people, but considering the craziness he'd seen already, it would be unwise to doubt he would pull the trigger. "Dem call I Scully. I am from de island. I don't wan' no trouble in dis place, mon."

"Why are you here then?"

"I comin' here wid my friend, Grant. He seh dis he cabin, mon."

"I know who he is and I know this is his cabin. He was supposed to be here with two girls, Casey and Jessica, when we got here. But the first we've seen of him was today, and he was alone. So if you are with him, why weren't you in the canoe when he got here?"

"I waitin' in de boat wid de motor, mon. I waitin' while Grant check out de cabin wid de canoe. Nevah know what trouble you find in dese times, mon. I waitin' an' I hear de gunshot an' when Grant he not comin' bok, I walkin' here to see."

"I know about the boat. We heard the motor coming upriver. Joey and Grant have gone to get it. But Grant didn't say anything about *you* being with him. So where are Jessica and Casey?"

"De girls not wid us, mon. De girls dem wait down de river on de big boat. He only want to come here to an' get supplies he havin' in de cabin. We not lookin' for trouble, mon. Only comin' here for de t'ings dat belong to Grant."

The young man's reply was interrupted by the sound of the outboard motor starting up in the distance. Scully realized this man must have been telling the truth about his friend and Grant going back downstream to get the boat. Right after it cranked he could tell the boat was running back upriver as fast as the motor would go.

"You stay where you are and don't move. I'll shoot if you try anything."

Scully did as he was told and waited. It was only a matter of minutes before the boat reached the bank in front of the cabin, and from where he was lying on the ground he could see that Grant was at the helm of the outboard, while another young white man sat in the bow, covering him with the lever-action carbine Grant had been carrying earlier. Scully knew he must be this Joey that the other one spoke of. When the bow of the boat ran up on the sand, he hopped out with the gun and told Grant to shut down the engine. Grant's face fell as he took in the scene and saw Scully's predicament.

The one called Joey seemed just as shocked. Scully realized he must have thought Grant was alone. He ordered Grant out of the boat, still pointing the carbine at him. "Who is this, Zach?"

"I don't know, he says he's with Grant. He says he's from some island I've never heard of."

"Dominica," Scully said, meeting Joey's eyes as the white man walked closer, scrutinizing him as he apparently tried to decide if he believed this or not. Joey then turned back to Grant.

"Is this true? Why didn't you mention this freak earlier, when you told me all that bullshit about how you were by yourself? Why should I believe anything you told me is true if you were lying about that?"

"I told you all I know about Jessica and Casey. Yeah, this is Scully, that's about all I know about him, I don't even know his last name. I just met him on the river yesterday.

He's here because he has a boat; it's as simple as that. I told you I found the boat, but truth is, Scully found me. I was wasn't getting anywhere fast trying to paddle against the current up this river, and then he came along in that boat and when he saw me, he stopped to talk. When I told him my parents owned a cabin up here stocked with food and supplies, he offered me a ride the rest of the way in exchange for a few days' worth of food. He's stranded here in this country because of the pulse, and he is just trying to survive."

Scully watched as Joey reached down to pick up the Mossberg that was still lying on the muddy ground where he'd dropped it at Zach's orders.

"Is he telling the truth? Why were you here in America in the first place? Are you an illegal or something? And where did you get that boat and motor? And what about this shotgun? Did you steal all this shit?"

From what Grant said to the one called Joey, Scully quickly picked up on the fact that the two of them somehow knew each other, and that Grant didn't want him to know their plan or that the two of them were more than chance acquaintances. Ever quick-witted and experienced in maintaining a calm composure under the stress of dealing with the police and other officials, Scully lost no time filling in the blanks with a story of his own:

"I am from Dominica, mon. I don' know not'ing about dis country. First time I comin' here; working crew on de container ship, mon. An' den all de lights go out before de ship, she leave New Orleans. No GPS an' no radio, so de coptain, he seh we cannot sail. Some of de crew dem stay in de port, but lots of problem an' de men fighting an' stealin' food. I an' I knowin' a mon is not safe in dat city, but I see de mouth to dis big river on de way in an' a mon in de crew who know dat place seh on dis river is not'ing but de bush. I comin' here because to me, de bush is home, mon."

"So you stole a gun and a boat?"

"No mon, I don' steal it. I havin' American dollars and some ganja, too, in my seabag. I bought de gun an' de boat from some mon who live by de lake in dat place. He got a lotta boat an' dat boat de oldest he got an' he don' need her. He got a lotta gun too, but he like de ganja smoke so we make de trade on dat Mossberg."

"I can't imagine anybody would be stupid enough to sell a boat or a gun right now, but I couldn't care less whether you stole it or not. I just want to know the truth about why you're here and I want to know where Jessica and Casey are."

"He said they're downriver waiting on a boat," Zach said.

"*What?* What the fuck did you just say, Zach?"

Scully saw the look of surprise on Joey's face. That's when he knew Grant had told him something completely different.

"I said he told me that Jessica and Casey were somewhere downriver, waiting on a boat. When he came sneaking up in the yard with that shotgun, I got the drop on him and asked him who the fuck he was and what the fuck he was doing here, and he said he was with Grant, and that this was Grant's cabin. I told him I knew that and we were here looking for Jessica and Casey, and he knew exactly who I was talking about. He said they weren't here, but were downriver, waiting on a boat."

At this, Joey turned on Grant with the shotgun leveled at his chest, calling him a liar and ordering them both into the cabin. Scully had no choice but to follow Grant inside. He felt really stupid for what he had done, carelessly approaching the cabin and letting such a young and inexperienced man, really just a boy, get the drop on him. He knew that if they couldn't talk their way out of this they were going to have to turn the tables somehow, but he hoped it wouldn't come to that.

When they entered the dark interior of the cabin, the first thing Scully noticed in the muted light streaming through two small windows was the motorcycle, and he correctly deduced that it was how these two had gotten here from New Orleans. There was a simple wooden table with matching benches that had been pushed aside to make room for the bike, and Joey motioned for them to sit while he and his friend stood, their weapons still in hand.

Scully remembered Grant telling him about trouble with Jessica's boyfriend in New Orleans. From what he'd said, he never expected to see him again, especially not way out here. Jessica had left him behind in the city to go with Grant and Casey, and now, after meeting him, Scully could certainly see why. Grant had made up some story to tell him and Joey would have believed it if he had not screwed it up by letting the other one know he knew the girls, too. Scully felt bad about making the situation worse, but Grant had said little of the boyfriend other than that there had been an argument, and had not mentioned his name, so he had no way of knowing what he should or shouldn't say when confronted by the other one. He listened as Grant answered Joey's questions that were essentially an interrogation at gunpoint.

It quickly became apparent that even though he'd refused to leave with them in the beginning, when Grant had invited him to join them here, Joey was now obsessed with getting back with Jessica and believed she wanted him back just as much. Scully knew why he was so attracted to her. She was gorgeous, and men would do crazy things to be with a woman like that, but Scully could tell that his motivation was more jealousy and anger than anything else. Joey was enraged that she'd left with Grant, that she'd trusted his judgment more than his own, yet Grant had not succeeded in getting her here. Joey had come because he couldn't stand it that she'd defied him, and also because his world was crumbling around him and he had no idea how to deal with it. Now he was demanding to know where she was, and if she was not okay then Grant was going to be the one he blamed and held accountable. Like most of the Americans he'd encountered since they arrived on these shores, Joey and his friend Zach were completely unhinged by the circumstances they found themselves in and practically on the edge of breakdown. Scully knew they were liable to do anything if Joey didn't get the one thing he wanted: *Jessica*.

EIGHT

When Grant had closed the door to the cabin and made his way back down the riverbank to where he'd left the canoe, he thought that whoever had been living there wasn't around and that his quick investigation had gone unseen. He was about to shove off to go tell Scully what he'd found when a bullet tore into the water next to him in a huge splash and a rifle shot rang out from somewhere in the woods above. Grant realized in an instant that he'd made a big mistake and had not been cautious enough. He glanced at the carbine he'd already laid in the bottom of the canoe but thought better of reaching for it and instead threw himself to the ground, crawling across the wet sand to try to find cover under the riverbank.

But the shout that followed the rifle report was even more shocking than having a bullet strike the water so close by. Whoever had fired it knew his name! He lifted his head just enough to see two figures emerge from the woods and start down the bank in his direction. One of then looked vaguely familiar, but he couldn't place him; but the other one—the one carrying the rifle that had just missed him, whether intentionally or not—was Jessica's ex-boyfriend, Joey! The barrel was even then pointed right at him, and Grant wondered if Joey was walking closer simply to ensure that he would not miss the second time. It was easy to imagine that he might do such a thing, considering the terms on which they'd parted the last time they'd met. But Joey didn't shoot; he wanted answers instead. At the time, Grant thought he did a good job of throwing him off, as the last thing he wanted was for these two to know where Jessica and Casey really were.

"I've been wondering where you were," Joey had said. "We were expecting to find you and Jessica and Casey here when we got here, but I could tell as soon as we looked around that no one's been here since the blackout. So where is she?"

"She's safe, I'm sure of that, but I haven't seen her or Casey in over a week."

"What do you mean you haven't seen them in over a week? If you haven't seen them, how the fuck do you know she's safe? The only reason they left New Orleans was to come here with you, so why aren't they with you?"

"We did leave New Orleans together. And we almost made it all the way here, too, but we couldn't cross the state line into Mississippi on the bicycles. There was a roadblock."

"Zach and I didn't see a roadblock, and we rode all the way here on a motorcycle."

"Well, you probably got through before they set it up. I don't know when you left New Orleans, but it took us three days to get to the state line." Grant could tell Joey was thinking about this, considering whether it was possible he was telling the truth. It was plausible, because even if the two of them had left the city a day or two after he left with the girls, they could have traveled this far in just a few hours on a motorbike, even considering the stalled cars and other obstacles that would be easy enough to get around on a two-wheeler. Grant didn't know for sure when the road-block that really had stopped them had been set up, but it was possible it wasn't there when Joey and his friend rode across the state line. It was also easy to imagine that the two of them passed along the same road he and the girls were on without seeing them, perhaps after they'd turned off one evening to camp, as they had done more than once.

"So what happened at the roadblock? Why are you here in a canoe and why aren't Jessica and Casey with you?"

"They told us they weren't permitting anyone across the state line from Louisiana unless they had a picture I.D. to prove they were residents here. None of us did, of course, so they wouldn't let us in even though my parents own this cabin and land, which is obviously in Mississippi. They told us about a shelter south of here on the Louisiana side that had been set up for refugees from New Orleans and the rest of the region, and said we could stay there and that there was food, water, and security. I was against the idea, but since we couldn't continue on to the cabin on the bikes, Casey and Jessica insisted that we go check it out. They were really getting scared after all that we had seen on the ride north, and with the promise of a safe refuge, they out-voted my plan to try to get here some other way. I told them I was sure we could find a canoe somewhere and paddle upriver to get here, but they didn't want to try that."

"So, you're telling me that's where they are now?" Joey demanded.

Grant had been thinking fast at the time, making up the story as he went along. He had to come up with a believable explanation of how he got separated from the girls. The last thing he wanted to do was let these two find out about the catamaran, and that all of them were planning to sail away from America for the foreseeable future. He didn't want them to think he'd abandoned them or that something had happened to them, either, especially not to Jessica. If Joey thought he was to blame, Grant knew there was no telling what he might do. An official shelter seemed like the most logical explanation, even though, to his knowledge, no such shelters had really been opened.

"Yes, as far as I know. I rode there with them even though I didn't want to go near a place like that. I tried to talk them out of it, but they weren't interested in my plan. I told them I didn't think the officials would be watching the river, and that I knew where we could probably find a canoe. I thought it would be possible to paddle upstream from the Louisiana side and get here, but they didn't want to try it, and I couldn't change their minds. So we rode on and when we got close to the shelter we hid the bikes in the woods and walked the rest of the way. The shelter was on the campus of a high school. It was crowded and noisy, but there was food and water. I had been in a shelter like that after Hurricane Katrina and I had hated all the rules and the crowded conditions then. I stayed there for nearly a week, trying to get them to change their minds and come with me, but they felt safe and didn't want to leave. I didn't want us to split up, but I had to get out of there; I just couldn't take it. I managed to sneak out at night and then I got back to my bike and rode until I came to the first bridge crossing over the Bogue Chitto. I thought I would be able to find a canoe at somebody's abandoned river camp, and I did. I found this one and here I am."

"Bullshit! You didn't paddle all the way up here against that current. We heard a motor, Grant. Where is the boat? Are Jessica and Casey in it right now?"

"Okay, look, Joey. There is a Johnboat. I didn't mention it because I *am* here in the canoe. Shortly after I found the canoe, I was having a hell of a time fighting my way upstream paddling by myself. As luck would have it, the second day I found a Johnboat with an old outboard at another deserted camp and managed to get it running. I towed the canoe behind it, just in case, and it was a good thing I did, since the motor just ran out of gas right before I got here. That's why you heard it. It's just a short distance downstream, but no, Jessica and Casey are not with me, I swear. I'm telling you the truth about that, Joey."

Grant had thought that Joey bought the story. He was clearly disappointed, as he had obviously concluded that

Grant's arrival here meant Jessica must be nearby. Grant didn't know what was going to happen next, but he had a feeling Joey and his friend weren't going to simply go away just because Jessica wasn't with him. They needed the cabin and its supplies and weren't going to give them up, whether the rightful owner was there to claim them or not. Now Joey also wanted the boat he'd heard, and Grant regretted that he had not shut down the engine much farther downstream, out of earshot. Then he could have omitted that part of his story and his claim to have paddled all the way might have been believable. But what was done was done. Joey picked up the lever-action carbine from the canoe and passed his scoped rifle to his friend, telling him to keep an eye on the cabin until he got back.

"Okay, dickhead. Let's go get that motorboat first. We'll tow it up here behind the canoe if we have to. Then you can tell me exactly how to get to that fuckin' shelter. Jessica is obviously just confused and needs someone to explain the situation to her. She'll be glad to come here now that she knows I'm here."

When they had left, with Zach guarding the cabin and Joey sitting in the stern of the canoe with the carbine covering Grant in the bow, Grant had deliberately made as much noise as he could get away with, splashing the paddle and talking loudly. He had hoped this would give Scully enough of a heads-up so that he would be ready when they got to where he was supposed to be waiting in the John-boat. Of course, when they got there, the boat was empty and Scully was nowhere in sight. And although Grant had claimed the outboard engine had run out of gas and quit on its own, when Joey hopped aboard and checked the tank he found out otherwise. He pulled the starter rope and it fired right up, causing him to look at Grant with renewed distrust. With the canoe trailing behind, they had motored back to the cabin where both were quite surprised to see Zach standing there with his rifle pointed at a dark figure lying spread-eagled on the ground, wild dreadlocks draping about his face as he raised his head enough to see them get out of the boat.

When Zach told Joey what had happened and what Scully had already said, Grant knew he had a problem. Their stories didn't match regarding the Johnboat or the whereabouts of Jessica and Casey, but it wasn't Scully's fault. He didn't know anything of Joey or Jessica's history with him. Grant simply hadn't thought about Joey anymore after he left New Orleans until today, and there had been so many other things to talk about in the short time he had spent with Scully. Even when he told him of her having a fight with her boyfriend before they left the city, he'd never mentioned Joey by name because he didn't think it mattered.

It now became apparent to Grant that his elaborate story about the refugee shelter had fallen apart in the face of what Scully had already let slip to Zach. Having no way of knowing Zach's friend was the boyfriend Jessica had left in New Orleans, when he heard their names mentioned along with Grant's he naturally assumed they all knew each other and casually said they were waiting on the boat. Of course that was completely different from Grant's version of where they were, so now they were both seated in the cabin, facing an enraged Joey with his armed accomplice, and the game was up.

"You're a lying son of a bitch, Grant! I should have beaten the crap out of you in New Orleans and never let Jessica out of my sight."

"Look, Joey. I'm sorry about what happened in New Orleans, but I was just trying to help Casey and Jessica get away from an impossible situation there. You know how it was. That's why you and your friend left, too. You can see for yourself how isolated this place is, and you know by now that what I said about having everything we need here is true."

"Well what good is it doing them, Grant? Why weren't the three of you here when we got here, like the note Casey left for her dad said you would be? The only reason I came here was because of Jessica. Otherwise, Zach and I could have gone anywhere we wanted with that motorcycle."

"You could have come with us in the first place when we were all trying to get you to. That's what Jessica wanted. Now you can see why I wanted to bring them here; there's plenty of food here and it's still relatively safe. Hey, I don't mind that you're using the place and the supplies. There's enough to share. I just came here to get what we could carry in that boat and canoe because it's going to help Jessica and Casey survive."

"So why the fuck did you make up all that bullshit about them being in a refugee camp if you knew they were somewhere else all along?"

Grant knew there wasn't any point in trying to create another story. He decided to tell the truth, because in the end, it was Jessica's decision if she wanted to give Joey the time of day again or not. He didn't need to waste time here with these two idiots pointing guns at him and Scully when they had a ride waiting for them downriver. No matter what he did or said, it was clear that it was not going to be easy for him to extricate himself and Scully from this messy situation. Maybe it would be best to let the men come along to the boat. Then they would have to face Artie and Larry, both of whom were armed; not to mention an angry Jessica, whom Grant was certain would not be happy to see this clown again, much less let him come aboard with them. So he decided to tell Joey the truth.

"Okay, I didn't really know what to do, to tell you the truth. What would you do if somebody shot a rifle bullet right past your head into the water and then came out of the woods pointing a gun at you? I didn't know what to tell you. But truth is, Jessica and Casey are fine. Casey's father and her uncle have sailed all the way here from the Virgin Islands to find her. If you've been dating Jessica long at all, you know she went down there last summer with Casey for a week of sailing with Casey's Uncle Larry. Anyway, he's got some kind of big ocean-going catamaran, and that's what they came here on. Scully came with them."

"Another fuckin' lie, huh? All that stuff about working on a container ship and buying that boat and shotgun, that was just a lie, huh, *Scully?*"

"Yeah, it's a lie," Grant said. "Scully is a good friend of Casey's Uncle Larry. But what I told you about us not being able to get to the cabin on the bicycles was true. A lot happened in the meantime, but basically we ended up on the lower Pearl River in canoes and that's where Casey's dad and Scully found us. They were on their way to this cabin when they did, because they first went to New Orleans and found the note Casey left for her dad with the map I drew to the cabin on it."

"So where exactly are they now, and you better not make up any more bullshit. I'm not fuckin' around, Grant."

"They're with Casey's dad, and the three of them should be on her Uncle Larry's boat by now. It was not far downriver from where we met up. The plan was that they would wait there while Scully and I made the run up here to the cabin in the Johnboat. With all of us on the catamaran, we knew we would need any extra food we could get."

"The catamaran is in the river? How far downriver?"

"I don't know exactly, maybe a hundred miles, or a little more with all the twists and turns. Scully knows where it is, I haven't seen it; but it's on the lower Pearl River, in the area called the Honey Island Swamp."

"I've been there," Zach said, "a long time ago, fishing with my grandpa."

"It took us all day yesterday and most of today to get here motoring upstream," Grant continued. "There are lots of shoals and logs across the channel in this upper part of the Bogue Chitto, but once it runs into the Pearl it's deep and wide open. We planned on staying here overnight and getting back down there to the boat tomorrow."

"Well, just how big *is* this catamaran?"

"Scully can answer that better than I can. Like I said, I haven't seen it, but they sailed it across the Caribbean and the Gulf of Mexico to get to New Orleans, so it's big enough."

"De boat thirty-six feet long an' twenty-two feet on de beam. She got de cabin in both hull, but she got lotta deck, too."

"So, it's big enough that all of you were going to sail away on it? That's what, six of you, with Casey's dad and uncle?"

"Yes," Grant said. "Artie said it was big enough."

"That's a lot of people living on one fuckin' boat for a long time, but whatever. Anyway, here's what we're going to do. We're going to load everything from the cabin we can fit into that canoe and tow it just like you planned. Whatever won't fit you can keep. Like you said, it's your stuff anyway and this is your home away from home. If you don't try to fuck with me I'm not even going to give you the ass whipping you deserve for all the trouble you've caused me and the lies you just told me to my face. No, I'm just going to forget all that and leave you here where you wanted to be so bad ever since the power went out. But Rastaman here goes with us. He knows where that catamaran is and he's going to show us, if he values his life." Joey glared at Scully: "You got that, Bob Marley?"

"That's crazy, Joey! If you leave me here, what are you going to tell Jessica? You think she's just going to want you back after what happened in New Orleans? How are you going to explain why you and your buddy Zach are in the boat with Scully and I'm not with you?"

"Easy! You had an accident and it was really awful, but there was nothing anyone could do. Mr. Scully may have one, too, if he doesn't do what we tell him."

"They'll never believe that horseshit. They're going to know immediately you're lying and they're going to think you killed me to get that Johnboat. Casey's dad and uncle are not going to want you two on board anyway, even if Jessica did. What do you know about sailing?"

"I don't know jack shit about it, but they're gonna want us on board, trust me. I've got something they're gonna need when they get where they're going. Toss me the bag, Zach!"

Zach reached for a small canvas shoulder bag that was piled up with their gear and pitched it to Joey. When he unzipped it, he held the open top at an angle so Grant could see. Inside the bag was a plastic freezer bag full of cash; several packages of crisp twenties as well as a fat wad of hundreds. Grant figured it was several thousand dollars, at least. Where he got so much cash was anyone's guess, but Jessica had told him that Joey came from a wealthy family. Maybe for him it was just gambling money he kept in his house for weekend trips to the casinos in Biloxi.

"This may not be much good around here, but there's gotta be somewhere that wasn't affected by this blackout. If Casey's uncle is the sailor they claim he is, he'll know that, and he'll know where to go. And he'll know that when he gets there, he's going to need some of this to live."

There was no doubt it was a sizeable stash, but Grant knew it wouldn't matter. From what they'd discussed that one night they all camped together on the riverbank, where Larry Drager was planning to go, money wouldn't be all that useful even in normal times. Besides that, the collapse of the grid was likely so widespread that paper currency was worthless everywhere.

"He's not going to care about your fucking money, and neither is Jessica!"

"We'll see. Meanwhile, you can enjoy your cabin in the woods and think about how much fun Zach and I are going to be having with your two girlfriends on some nice beach on the islands."

Grant knew that Joey was leaving him there because he didn't want him around Jessica or Casey. But he had another good reason for taking just Scully. Scully knew exactly where the catamaran was anchored because he'd seen it, and it would be a lot easier for the two of them to keep one man under guard than two, especially on a long river trip in a small boat. Joey wasn't taking any chances, or so he thought. But Grant was already thinking fast and he knew Joey was making at least one major mistake, and that was leaving him here alive and unhurt. The other mistake was that he was vastly underestimating Scully. Grant already knew from what little time he'd spent with him that the islander was a man of diverse skills and knowledge, a resourceful survivor who would likely find a way to prevail, even outnumbered two to one. He had to keep reminding himself of these two things and refrain from protesting the arrangement too much. It was best to let Joey think he was resigned to his fate of being stranded here. If Joey thought he had won already, he would go away sooner.

Before they left the cabin, Zach disconnected the fuel line from the carburetor of the motorcycle, draining the gas from the three-gallon tank into the plastic tank for the outboard. The idiots had already burned all the gas he had stashed there for the generator, probably running it to power a fan and lights twenty-four/seven. Grant knew he was doing it not only to make sure they had as much gasoline as possible for their trip downriver, but also to keep him from using the bike to leave. Joey also made a point of showing him the one and only key to the bike before dropping it into the bag with the money and closing the zipper.

"Don't be fucking with my Harley! I might come back for it some day."

Of course Joey and Zach also took the Mossberg shotgun Scully had been ordered to drop, as well as the lever-action carbine he had brought. Then they quickly loaded the canoe with canned goods and other non-perishables that were in the cabin, as well as the camp stove and all the propane, and tied it on a short towline behind the Johnboat. When they were ready to leave, all Grant could do was wish Scully luck. He stood and watched as Joey started the engine while Zach sat in the bow facing backwards, the shotgun pointed at Scully, who sat on the middle seat between them. That they chose such an idiotic seating arrangement showed their incompetence right from the start. If Scully *did* try something, Zach was just as likely to shoot Joey, who was right behind him in the line of fire, as he was to stop their prisoner from escaping. Seeing this gave him confidence that Scully would figure out something before they got very far.

Grant did nothing to give away his intentions while they were watching, but as soon as they were out of sight around the bend, he hurried back into the cabin. He opened the cabinet doors under the sink and found the Phillips screwdriver in a small toolbox that he kept in there in alongside a bottle of bleach and other cleaning supplies. Then, with the screwdriver in hand, he rushed over to the wall next to the built-in bunk beds and went to work removing the six deck screws that held one of the interior paneling boards in place between the bed and the window. He could tell the screws had not been disturbed since the last time he'd tightened them, some two months before the blackout.

When they were all loose, he gently pried the board out to reveal his cache, and the sight of his familiar Ruger

10/22 with the well-worn walnut stock brought a smile to his face despite all the other disappointments of the day. Grant took it out and checked the magazine to be sure it was fully loaded. He grabbed the big Ziploc bag next to it that held two spare magazines and several boxes of .22LR hollow points and stuffed all of it into a small canvas tote bag that had been left on the floor when Joey and Zach ransacked the cabin. Grant hurriedly looked through what little food they had left and put some packages of ramen noodles, a box of pancake mix and a small bag of cornmeal in the sack with the ammo. Joey and Zach had ransacked his other gear, including most of his camping equipment, but he found a Nalgene water bottle and a spare bottle of Polar Pure, his favorite water purification treatment, as well as another butane lighter. He still had the Bic in his pocket that he'd been using to start fires every day, along with the Swiss Army Knife he always carried. He was down to the basics, but he knew he could make it work. He filled the water bottle from the well pump, put it in the bag with the food and ammo, and then he was out the door and on his way.

The Bogue Chitto in these upper reaches was swift, and he knew that even a canoe would be moving faster than he could force his way on foot through the dense forest and choking undergrowth along the bank. He could never hope to catch up with the outboard-powered boat, despite the shoals that would slow them down in many places. Grant had another idea, though, and he immediately set off at a moderate jog down the gravel road, keeping a pace he knew he could maintain for at least a few miles, fairly confident that what he needed would still be there when he arrived.

NINE

Artie Drager was beginning to wonder how any of them would survive if they didn't hurry up and get away from the crazy desperation that seemed to have gripped every place he'd been since the grid went down. As he sat in the cockpit at dawn the next morning drinking coffee with Larry, he was troubled by the thought of how close he'd twice come to losing his brother to violent attacks in such a relatively short time. When he'd first seen Larry lying there in the mud, half in and half out of the murky river water, it had scared the hell out of him, as he was certain his little brother was already gone. Considering the remoteness of the location and the utter lawlessness that prevailed, he realized it was practically a miracle that the men who'd done this had not simply shot him dead. The only thing he could figure was that they thought it would be more fun to leave him to suffer and die slowly. After all Larry had done to make it possible for him to get to this place and find his precious Casey, it would have been utterly tragic to lose him before he even got to see that they had succeeded in their quest. Artie realized more than ever that in this new reality, nothing could be taken for granted, and that no matter how bad things were now, there was no telling what would happen next.

Before all this happened, he would have never believed that he, a man who'd spent all his career trying to heal others and prolong lives, would be making plans alongside his brother and only daughter to ambush and murder four men. *What in the hell has the world come to?* He wondered. That same daughter, the sweet and pretty twenty-year-old that he would always think of as his little girl, grown young woman or not, had already been forced to take another person's life. And Artie knew that what she had said about the need to turn the tables on these rogue fishermen-turned-pirates was correct. Their only chance of saving their boat was to take the initiative and attack first, rather than be caught helpless in a futile attempt to escape down the river with no engine and no real possibility of sailing before they reached the Gulf.

It appeared that a fight was inevitable, whether here and now, where surprise might work to their advantage, or someplace later on, where the odds might be considerably less favorable. Artie knew he couldn't take a chance that Casey or Jessica would be hurt or killed, and the best way to avoid that was to attack first and make that attack decisive and complete. Talking it over with Larry, he felt they had a reasonable chance of pulling it off; after all, there were four of them, and thanks to Casey's haul from her abductor's camp, enough weapons and ammo to arm them all. And if Scully and Grant made it back in time, the odds would really be in their favor. At this point it was quite clear that the only way they could avoid such a confrontation would be if the men in the fishing boat simply did not come back for whatever reason, or if, when they did, they left the catamaran alone and continued on downriver. Artie didn't think either scenario was likely after what his brother said he'd overheard.

"When they come, we need to be ready to get to our positions as soon as possible. Like Casey said, we want them to think the boat is empty, just as they left it, and that I'm already dead, likely pulled under to some gator's lair by now."

"I still don't see why they would want to bother with taking our boat," Jessica said. "Why would they need it when they've got a bigger boat with a working motor? Maybe they'll just forget about it."

"No, they plan to get it. I told you I heard them talking about it. They'll tow it to the coast. There's no telling what their plans are, but they've got to know that finding more diesel is not going to get easier. A lot of people these days are going to start understanding the advantages of sails."

"If they're trying to steal our boat and we shoot all of them, what are we going to do with their boat then? Shouldn't we take it instead of this one?" Jessica asked. "Won't it be faster than the catamaran, since it's got an engine? Couldn't *we* tow the catamaran, too, until we run out of fuel, and then switch over and sail when we have to?"

"We could, but there's no point in that," Larry said. "That fishing boat is designed for coastal waters, not off-shore. Once we get out of this river and out of the Missis-sippi Sound, we're going to be setting sail across the open Gulf. We need the seaworthiness of the cat, and besides, out there where there's wind, it'll be as fast anyway."

"So we'll just leave it here?"

"Sure, why not? We'll get our things they stole back off of it, and any other useful supplies, of course."

"I just wish Scully and Grant were with us now so we could leave without having to do all this."

Artie wished the same. But then again, if all of them had come this way together this morning, with the John-boat and the two canoes, chances are they wouldn't have heard the fishing boat soon enough over the sound of their own outboard, and they might been caught out on the open river with no place to hide. After seeing what these men had done to Larry, Artie shuddered to think what they would do if they found two pretty young women on the river. He was confident that Scully and Grant would arrive as planned either late today or sometime tomorrow. In the meantime, they had preparations and repairs to make.

"I don't want to start any work on the damage until this is over," Larry said. "The boat needs to look just as it did when they left it, if this is going to work. We can stop some-where off the coast, maybe at one of those barrier islands we passed on the way to New Orleans, and fix the hull before we set out. What we need to do now is decide where we are going to hide when they come."

"Shouldn't we go upriver a bit, and start shooting before they get to the boat, while they are still focusing on their navigation?" Casey asked.

"That could work," Larry said, "but the problem with that is that they will be moving targets as long as their boat is moving, and if we don't kill all of them at once, any that survive will have places to duck for cover in the pilothouse or down below. It would give them a chance to shoot back. And besides, as much as I would like to kill them at first sight, you all will feel more justified in doing it and will probably sleep better afterwards if we do it while they are in the actual act of stealing our boat. As far as I am concerned, I've already got just reason to annihilate those sons of bitches, but we all will if they are trying to take our only means of survival."

"I agree, that is the best way to handle it. If we wait until they are preoccupied with taking our boat that gives us more of an edge." Artie did feel better about waiting. There was a chance, no matter how slim, that just maybe the fishermen would change their minds by the time they got back here, and would pass the catamaran by.

"So anyway, we need to choose our positions based on having clear lines of fire at them once they are aboard the *Casey Nicole*. They'll probably come alongside with their boat from the same approach as before, tying to our starboard stern quarter to keep from doing more damage, so we need to take that into account in laying out our positions. We probably should split up in teams of two and set up so that we catch them from two intersecting angles, in a crossfire, like this:" He drew imaginary lines in the air to show what he meant.

Artie wondered if his younger brother got these ideas from watching movies or if he had actually learned such tactics from experience. He certainly had no military training, but he'd been living pretty unconventionally all his adult life. It wasn't beyond the realm of possibility that he and Scully had made a few deliveries of something other than empty boats all those years he'd been sailing back and forth across the Caribbean. But whether Larry had tested his ideas or not, Artie agreed it sounded like a reasonable plan and he couldn't think of a better one. The first order of business was sorting out the weapons and deciding who was best suited for each. Artie hoisted the duffel bag of guns and ammo from the canoe to the deck of the *Casey Nicole* and laid them out for viewing. Larry whistled when he picked the Saiga AK-47 with the folding stock.

"Now, this is sweet! You can sure lay down some fire with this, even if it *is* only semiautomatic," he said, as he popped the mag release and checked to see what kind of ammo it was loaded with. "Perfect! This full-metal-jacket stuff will go through just about anywhere they've got to hide on a wooden boat, if they even have a chance to dive for cover."

"Just don't shoot your own boat full of holes, little brother."

"It wouldn't be anything epoxy couldn't fix, Doc. You've seen that already. Now what have we got here, a .308?"

"Yeah, I remember now, that's what Derek said it was," Casey answered. "He said it was one of his deer rifles but he never took it hunting. He always had that Winchester cowboy gun with him."

"Grant took that one though," Artie said, when he saw Larry's face light up again.

"Oh, well, it looks like we've got enough anyway. What's this, a Marlin bolt-action .22? Not much of a fighting rifle, but it's a good squirrel gun. And then there's your .22 pistol. So how do you want to do this? Those .22s won't be great at any kind of distance, but they'll still add to the noise and the amount of firepower we can deliver. With all four of us opening up, even if they survive long enough to know they're under fire, they're going to freak out and not know what the heck to do with so many different weapons shooting at them."

"Well why don't you take the AK? You seem to be familiar with it. I've never shot one before, but I know I can handle that .308."

"That's fine with me, Doc. But whoever's got the .308 needs to fire the first round. With that scope on it, it's the most accurate weapon we've got, and you need to take the first man down with the first shot. That'll be the signal to the rest of us that there'll only be three of them left, unless they're bringing more from wherever they went upriver. Can you do it?"

Artie let that sink in for a minute. Not only was he going to be participating in an ambush on unsuspecting fellow human beings, he was actually going to be the one initiating it—the one making the first kill. He didn't know if it might bother him later, but he was resolved to do what he had to do now. He was fast learning that this whole ordeal was about getting through one day at a time. "Okay, as long as I've got a clear shot and that scope is zeroed in, I'm sure I can hit whomever I'm shooting at, but how do I pick which one?"

"Just take out the first one who tries to pull up our anchor or put a towline on the *Casey Nicole*."

That seemed simple enough to Artie. At least once one of them committed to the act of actually trying to move the catamaran it would be clear that piracy was their intention. He was doubtful of the role the girls could play in this, knowing that the .22 caliber weapons were minimally effective at any kind of distance, but he also knew that Casey, especially, would want to do her part. "Casey, you've had plenty of experience with my pistol, so why don't you take it and let Jessica use the .22 rifle? The two of you can back us up in case we miss, and if you keep firing at a steady rate, they won't have a chance to fire back or take cover."

"I've never even shot a real gun," Jessica said.

"Don't worry, it won't kick or anything, and it's not even all that loud," Larry said. "It will feel about the same as shooting a BB or pellet gun. I wish we could all practice first, but we can't afford to make the noise. Anyway, all you've got to do is cock it like this each time before you shoot, take aim by lining up the sights, and then just pull the trigger." He showed her how to work the bolt and switch the safety off, and how the sights were supposed to be aligned on target. "The cartridges are inside this tube under the barrel. But you don't have to worry about reloading because if this goes as planned it'll be over before you shoot half of the fifteen rounds already in there."

"I just wish we didn't have to do this at all. I wish those men wouldn't come back. I just want Grant and Scully to be back so we can go."

"Me too, Jessica, believe me, but let's just focus on what we've got to do. This will all be over soon and Grant and Scully *will* be back and we *will* sail away from this mess. But right now, you and Casey stay here and keep watch while I go with Doc in the canoe to try and find a couple of places to set up. It shouldn't take long but we need to do it now and not at the last minute."

Artie did most of the paddling, as Larry's injured arm was still useless for strenuous work and was a long way from completely healing. He was complaining about a headache too, and Artie had woken him several times during the night, fearing he might have a serious concussion. But he refused to let the rest of them do everything, so as they worked their way around the edge of the dead lake, he hopped out on the muddy bank several times to reconnoiter. He walked back and forth among the trees and understory thickets of red bay and palmetto, deep in thought, looking for spots that would offer both concealment and a decent angle of fire back in the direction of the anchored catamaran. The lake was small and every part of the shore was in easy range of the AK and especially the .308, but none of it was ideal, as all the surrounding solid ground was low and swampy, the vegetation so thick they would have to shoot from practically right at the water's edge. Larry said it was okay from an offensive standpoint, but that it would suck if they were taking return fire. "And that's why we've got to make every shot count."

Once Larry was satisfied that they'd investigated every option, they returned to the boat. The two positions Larry had picked out were about ninety degrees apart, enough to create an effective crossfire without either team endangering the other with stray rounds. Jessica would go with Larry, and Casey would be teammates with Artie. Artie hoped he and Larry could take care of what needed doing quickly and without the help of the girls, but he was glad his daughter would be right beside him because if anything went wrong he would be ready to take a bullet for her without hesitation.

After all this was settled, the afternoon hours dragged by with no sign of Grant, Scully, or the men in the fishing boat. Although the galley was a wreck of scattered dishes and cookware, the alcohol stove had been left where it was mounted in the counter, and its fuel tank was still half full as it had been when Larry had made coffee that morning before the attack. They cooked rice and canned beans from the stash of supplies Casey had liberated from Derek's camp and then had hot tea, which was among the few supply items the thieves had left aboard when they looted the boat. Needless to say, all of Larry's rum supply was gone.

"I may never see another bottle of 10 Cane again," he grumbled.

"I'm sure that wherever we end up eventually, we can figure out a way to trade for something drinkable."

"Yeah, I guess. That reminds me though, before all this happened, I was using my alone time on the boat to go over my charts. I've been thinking about where we might go."

"And?"

"Well, I had first thought about some of the cays along the Caribbean coast of the Yucatán. There are some really isolated ones out there along the barrier reef, both in Mexico and Belize, but the more I think about it, I don't know. That area is pretty easy to get to from Florida, not to mention Cuba and the bigger resort towns in Mexico. There may be too many other boats there already. It's not really remote enough.

"I thought about going farther south, too, like maybe the cays of Nicaragua or the San Blas Islands of Panama. A lot of them are inhabited by indigenous people, but those people were already living off the grid before it went down. I thought maybe we could trade with them, or at least work out something where they'll leave us alone."

Scott B. Williams

"Nicaragua or Panama?" Jessica asked, a look of disbelief on her face. "Why do we have to go so far? How long will that take?"

"Not as long as you'd think, Jessica. I know your and Casey's only experience sailing was knocking around with me in the Virgin Islands last summer, but that was a slower boat, and when you're day sailing, there's the getting underway every morning and then anchoring down every night that eats up a lot of your time. Offshore is different. The boat is underway twenty-four/seven. With any decent wind at all, we can reel off up to 200 miles a day. We could be in the Canal Zone in a week if we are lucky. Unfortunately, going through it is probably not an option, but I sure wish it were. Life would be easier for us on the Pacific."

"If we were on the Pacific, you could drop me off in Los Angeles."

Artie saw the look of sadness come over Jessica's face. Her parents were in Los Angeles. She had no way of knowing if they were dead or alive. Of course none of them had any way of knowing if the West Coast of the continent was affected the same way as the Southeast, but it seemed likely it was.

"Yeah, I wish we could, Jessica. I wish we could…. But anyway, to answer your other question, we need to go far to get away from the main sailing routes and stopovers most boats use. Places like the islands of the Eastern Caribbean, the Bahamas, Caymans, and the rest are likely to be destinations for a lot of people who had anything resembling a seaworthy boat when this happened. We're not the only ones with the idea of sailing away, believe me. We need to get off the beaten path, not only to avoid the others, but to find places that aren't fished out and that have a water source. The more I've thought about it, though, the more I think the tropics may not be the answer. Like I said, if we could get to the Pacific, we'd be set. We could sail north to British Columbia or Alaska, where we'd have the whole Inside Passage to cruise and hide out in. That place is a paradise of wilderness that's full of fish, game, and fresh water. But we can't get there."

"So what are our other options?" Casey asked.

"There are a lot, but none of them are easy to get to. Another downside of the Nicaragua and Panama area is that those coasts are on the leeward side of the Caribbean. Getting away from there to go anywhere else would be a difficult upwind beat. There are a lot of people in those countries, and even though much of the area is still jungle and swamp, by now many of those people may be making their way to the uninhabited areas with the same idea of living off the land as we have. If we get there and find it too crowded, it would be a difficult sail upwind to leave and go anywhere else."

"Where else do you have in mind?" Artie asked.

"Well, there's always the North Atlantic. We could head to the Maritime Provinces of Canada, somewhere like New Brunswick or Labrador, or we could head out into the ocean and sail far enough east to catch a favorable wind and then cross back to the east side of South America. There are still some extremely remote places on the coasts of Brazil and the Guyanas."

"I'm betting Scully will be in favor of the latter," Artie said. "From what he told me, he hates the cold!"

"Grant would like the second option better, too!" Casey said. "He spent all last summer in Guyana. That's where he did his graduate fieldwork. Hey, maybe we can go stay with that tribe he lived with! It was somewhere along a big river in the jungle. I'll bet it was a lot like this place."

"I'll talk to him about it. I don't have detailed charts for that coast, but it's a possibility. It would be a long, hard sail, but so would anywhere remote enough to consider a real refuge. One thing is for certain, though, anywhere would be better than here. We just *have* to get away from the U.S. mainland."

⊙ ⊙ ⊙

When the sun finally set and dusk turned to full darkness with no sign of Grant and Scully, Larry had to once again remind Casey and Jessica that it was unlikely they were in imminent danger. He said that even aside from the grid going down, they were on river time and traveling by boat, so schedules meant little. An extra day's delay could be something as simple as engine problems or log jams they were dealing with trying to get to the cabin. It was a long way upstream on a much smaller tributary than the main

Pearl, after all. Artie pointed out, too, that Grant and Scully were both competent woodsmen and travelers.

Even after this pep talk, sleep did not come easily that night for any of them. Every hour that Grant and Scully were overdue increased their anxiety, and Artie found himself in a mental battle fighting to push away possible scenarios that kept playing in his mind. When dawn broke he had probably slept less than two hours, but he was up on deck at first light watching and listening with Casey, hoping to hear the little outboard approaching from the north. But there was nothing but the normal sounds of the wild inhabitants of the swamp until mid-morning, when Casey hushed them all to silence.

"Listen! Do you hear that?"

At first, Artie thought she was just hearing things, but half a minute later, he heard it too: a faint, mechanical throbbing, far in the distance to the north, clearly somewhere upriver. It was not the erratic, high-revving whine of an outboard, he knew that immediately, and there was no mistaking what it was or what it meant.

"They're coming!" Larry said. "Let's get moving!"

Artie felt his stomach twist into knots at his brother's words. All the talk and planning had come to an end. It was time to act.

TEN

Once they were a few bends down the river from the cabin and well out of Grant's sight, Joey slowed the outboard to idle and eased the Johnboat ashore on a small sandbar. He found it annoying having Scully sitting in the middle of the boat, with Zach at the bow facing aft to cover him and unable to help scout the waters ahead for obstructions. He decided it would be better to put their hostage in the bow. That way he and Zach would both be facing forward and could talk without going through Scully. This done, they were back in the river a few minutes later, Joey running the motor about half speed, which was as fast as he dared with all the snags and shallows that made staying in the channel a constant worry.

"How long is it going to take to get to the sailboat, Island Man? This river is so damned crooked it feels like we're going two miles sideways for every mile we go forward."

"Grant said they were planning on going back tomorrow, Joey. It took them almost two full days to get up here. It's going to be dark in a couple of hours, maybe we should have waited and left in the morning."

"Nevah gonna see dat boat before tomorrow. Got to go slow on de river in de night. Lotta log, shoal, and bad place, mon."

"See what I mean, even he says it's not a good idea. We should have waited."

"And sit there all night trying to guard two people? No, I didn't want to have to look at Grant another minute. I should have just shot him, but I'd rather he sit there in that cabin thinking about us sailing away with his girlfriends. Besides, I'm not worried about running the river at night. We'll have moonlight, and people fish at night, don't they? We'll just have to go slow. But I want to get there."

"I hope you're not wasting your time. I just wish Jessica and Casey had been with Grant today. We could have run him and Rastaman off and just stayed there. I would rather be in that cabin than out here any day."

"You've got to look at the big picture, Zach. That cabin is fine for now, and we haven't had any trouble, but you can bet that people are going to start showing up there. They have to. There are too many people looking for anywhere they can go to hide and stay alive. We couldn't have stayed there much longer even if Jessica and Casey *were* there."

"I get that, but this idea of sailing away sounds risky, too. And you heard what Grant said about Casey's dad and uncle. I'm betting they're not going to be too excited to see us show up looking to crew for them, even if Jessica does listen to what you've got to say."

"We'll see," Joey said, giving Zach a look that said he didn't want to discuss this aspect of their plan in front of Scully. "Just help me keep an eye out for logs. If we hit something and fuck up the motor we're screwed."

"I'm watching, but you need to take it easy until we get to deep water. The Pearl River is a lot bigger, and down there in the swamp we can run wide open, or at least we could in the daytime."

"I'm not scared of the dark. It's probably better to travel this river at night anyway. You never know when some yahoo with a rifle might take a pot shot at us going by. There's got to be a lot of people out in these woods that would like to have a boat and motor, even if it is a worn-out piece of shit."

But they quickly found that Scully wasn't joking about shoals and logs in those upper reaches of the Bogue Chitto. Joey constantly had to shift the outboard to neutral and tilt it forward to lift the prop so they could slide over some log or gravel bar covered with just inches of water. In a few places they had to actually get out of the boat and drag it. The late afternoon light faded as they worked through this section. By the time they passed under the first bridge below the cabin, it was already dark, but the almost-full moon was rising, casting a pale light through the trees that reflected in the current of the channel. There was a long beach of white sand that stood out in contrast to the black backdrop of woods, running for a good 200 yards north of the bridge on the east side of the river. The sandbar was deserted and nothing moved in the vicinity of the bridge or on the roadway above. Another half mile downstream, they passed a large vacation home situated on a high bluff overlooking the river. The absence of candlelight from the windows or campfire outside meant it was likely deserted.

"Looks like a nicer cabin than Grant's," Zach said as they motored by. "I'll bet there's all kinds of stuff in there we could get."

"Maybe, but we don't have time to stop. That close to a bridge, somebody's probably looted it already. I'm surprised it hasn't been burned."

"There are some canoes up there, too. Look."

Joey could see a separate shed bathed in moonlight, and under the tin roof a couple of canoes and what looked like a kayak of some kind, all against one side in racks. "Yeah, who the hell wants 'em? Too fucking slow and only good for going downstream. That's why they're still there."

"Well, this one we're pulling is good for something. At least for hauling stuff."

"Yeah, but I also didn't want Grant to get any ideas about following us, not that it would do him any good to try and keep up with us without a motor. But he's so stupid, he'll probably try to walk all the way down the river to get back to Casey and Jessica. And we'll all be long gone way before he does, if he even makes it that far."

They had gone another mile when Joey noticed something different about the reflections on the water ahead. He throttled the engine back to idle and slowed down. With the outboard running more quietly, all of them could now hear the sound of rushing water ahead. "Hey, what have we got here? Can you tell what it is?"

"It sounds like rapids, but I can't see where they are."

Joey yelled at Scully: "How bad is this place? Can we get through it? You and Grant did, right?"

"Coming through in de day, no problem, mon. But de current she strong and lotta snag sticking up in de river. Gotta be careful, de boat she don't go sideways and flip!"

"Watch out, Joey, it looks pretty swift!" Zach yelled as they rounded the bend and saw the source of all the noise.

"Shit! We're already too close to turn back and look it over with that damned canoe tied behind us. The last thing I want to do is get the line tangled up in the prop. Fuck!"

Joey tried to steer through the deepest part of the current ahead, but in the dark it was impossible to discern the channel from the shoals, much less pick out all the protruding snags and logs in time to avoid them. The rapids area was only a minor drop of a few feet over a distance of about a hundred yards, but it reached from bank to bank so there was no avoiding it. Joey was afraid to apply too much power to the throttle because the river was moving faster than he was comfortable with even drifting, but without enough thrust from the engine to maintain steerage, it was impossible to maneuver around the obstructions. The Johnboat first slammed into one protruding tree branch and then another, causing it to spin around until they were actually going stern first. Joey yelled and screamed at Zach to try the paddle, but neither of them really knew enough about boat handling for paddling to make a difference, and they would have found this stretch of river challenging even in daylight. It was hopeless in the dark, and Scully didn't even attempt to help.

Joey thought getting spun around stern-first was bad, but then the line between the canoe and the boat snagged on the jagged end of a protruding log, causing both boats to suddenly slam to a stop, the canoe flipping and the stern of the Johnboat dipping low enough to swamp the entire boat. Joey screamed in rage as the water flooded over his seat in the stern and the engine submerged and finally sputtered and died. The next thing he knew, he was in the water, clinging to the side of the boat with one hand and the Mossberg shotgun with the other. All the supplies in the capsized canoe were floating away in the current and everything that would not float immediately sank to the bottom. Joey focused on hanging onto the Johnboat, which finally came free of the log when both boats shifted to one side in the current, allowing the towline between them to slip off the projection it had snagged. As soon as the line was free, the two boats continued to be swept downstream. Joey turned to see Zach swimming beside the boat, desperately trying to grab some of the floating bags of food and gear. He expected to see Scully as well, but though he scanned the dark waters as far as he could see around a 360-degree arc, he saw no sign of the dreadlocked islander.

"Zach! Where did that son of a bitch go? Do you see him?

Zach did not. He had been so busy trying to grab their stuff before it floated away that he didn't even realize their hostage was missing. Both of them were now looking for him as they wrestled the two boats into an eddy, and then into still water, where they finally stopped drifting. Joey was furious. The boat was too full of water to climb back in without bailing it out, but, much to his surprise, when he put his feet straight down, he found the bottom and discovered the water was only chest deep. Forgetting the boat for the moment, he raised the shotgun to his shoulder and pointed it back upriver in the direction of the rapids. He had managed to keep the muzzle above water the whole time, so he didn't hesitate to quickly unleash three rounds in the general direction they had last seen Scully, just as fast as he could work the pump-action slide. When the echoes of the blasts died away, there was only the sound of the rushing water, and they still had seen no movement or anything else to indicate anyone was there.

"Where are you, you motherfucker?"

"Maybe he just fell in and drowned," Zach said.

"No fuckin' way. That dude lived on boats. You heard what Grant said. He didn't fall in; he jumped in when we were busy trying to save the boats. The son of a bitch is probably already in the woods by now."

"So what are we gonna do about it?"

"There's nothing we *can* do, we just have to bail the boats out and keep going. At least he knows I've still got the shotgun, in case he thought he was going to try something." Joey fired another wild shot into the woods just for good measure. "If I see your face again, you're dead! You got that, island man?"

● ● ●

Grant hoped he was making the right decision as he jogged down the deserted gravel road leading away from the cabin. Even before they left, as Joey and Zach were loading the Johnboat and canoe with most of the supplies from the cabin, Grant was quickly weighing his options. Although none of them was ideal, at least they were leaving him free and unhurt. He knew he was lucky Joey or Zach had not shot him and Scully, too. Somehow they'd been stupid enough to believe that they were effectively stranding him and that Scully was going to lead them right to the catamaran.

The motorcycle the two of them had ridden there from New Orleans was a possibility, despite the fact that Joey had taken the key and drained the gas. The lack of a key was hardly a deterrent. Grant was no mechanic by any means, but he'd owned a couple of dirt bikes when he was a teenager and he knew he could bypass the switch and push start the bike by rolling it down the hill behind the cabin if necessary. The Harley Sportster didn't even come with a steering lock, making it a very easy bike to steal.

The empty fuel tank wouldn't stop him either if he really wanted to use it. He was certain he could find some gas easily enough in the tank of an abandoned vehicle on the nearby road. But tempting as it was to be able to travel at the speed of a motorcycle, Grant knew it wasn't practical. First of all, there was the matter of the roadblock at the state line that he had to assume was still in place, even though it was possible it had been dismantled in the weeks since they'd first found out about it. But even if it were possible to get through and ride south, there were all the dangers of travel by road that he and the girls had already dealt with on the bicycles. A running motorcycle would be a much more desirable target than a bicycle, and as it was a Harley, Grant knew it would be loud, giving anyone on the road ahead plenty of time to hear him coming and set up an ambush.

He thought the bicycles they'd hidden near the bridge south of the state line were probably still there, too, covered in brush in the dense canebrake and ready to ride, but even though he could travel quietly and still make good time on a pedal bike, there was still a major problem. He had canoed the entire waterway to the coast once, before all this happened, and was familiar with the terrain, even if he didn't know the exact location of the anchorage Casey's uncle had chosen. No road passed anywhere near that part of the river, and the surrounding swamps were impassable even on foot for the most part. He would still need a boat of some kind long before he got close, anyway, and he knew it might be harder to get one farther south where other refugees might have already taken any that might be available. That left getting one now, in the one place where he knew for sure he could find one that would work.

The road he was running on now would only take him part of the way there. It was on the wrong side of the river, for one thing, and a couple of miles south it turned away from the river valley and ran west until it intersected a nearby paved county road. Grant was only using it to make some time while it roughly paralleled the river. Once he reached the point where it diverged, he would plunge back into the woods to stay close to the riverbank. This would be the hard part; three or four miles of pushing through dense undergrowth, bypassing sloughs and thickets and keeping an eye on where he placed each step to avoid water moccasins or rattlesnakes as the light under the canopy faded. Grant knew he wouldn't get there before dark, but he pushed himself as hard as he could. He could catch his breath later, in the boat, as there would be places where the current would keep him moving at a good clip even if he weren't paddling.

His mind was racing faster than his body could move as he tried to process all that had happened this afternoon since he and Scully had approached the cabin. Joey was absolutely the last person Grant had ever expected to see again, and he had scarcely given the incident with him in New Orleans another thought since they'd left. He had just assumed that when Jessica slapped the hell out of him and told him she was through, that would be that. At the time, he hadn't thought Joey had either the motivation or the ability to get out of the city, much less make his way all the way to the cabin. Thinking about it now, though, he realized he should have known that the note and map would be an open invitation to anyone who found them, even though it was intended solely for Casey's father. Now it made sense that Joey would cool off after the altercation and seek out Jessica in an attempt to talk to her and reconcile. Maybe he'd changed his mind and decided he wanted to go with them, as she'd first urged him to do, but by the time he'd gone to the apartment she'd shared with Casey, he had been too late. By then he must have surely realized survival in New Orleans was dicey, and having nowhere else to go, he and his friend had used the map on the note to find their way out here. Joey was still clinging to a delusion that Jessica wanted him, and, unbelievably, thought she would welcome him back with open arms after all this time. Grant wondered how Joey intended to explain how he'd found them, when and if he and Zach reached the boat. But he had no doubt Joey would do what he'd said he would, fabricate some bullshit story about how he'd had an accident, probably telling them he was dead. Thinking of this, Grant was worried about what would become of Scully. Once they knew where they were going and knew where the boat was anchored, they wouldn't need him anymore and it would be inconvenient to have him along, contradicting whatever narrative Joey had concocted for Jessica and the rest of them by then. Was Joey deranged enough to simply kill him to cover his lie? Grant figured it was certainly possible.

He doubted he could catch up with them, and had little hope of preventing them from reaching the sailboat where Jessica and Casey were waiting, but he was determined to get there as fast as he could. He was certain that Casey's father and especially her uncle would be hesitant to take those two on, and he hoped they would question any story they presented to explain his and Scully's absence. He just had to get there before the boat sailed, no matter what.

He pushed through the undergrowth as fast as he could without getting hurt. It was nearly twilight when he came to an opening on the riverbank at a place where there was a sandbar on either side. It was as good a place to cross as he was likely to find. After pausing to look and listen to be sure he was alone in the forest, he sprinted across the open sand and splashed into the water until it was chest deep. The main channel was less than fifteen feet wide at this point and the low bank on the other side was close enough that he could gently toss his rifle and bag across to keep from getting them wet. Then he swam the rest of the way and resumed his downstream trek, feeling his way through vegetation that now cut his visibility to a little more than arm's length in the darkness.

Grant was not uncomfortable in the woods at night, and had no fear of the dark other than the increased chance of stepping on a poisonous snake because he couldn't see it. To lessen the odds of that happening, he made just enough noise as he walked to scare any reptiles directly in his path, but not enough to be heard by someone on the river or elsewhere in the vicinity. An hour after his crossing he emerged from the trees onto another sandbar, much longer and broader than most on the river. The white quartz sand glowed in the light of the rising moon, and Grant knew exactly where he was. It was the upper end of the long beach that wrapped around a gentle bend just upstream from the Highway 438 bridge. He knew he was now in Louisiana, and standing near the very spot where Casey had been abducted by the deranged survivalist after taking a bath in the river. The bicycles were hidden in the canebrake just past the bridge, and a short distance below that, was the vacation home where he and Jessica had "borrowed" the canoe from among those stored in the boat shed beside it. Grant knew the other boats were still there, as he had just seen them earlier that very day, when he and Scully had motored past the property on their way upriver. Relieved at having made it to the bridge, he pushed on past it without bothering to see if the bikes were there. He couldn't wait to get back on the river, and wrap his hands around a paddle. Driven by his desire to get to Casey and Jessica as fast as possible, he felt no fatigue and had no intention of resting, nighttime or not.

ELEVEN

Casey crouched in the mud next to her dad, the two of them looking out from either side of a buttressed cypress trunk onto the dead lake where the *Casey Nicole* was lying quietly at anchor. The canoe was hidden in the palmetto thicket behind them, and Jessica and her Uncle Larry were likewise concealed and waiting, approximately one hundred yards away, where the shoreline curved around close to the entrance to the main river. Larry had carefully picked these positions to allow them to lay down crossfire on anyone boarding the catamaran. Her dad's job was to take the first shot, so the two of them were set up on the side facing the bow of the catamaran, where one of the men would likely be exposed if he began hauling in the anchor rode. If her dad's first shot found its mark, that first guy would never know what hit him and Larry would cut down the other three quickly with the semiautomatic AK. It seemed like a foolproof plan to Casey, but her uncle had convinced her nothing was foolproof in a gunfight, so she nervously checked the chamber of the Colt .22 automatic handgun that was her designated weapon, determined to do her part to keep these guys from shooting back.

The sound of the *Miss Lucy*'s powerful diesel was getting louder as the vessel worked its way around the big looping bends of the river. It would be in view in a matter of minutes. Once the men tied it alongside the catamaran and boarded, there would be no turning back in their plan to kill them all. Casey wished it didn't have to be this way. She wished Grant and Scully were already back with supplies from the cabin and that the fishermen had never boarded and looted their boat. She wished they hadn't knocked her uncle unconscious and left him tied up to die in the swamp. Casey wished a lot of things, mainly that this whole nightmare of a changed world really was just that: a nightmare she would wake up from. But she knew wishing wasn't going to make it so, and that these were really bad men who stood in the way of her own survival. Just like Derek, they had chosen a path that could only lead to death. That was not her fault.

"Are you okay, Dad?" she whispered while they still had time. "Do you have a clear shot?"

"Yes. As good as I could hope for, as long as they tie up on the same side of the boat they already rammed. Casey, you stay behind this tree no matter what happens!"

"I'll be all right, Dad. Don't worry about me. Just focus on your shot and know I'm right here to back you up."

She gave him a quick hug and moved back to her side of the tree. They didn't have to wait but a couple more minutes before the big blue and white wooden boat steamed into view, looking almost as out of place against the green backdrop of forest as the *Casey Nicole*. For a moment, Casey held out hope that the fishermen would cruise on by, leaving the catamaran alone, but it was not to be. She heard the engine throttle back and then the clunk of the prop shifting to reverse as the captain did a quick maneuver to point his bow into the opening of the small lake. Then the boat moved forward again, though much more slowly, and, as Larry had predicted, the captain aimed for the same spot along the starboard hull he'd already damaged with his last boarding. Casey watched as he approached with the engine now at idle, and a tanned, shirtless man hopped from the rail of the fishing boat to the decks of the *Casey Nicole* with a line in hand. It only took him a few seconds to tie it off. Then she saw another man step aboard, and then, finally, the third one emerged from the pilothouse and climbed down to the main deck. That made three, but Larry had said there were four. Where was the other one? Casey wondered if maybe he'd gotten off at whatever place they'd gone to upriver. Maybe that was the purpose of their trip. But she didn't dismiss the possibility that he could still be somewhere in the cabin, either.

Casey noticed that the captain had left the engine running. So they didn't plan on taking long, probably just long enough to haul in the anchor and rig the catamaran with a towline. Her heart raced as she waited to see if the fourth one would show, but when the captain stepped aboard the catamaran, too, and all three of them stood there apparently discussing how they were going to carry out the towing operation, she assumed there was no one else on board the fishing boat.

She felt herself tense as one of the men moved forward onto the slatted foredeck between the catamaran's twin bows and bent to untie the cleat knot securing the anchor rode. Although she couldn't see him because of the tree standing between them, she knew her dad must be equally tense as he brought the crosshairs of the rifle's scope to bear on this man, who by stepping up the anchor made himself the first target. Casey had no doubt her dad would make his shot count, even though she knew he'd never fired at another human being before. The range was only about seventy-five yards, and they both had a clear field of fire in the direction of the boat. She aimed her pistol squarely at the one from the pilothouse, who was standing by, and though she knew it was a long shot for a .22, she was determined to do her part in adding to the firepower of the attack. She steadied her aim as the first one bent to begin hauling in the line, and the other crew member reached to help him. When he had pulled in maybe ten feet of the rode, Casey braced for the sound of the rifle shot she knew was coming any second.

She flinched when it did, even though she was expecting it, but she saw the man go down and she squeezed the trigger to fire the first round from her pistol. She had no idea if it had any effect or not, because her dad's first shot was immediately echoed by a rapid series of deafening rifle shots from another part of the shore. Uncle Larry was unloading part of a thirty-round magazine as fast as he could pull the trigger of the semi-automatic AK. The other two men standing on the deck didn't have a chance. Casey kept shooting into them, too, and heard her dad fire at least twice more as well. All three of the men aboard the catamaran were down and only one was moving, trying to crawl back to the trawler. He didn't make it; another double tap from Larry's AK saw to that.

Casey's ears were ringing from the shock of the .308 fired so near her head, but when the shooting stopped she stayed focused and watched both boats, just as they had agreed to do, until they knew there was no longer a threat. Only one of the three who had been shot was carrying a weapon at the time; a shotgun slung out of the way behind his back. As it turned out, it wouldn't have mattered for him how he carried it, so complete was the surprise of their ambush.

She had just crept around to her dad's side of the tree and put an arm around his shoulder when from below decks in the aft cabin of the fishing boat, a figure suddenly dashed up the ladder to the pilothouse door and disappeared inside. Casey heard Larry open up again with the AK-47, but not before the engine revved to what must have been full throttle. Whoever was at the controls managed to put it in reverse in an attempt to back down with the anchored catamaran still tied fast to the bow. It was a desperate and futile maneuver, and Casey saw that the glass windows of the pilothouse had disintegrated in the fusillade of bullets. She knew anyone inside could not have survived that, but the powerful diesel was still running wide open with no one to throttle it back or control the helm. She saw the anchor line stretch taut as the mooring line the men had used to secure their boat to the catamaran held fast. The fishing boat veered wildly back and forth against the restraint, grinding against the catamaran hull and surely doing even more damage. Casey wondered how long the anchor would hold against such a relentless force.

"Come on, Casey, we've got to shut that engine down!"

She knew he was right; it was up to the two of them. They had the canoe, so there was nothing Larry or Jessica could do. She jumped up and helped her dad slide it into the water. As they began paddling towards the two boats, she saw Larry emerge from the woods with the AK still aimed at the pilothouse.

"I'll try and shut it down!" her dad yelled to him.

"Okay, be careful," her uncle yelled back. "I've got you covered, Doc!"

Just as Larry shouted this, Casey saw that both boats were beginning to move away from them. The heavy nylon anchor line and the connecting mooring had not parted, but the anchor was dragging in the soft river bottom mud, unable to resist the pull of so much raw horsepower. Casey and her dad paddled as hard as they could. They desperately needed to catch the two boats and get that engine stopped before the fishing boat tore the lighter catamaran apart. They succeeded just before the anchor broke completely free, finally reaching the side of the catamaran's port hull.

"Grab the rail and just hold us steady! Stay in the canoe while I climb up there and see if I can stop it."

Casey did as he asked, catching the toe rail with both hands and pulling the canoe tight alongside, careful to keep her center of gravity over the narrow hull beneath her so that it wouldn't roll as the bigger boat continued to be pulled in an erratic sideways motion.

Before he boarded the boat, she and her dad both looked to make sure the men lying on the deck were no longer a threat. It only took a glance to confirm this, and then Casey had to look away. The high-velocity rifle bullets had made a messy job of what had to be done, especially the .308 round that had killed the first man.

She glanced back to the shore and saw Larry standing there with the AK aimed squarely at the pilothouse, ready to open fire if needed. Jessica was right behind him, clinging to her .22 rifle. Casey wondered if she had fired it alongside Larry, but it didn't matter in the end, anyway. Her dad had made his way into the pilothouse; she assumed he was trying to figure out how to shut off the engine. First he backed down the throttle and the dragging slowed, then she felt the tension on the anchor ease completely as he found the shifter and dropped the transmission into neutral. The engine ran at idle for a few more seconds, then sputtered and died. He had found the kill switch and both boats came to rest once again.

"Dad?"

"I'm okay, Casey. Just stay where you are!"

She waited until he emerged from the pilothouse and shut the door behind him, his face pale and his knees shaky and weak.

"Dad, are you okay?"

"I'm all right, Casey. Just don't go up there; you don't need to see that."

Casey wondered what could be worse than the three shot-up bodies sprawled on the decks of the catamaran, mere feet from where she waited as he carefully stepped over pools of their blood on the deck and climbed back into the canoe.

"Let's paddle back to the bank. Your Uncle Larry and I will move these men and clean up the boat. You and Jessica can wait ashore until we're done."

"I can help, Dad."

"I know you could, but Larry and I can do it."

When they rejoined Larry and Jessica on the bank, Casey heard what her dad whispered to Larry and knew why he didn't want her to help move the bodies. The fourth person who darted up to the pilothouse from below decks had looked like another man, but was really just a kid; a teenager younger than she and Jessica, who would probably be in school today if not for this accursed blackout. Her dad was having a hard time with the image of what those AK-47 bullets had done to him.

"You couldn't have known, though," she heard him tell Uncle Larry. "We had to take them all out. There wasn't any other way, and besides, he could have destroyed the *Casey Nicole* backing out of there like that."

She and Jessica sat huddled side by side, solemnly watching, as the brothers paddled back over to the two boats. There was no reasonable way to move the dead men ashore or bury them. Aside from the difficulty of getting them off the decks, into the canoe and over to the bank, digging four graves in the swampy forest soil that was surely entwined with heavy roots would be exhausting and far too time consuming. They had enough to do just getting the boat cleaned up and ready to move downriver.

They watched as Larry and Artie searched the fishing boat, going through the tackle and gear and coming back aboard the catamaran with several lengths of heavy anchor chain. One by one, they heard the splashes as the dead men were committed to the muddy waters of the Pearl. Then, with buckets and brushes, the two brothers scrubbed the decks of the catamaran of blood before Artie paddled back to the bank alone to get the two of them.

"Are you two okay?" he asked.

"We're fine, Dad. We know that this had to be done. There was no other way."

"You're right. I'm just glad it's over. A lot could have gone wrong."

"What about the boat? Did the bigger one smash it more? Are there many bullet holes?"

"It's not too bad. Uncle Larry said it could have been a lot worse. Don't forget, though, he built the whole thing, so there's nothing on it he can't fix or replace as long as he has the time and materials. Since these guys came back with all the stuff they stole plus other things of use they already had on their boat, Larry says we're going to be fine. We'll load on everything we can and get down to the coast first, and then he'll do the repairs somewhere safer. Larry hates being in these woods where he can't see the horizon and can't raise a sail."

"But with those men dead, I don't see why we still have to be in a hurry to leave," Jessica said to Larry when they were all back aboard the *Casey Nicole*. "We might as well wait and give Grant and Scully time to get here."

"Yes, those four are no longer a threat, Jessica, but I'm convinced they weren't the rightful owners of the *Miss Lucy* anyway. I'm pretty sure they weren't fishermen, and that they probably stole the boat somewhere on the coast and maybe killed the owners, too, whoever they were. We don't know who else might come along that might want to do the same. I'm just not taking the risk when we have better options.

"Maybe they will get here anytime now, anyway," Casey said. "They've got to. They've had plenty of time."

"She's right, Jessica," Artie said. "Let's just help Larry do what has to be done to get the boat ready to go. I'll bet

Grant and Scully show up before we even get finished. I'm sure they'll be here way before dark today."

But despite her dad's optimism, Grant and Scully did not show up that day either. All throughout the afternoon the four of them listened for the outboard while they worked at reorganizing the ship's stores and equipment and moving their stolen goods back from the *Miss Lucy*. All of them were still on edge from the ambush earlier, and everyone agreed they did not want to spend the night tied to the shot-up fishing boat or anchored over the spot where the bodies had been dumped. They set one of the trawler's anchors to keep it in place until they could decide what to do with it and then set up Larry's tandem sea kayak that the men had taken with a towline so Artie and Casey could pull the catamaran back out of the main channel of the river and into the lake where it had been before. Casey was surprised at how easy it was for the two of them to pull the much bigger sailboat with just paddle power, but Larry said it was because the extremely narrow, knife-like hulls of the catamaran presented little resistance to the water. Moving it a short distance in a calm with only the kayak was no problem; but still, the afternoon was fading to twilight by the time all these tasks were done.

"They are certainly overdue now," Larry said, as he poured himself a shot of rum from one of his stolen bottles of 10 Cane that he had recovered from the other boat. "Something has held them up, that's for sure. It could be that damned worn-out outboard, but Scully ought to be able to keep it running, unless they hit something in the river and knocked it off the transom of that old, broken-down Johnboat."

"I'm worried about them," Casey said.

"I'm not so much worried about their safety," Larry said. "I'm sure they're okay. You don't have to worry about Grant as long as he's with Scully. I just think something has seriously slowed them down. But as I said before, we can't hang around here indefinitely, especially after what happened today. Besides, we're helpless here on a sailboat that can't sail, and any big boat that obviously has supplies and goods is a target of opportunity for whoever comes up that river next. That ought to be obvious to you all now. We've got to move downstream to the Gulf before it's too late."

"But I don't understand how they're ever going to find us. Everything out here looks the same, and that's just in the river. When we get to the coast it'll be ten times harder. We can't just leave them with no way of knowing where we are!"

"I'm not suggesting leaving them behind and sailing away; not on your life, Jessica! Scully's my best friend in the whole world. Well, at least he was before my brother here finally decided to come down to the islands and spend some time with me. I wouldn't leave Scully for anything, or Grant either, considering what he did for you two, but that doesn't mean we have to sit here at great risk to our lives and the boat, which is our lifeline to get out of this hell we're stuck in. That fishing boat over there has given me an idea, and it gives us another option besides waiting here."

"I thought you said it wouldn't do us any good. You said it wasn't as good in the ocean as the catamaran and that the catamaran would be faster anyway when there was wind."

"That's right, I did say that, and it's true. We don't need that boat, but since it's here, that means we don't have to wait."

"I don't understand," Artie said.

"Doc, do you remember where we stopped when we first crossed the Gulf from the Florida Keys, before we approached New Orleans? Do you remember that barrier island off the Mississippi coast, the one with the old fort, where we spent the night anchored?"

"Of course. That's where we helped that young guy who had run aground in his little sailboat, right?"

"Exactly. That's Ship Island; actually it's West Ship Island, because there is an East Ship as well. It's about ten or so miles off the mainland, and if you remember, mostly out of sight from shore because it's so low. That island is part of a chain of barrier islands along the coast. All of them are uninhabited because they are protected areas, part of a national seashore or something. In normal times they are patrolled by park rangers, but not likely now. There may be a few refugees hanging around them, like that guy we towed off the sandbar, but it's a big area and would be relatively safe for a short time, compared to anywhere near the mainland, or especially here."

"So what are you saying?" Casey wanted to know.

"I'm saying we need to get down this river to open water and then sail out to that island chain, ASAP."

"But what about Grant and Scully?"

"That's where the *Miss Lucy* comes in," Larry said. "Scully knows exactly where we're supposed to be, anchored right here in this dead lake off the river channel. When they get here, he's going to see a fishing trawler anchored here instead. Naturally, he will investigate. All we have to do is leave him and Grant a note aboard it telling them of our intentions, and they can use it to come out to those islands and join us."

"That's crazy!" Jessica said. "What if someone takes the note? What if they take the whole boat?"

"There's a small chance of that, but there are things we can do to make it less likely. First of all, the note doesn't have to be on a piece of paper. We can paint it on the side of the damn hull for that matter. I can word it in a way that it won't make sense to anyone else who might see it. And as for the boat, yeah, it's possible someone could tow it away, but only if they've got a damned good boat and motor already, which is less likely."

"Why couldn't they just fire up the diesel and drive it away?"

"Because I intend to 'fix' the engine so they can't, Doc. Scully and I have used this trick before, in our business endeavors on the islands. He'll know exactly what to do to get it running again, but anyone else who finds it won't stand a chance, unless it's someone who really knows die-sels. But the odds of anybody like that finding it before Scully and Grant do are slim to none."

Casey thought about what Larry said. She didn't like the idea of going anywhere without Grant and Scully, but she could see his point. She was also nervous about being in this place, especially now that night had fallen. It wasn't the sounds of the owls and pitch black of the surround-ing forest that bothered her. She was used to that by now after so many nights in this river bottom; but it was kind of spooky being out here at the scene of so much death, thinking about the men and the boy they'd killed just hours earlier, weighted to the muddy bottom by lengths of chain. Casey wanted to put this place behind her. She, too, wanted to see the open horizon of the sea, feel the sun on her face and smell the salt air. But she was worried about Grant and Scully, despite Larry's confidence in them. She knew he was right that they shouldn't wait here indefinitely, though. All she could hope for was that the two of them would show up in the morning, and they could all go down the river together.

TWELVE

Larry Drager slept little the night after the ambush of the fishing boat. He was wired from the stress of what they'd had to do, as well as the worry about the decision that had to be made next. Scully and Grant had not arrived during the night as he'd hoped they might, and now as he sat in the stillness of dawn drinking his coffee, he wondered if they might show up that morning. If not, then he was determined to get the catamaran moving downriver to the coast. Although he had already spoken of the need to do this, he knew that when he announced they had to go, Casey and especially Jessica would not be in favor of it, but he had to do what was best for his ship and the safety of his crew. He had to remind himself that the reason he had sailed here in the first place was to find his niece and get her to safety, and now that she was on board the first part of his task was complete. The last thing in the world he wanted to do was sail away and leave Scully behind, but he still had faith that his best friend would get here eventually, and, with the information he planned to leave for him, make it to the rendezvous point along with Grant.

When the others joined him on deck, he pulled out his chart showing the northern Gulf coast and approaches to New Orleans, and pointed to the chain of low-lying barrier islands he wanted to move the boat to.

"This is Cat Island," he said, pointing to a roughly tri-angular-shaped island to the west of West Ship Island. "It's the closest of the group to the mouth of the river where we are now, and is far enough off the coast that it should be relatively safe. There's a shallow anchorage here on the south side, which would give us quick access to the open Gulf if we need to make a fast escape for some reason." Larry pointed to a semiprotected area behind a long point of land on the island's south shore. "It doesn't show the detail on this chart, but it's called Smuggler's Cove. I've stopped there before, years ago, on a boat delivery from Fort Lauderdale to Slidell. When Scully and Grant get here and find the *Miss Lucy*, they will easily be able to easily run out to the island on her and it'll be easy for them to find us there if we get there before they catch up."

"What if they don't show up, even after we get out there? How long will we wait and what will we do?" Casey asked.

"We wait as long as it takes," Larry said. "If Smuggler's Cove is not safe, then we anchor somewhere else among the barrier islands. I'm not leaving the area until they come."

"I would rather go and look for them first. That would be better than going somewhere else even farther away and waiting," Jessica said.

"I would agree," Larry said, "if we had a means of going upriver quickly, but we don't. Our boat and *Miss Lucy* are both too big to go up the Bogue Chitto to where the cabin is. I could go in the sea kayak and probably make it in two days if my arm weren't out of commission from this cut, but none of you have enough paddling experience to make that kind of time in a kayak, and besides, it's too dangerous. The last thing we want to do is split up further. That's why we're in this dilemma now."

"I know, right? That's why I tried to talk Grant out of it," Jessica said.

"He was just doing what he thought best at the time," Artie said, "and I still have hope they're going to show up this morning. And even if they don't they'll probably show up in time to catch up with us before we get to the coast."

"That's right," Larry said. "It's going to take some doing to get this boat down the river without an engine, and we won't be traveling fast."

"Seeing how easily we towed it over here to anchor with the kayak, won't that work for pulling it downstream?"

"It will, but it's going to be hard work. I just wish I could do my share of it, but with this arm, I can't. You three are going to have to take turns, two of you in the kayak at a time. We'll just have to stop and rest when you get tired. That's all I know to do. The only other option is poling it from the deck, but there are going to be places too deep to reach the bottom, and that would be a lot slower than towing with the kayak. We need to stay in the deepest part of the river anyway to avoid running aground."

While they were waiting, half-expecting that Grant and Scully would show up any minute, Larry insisted they go ahead with preparations to leave. With Artie paddling, they went back to the *Miss Lucy* and climbed aboard. Larry had already mentioned that he planned to "fix" the inboard engine on the old boat so that anyone else who might come along and find it before Grant and Scully did would not be able to get it running and, he hoped, would leave it alone. Now he was going to show Artie what he meant. He led the way below decks to the engine room, where an ancient and rusty Perkins diesel was bolted to the heavy floor timbers.

"I'm surprised that thing will run at all," Artie said, as Larry shined a flashlight over it.

"Diesel engines are dead simple, Doc. That's why an old diesel like this would be completely unaffected by the electromagnetic pulse. All it needs is clean fuel and air to run. It's independent of any electrical circuits other than the starter and starting battery, and those wouldn't be affected either, nor would the alternator that keeps the starting battery charged once it's running."

"So, how will you disable it, then?"

"Basically, by interrupting the fuel supply, but in a way that's not obvious. For one part, I'll introduce air into the side of the system between the fuel tanks and the fuel pump. It won't run that way until someone who knows what they're doing bleeds the fuel lines to get all the air out.

But in case that's not enough, I'm also going to adjust the fuel shutoff valve on the high-pressure side of the injectors."

"If you say so. None of this makes sense to me."

"You know that knob you finally found up in the pilot-house, the one you pulled to shut down the engine?"

"Yeah, I finally figured it out after trying everything else."

"Right. That knob is nothing but a lever connected to a long cable that runs down here." Larry pointed to a small moving part connected to a stiff wire cable that looked like the throttle cable of a lawn mower. "When you pull it, it moves this little lever, which closes the valve and cuts the fuel supply. All I'm going to do is adjust the cable a bit so that the valve is always closed, even though it won't be apparent. Anyone up there looking at the shut-off knob won't be able to tell that it's activated."

"That's pretty slick. And you think Scully will be able to figure it out?"

"Of course. He's been working on boats at least as long as I have. And, I'll let him know in our message that I've 'locked her up.' He'll understand."

"I get the impression this is not the first time you've done this. I won't even ask why."

Larry just smiled as he went to work with the wrenches and screwdrivers he had brought from his tool kit on the *Casey Nicole*. It only took a few minutes before they were back on deck, the engine room hatch closed behind them after Larry checked to make sure that the trawler's tool box also contained everything Scully would need to fix the problems. Standing behind the main pilothouse bulkhead, Larry took two more items out his tool bag: a small paint-brush and a one-pint can of the black enamel he had used to paint the name *Casey Nicole* onto the primer-gray hulls of the catamaran before they'd set sail from the islands. The paint would stand out against the white surface of the bulkhead, and Larry made his letters big enough to be vis-ible from a distance, even to someone just passing by the anchored boat without coming aboard.

His message was deliberately vague, but clear enough that either Scully or Grant would understand, if for some reason only one of them made it here to the place the cata-maran was supposed to be. He painted a winding line rep-resenting the river, and at the end of it, the mouth where it entered the Gulf. On this rough map he drew the approxi-mate shapes of the five barrier islands that stretched away in a chain to the southeast of the river mouth, labeling them in order: Cat, West Ship, East Ship, Horn, and Petit Bois. The message was simple:

Casey Nicole, Cat Island. De boat lock!

"What do you think, Doc?"

"I guess that makes sense. Hopefully it won't make any sense to a stranger. But with any luck, Grant and Scully will find it before anyone else does, anyway."

"They may even find it today, Doc. If only we knew! I just don't want to take any chances, though. That's why I didn't want to make it easy for someone else to leave here with this boat."

Back aboard the *Casey Nicole,* Larry and Artie reassured Casey and Jessica that Grant and Scully would be able to find them, and that the old trawler was perfectly capable of carrying them out to Cat Island. They waited until noon, giving Grant and Scully a bit more time to show up, but when they did not, Larry said it was time to get moving. He said he didn't want to try towing the catamaran in the dark. At least until they had a workable system figured out. If they left now, he hoped, they could cover a few miles and then stop somewhere along the way to anchor for at least part of the night before continuing to the Gulf the following morning.

Jessica was on the verge of tears as Artie hauled in the anchor, but she volunteered to take the first turn with Artie in the kayak, as they set up the towline and prepared to move the big catamaran out of the lake and into the river. Larry wished he could help with the paddling, but he was grateful that all his crew were willing and able. He knew Casey was as sad as Jessica, even if she didn't show it. He was beginning to wonder himself what could have delayed Scully and Grant so long. It was possible that anything could have happened, but he tried to shut out thoughts of the worst and focus instead on steering the boat as it began to slowly gather way under its human-powered tow.

● ● ●

Scully never had any intention of letting the two American college boys take him all the way downriver to the catamaran. From the moment they'd left the cabin in the Johnboat, he had been thinking about his options. The first mistake they'd made was not tying him up hand and foot. The one called Zach had mentioned it before they left, but Grant had intervened, arguing that he would drown if something happened along the way and he was tied so that he couldn't swim. The two of them had foolishly heeded that warning, thinking they could keep him in control with one of them pointing a gun at him. And it did work in the daylight. Scully knew he could have probably tried something even then, but he also knew he didn't have to take unnecessary risks. Night was coming soon, and the darkness would be on his side.

In those first few miles down the river, he had contemplated what he might do. He didn't think even the two of them combined were a match for him in a hand-to-hand fight, but the fact that they'd chosen the Mossberg as the weapon with which to guard him gave him pause. Scully had a lot of respect for what a 12-gauge shotgun could do to a man at close range. It was a formidable weapon even in inexperienced hands, and he certainly didn't want to give either of them the opportunity to shoot at him with it. He wanted that shotgun back, as well as the boat and the motor that belonged aboard the *Casey Nicole*. Also, he wanted to stop these two idiots from going down the river at all, but his top priority was getting out of the hostage predicament he found himself in without getting shot.

Their inexperience in boat handling showed constantly through those first few miles down the river, as they struggled to avoid snags and other obstacles and awkwardly ran aground on the gravel shoals. With all the stopping and getting in and out of the boat, it was already dark by the time they passed the first bridge, the place where Grant had told him earlier that he had stashed the bicycles that he and the girls had ridden out of New Orleans. Not far below the bridge was the house where Grant had found the canoe that he had taken when they'd given up on reaching the cabin by road. Grant had said the place was just a weekend vacation getaway for someone, and that apparently no one had been back there since the pulse. At the time Scully had looked upon the mansion-like cabin with contempt. Who was rich enough to build a home this big and not even live in it? But he was no stranger to such part-time getaways for the wealthy, for they were found on the resort beaches throughout the Caribbean as well.

When they motored past the bridge and this house, Scully did not see a fire or any other sign that anyone was around. It was surprising that refugees had not yet taken up residence there, but after seeing how hopeless most of them were, Scully assumed most had died before getting this far out in the bush. Even the boats stored there for recreational use in normal times were untouched. That same day when he and Grant had passed going upriver, they had seen two canoes and a kayak still stored on racks under a shed.

With the night enveloping the river and the darkness of the surrounding forest closing in, leaving only moonlight reflecting on the water to guide their way, Scully smiled to himself at the incompetence and apprehension his captors displayed. When they reached an area of minor rapids, really just a long series of shoals where the channel was restricted, Scully had to force himself not to laugh at Joey's panic. Not knowing what to do, he let the boat get swept up in the current, then turn sideways and go completely backwards. Scully had never seen such foolishness, and, seeing it now, he knew he was about to get his chance. He had only seconds to wait until the towline to the canoe got caught on a log, capsizing the smaller vessel and dragging the stern of the Johnboat down until it filled with water and forced them all into the river. While Joey and Zach had their full attention focused on saving the two boats and their supplies, Scully took a deep breath and submerged, letting the river carry him downstream as he swam underwater to gain distance from the two of them.

Free-diving came as naturally to Scully as walking, and a lifetime of spearfishing and diving on the reefs made him completely comfortable underwater. He had no doubt he could hold his breath long enough to reach a dark area of the bank hidden in the shadows of overhanging bushes, but, unlike in the ocean, the visibility in this river water was practically zero at night, and he was making his way along the bottom by feel alone.

Focusing on getting as far from the scene as possible before surfacing again, Scully was swimming fast when he suddenly hit something solid. He felt a searing pain down the outside of his right leg, from mid-thigh all the way to his calf. Something hard and sharp had raked across the flesh, tearing it open as he moved across it. Scully stopped and felt blindly around him in the dark water as he drifted, his hand touching something hard and cold. His fingers closed around it, feeling its shape. The object seemed to be a piece of twisted steel angle iron. His other foot bumped into something else that felt like a piling. Coming into contact with even more immoveable objects, he realized he was in the midst of some kind of submerged manmade structure. Caught in the current, he suddenly feared he would get tangled up or trapped beneath the surface if he didn't come up to get his bearings.

His leg was burning in pain. Putting his hand to it, he knew it was bleeding profusely. Keeping both hands in front of him to protect his face, Scully surfaced slowly, careful to avoid making a splash. Turning in the water to see where he was, he looked upstream for Joey and Zach. He saw Joey standing in waist-deep water near the edge of the swift water, and heard him cursing before blasting several rounds from the shotgun randomly into the night. Satisfied that they were looking in the wrong direction for him,

Scully quickly assessed his surroundings and saw the tops of numerous wooden pilings protruding out of the river where he had struck the unseen object. It looked to him like the remnants of an old bridge that had collapsed and was now abandoned. He had not noticed it when he and Grant motored upriver, probably because what was left of it was well outside of the main channel. Moving as quietly as possible, with only his eyes above the water so he could see, Scully dog-paddled sideways across the current to a dark area of the bank near the base of a giant cypress tree.

He had to get out of the water and do something to stop the bleeding from his leg. It was impossible to know how bad it was as long as it was underwater, but he knew it needed attention. He also had to stay out of sight and be quiet as long as Joey was nearby with that shotgun. Scully was convinced that Joey was completely crazy, and that he was so angry now after dumping the boats there was no doubt he would shoot to kill. Scully had hoped both of them would lose their guns when they went in the water. It was bad news that Joey had managed to hang on to his. Along with this freak accident hurting his leg, it changed everything.

His plan had been to get away amid the confusion while the two of them were dealing with the rapids, and then take the Johnboat back, either by force or stealth, while they were busy trying to gather up all the stolen supplies that were floating away in the current. Now all he could do was watch from the dark shadows under the tree as the two of them splashed around grabbing what they could of the supplies and gear, their curses echoing from bank to bank. He waited until both of them were focused on bailing out the Johnboat; then he quickly pulled himself out of the water, grabbing roots and cypress knees until he was atop the bank, sitting on the forest floor. The blood was pouring down his leg and dripping onto leaves on the ground under him, most of it coming from the worst part of the gash, which he could now feel on the outside of his upper calf. Scully held pressure on it to slow down the bleeding, just as Doc had done for Larry when a machete slashed his forearm to the bone. Scully was sure his wound was not nearly as serious, but it still required immediate care, and he had little with which to work. He moved his hand away just for the couple of seconds it took to remove the T-shirt he was wearing, then used that to fashion a makeshift bandage he could tie tight enough around the calf to stop most of the flow. It was not enough, though; the shirt was not big enough to dress the entire gash. Scully needed something more, and he knew he wasn't going to find it on this part of the riverbank.

From where he sat he could make out Joey and Zach in the moonlight, still bailing and reorganizing the stuff in the Johnboat and the canoe from where they stood in knee-deep water outside of the channel. He had no doubt they would get underway again, but there was little he could do about that now. He needed to get to higher ground, because the trees he had seen that provided what he needed did not grow in the swampy bottoms. He didn't expect to have to go far, though; he'd seen them all along the way on this upper part of the Bogue Chitto in the daylight, standing tall on the drier ridges nearby.

Scully looked one last time at the two in the river and then turned his back on the scene, limping through the undergrowth, heading away from the stream. The jagged cut was painful, and he knew it would become more so before it got better, but he was grateful to Jah that he could at least walk. He crossed a bay thicket flat that extended some one hundred yards from the river. Then the vegetation changed slightly as the land began rising. He picked his way past giant oaks and other hardwoods. The T-shirt around his leg was completely drenched in blood, but at least it was still holding back the flow.

As the terrain began to rise, Scully hobbled painfully uphill, rewarded for his struggle by seeing what he was searching for: pine trees mixed in among the oaks. He climbed higher until the forest was almost nothing but pines, and from this point he could barely hear the sound of the fast-moving water where the boats had capsized. The pine groves here were open, and the light of the moon passed easily through their needle canopy, allowing him to see at least parts of their scaly trunks. Scully was looking for just the right pine tree; a pine tree with recent damage like so many he had noticed the day before. When he had asked about them, Grant said they blew down or broke easily in storms, sometimes by straight-line winds and sometimes by the powerful tornados he said were common here.

The reason for the downed trees didn't matter. What Scully needed was a wounded pine, and at last he found it—a formerly tall, straight-trunked specimen that had been split nearly in two from top to bottom by what could only have been a direct hit by lightning. Scully felt the places where the bark had been peeled back and almost literally blown off, and there he found what he sought—a sticky mess of oozing pine sap, as thick and difficult to wipe off the skin as the epoxy Larry used to build boats. He wiped away as much of the blood from his wound as possible, using the shirt, then applied a handful of the sap directly to the cut, starting with the deepest part. It was too dark to see how much blood was still coming out, but he knew that the more sap he packed onto it, the faster it would stop. His hand was now a gummy mess of blood and resin, as was his entire leg, but the sap was working. The wound was quickly sealed. Scully knew that as long as he didn't move quickly, the blood flow would slow and the bleeding would stop. He didn't think he'd lost enough blood to be a real problem, but without the pine sap to stop it, he knew he probably would. Not wanting to risk getting it started again, he sat down, his back to another nearby tree, closed his eyes, and tried to relax. At this point, it didn't make sense to get moving again before dawn, anyway, and when daylight came again, he was going to need his strength.

THIRTEEN

"There's no sense in wasting all our ammo! You'll never see him in the dark," Zach said, after watching Joey blast another round of buckshot wildly into the woods.

"Maybe, but I could have gotten lucky and hit him, anyway."

"Maybe you did, but maybe you didn't. He could be watching us and waiting for his chance to get the boats. I think we need to just get out of here."

"Yeah, I guess you're right. It just pisses me off that he got away. How in the fuck are we going to find the catamaran now?"

"It can't be that hard. From what they said, it sounds like it's a big-ass boat. There can't be many places on the river a freakin' sailboat like that could be. We'll find them; let's just get out of here first."

"How much stuff did we lose? Did you grab it all?"

"I don't know. I grabbed what I could. Shit was floating everywhere, except for all the heavy stuff that sank. I lost both of the damned rifles. The stove and all that canned shit sank, too."

"Fuck! What about the money? Where is the bag with the money?"

"I don't know. I didn't see it. I'm still looking, but some of those bags floated away before I could reach them."

"*Motherfucker!* There was almost ten grand in that bag!"

"I know, but fuck, don't blame me! You're the one that dumped the boat! I was just trying not to drown. Don't worry, we'll find it when we go downstream. It probably didn't sink."

Joey was furious, but after tying the canoe to the stern of the boat with a shorter towline to avoid a tangle like the one that had capsized it, the two of them got back in the Johnboat and let it drift back into the slower current downstream. Joey pulled the starter rope half a dozen times, but the outboard refused to even fire.

"*Motherfucker!*" he screamed at the night. "What the hell?"

"It got wet, didn't it? Didn't the whole top of the motor go under?"

"I guess. But so what? It's a fuckin' *boat* motor! Isn't it supposed to be able to handle getting wet?"

"Yeah, but it looks like an old worn-out piece of shit to me."

"Well, it got them up the river, and it was running fine before." Joey yanked on the starter cord again and again, but still the motor refused to start. He pulled the canoe alongside and untied the paddles that he had somehow had the foresight to lash to the thwarts. "Here, keep us in the middle!" he ordered, passing one to Zach. "I'm gonna get this bitch started if it's the last thing I do!"

But though he yanked the pull cord until his arm was tired, the result was the same every time. The outboard simply refused to start. Joey was so furious he considered unscrewing the mounting clamps and dumping it in the river, but then he thought better of it and settled for simply smashing the bottom of his fist down on top of it, cracking the plastic casing that covered the innards.

"Piece of fucking shit!" He muttered.

"I guess we paddle…." Zach said.

"And get there when, next month sometime?"

"You got a better idea? Maybe we can work on it in the daytime and get it running, I don't know. Why don't you take the cover off? Maybe that will dry the inside out and it'll start later. It can't hurt at this point."

Joey muttered under his breath but did as Zach suggested. Maybe it *would* start later. He sure hoped so. He picked up the other paddle and began stroking. If the motor didn't start, paddling down the whole river was going to suck. As he took out his frustrations on the paddle, he wondered what that crazy-looking dreadlocked Rastaman was doing, and where he could be. Joey didn't think it was likely he had drowned, as much as he would have liked to believe he did. The guy was an islander, after all, and probably a good swimmer. Hell, it was probably he who found the money while they were busy trying to get the boat out of deep water. The thought made him furious. Joey wondered if he could be watching them even now, following along from just inside the forest along the edge of the bank. It was certainly feasible, as they weren't going any faster than a man could walk. He eyed the shotgun, resting on the thwart in front of him, and was glad he hadn't lost it. The lever-action carbine he had taken from Grant, and the hunting rifle that had belonged to Zach's roommate had both gone into the river. Though he they had felt around on the bottom with their feet as they searched for the bag with the money, both weapons were lost, and they had given up on looking for them in the dark. It sucked to lose them, along with all that cash and half of their food supply, but nothing sucked as badly as the motor failing. They simply *had* to get it started again; but for right now, Joey just paddled as hard as he could, nervously scanning the black walls of forest on either side of the river as he did.

They went on like this until daylight, keeping an eye out for the canvas pack with the money as well as the other stuff that had floated away, but never saw any of it again. Joey hadn't spoken to Zach for more than an hour when his friend suddenly stopped paddling and turned around. "Hey, I just thought of something. Maybe water got in the carburetor somehow. We need to disconnect the fuel line and drain it."

Joey stopped and turned to look at the motor. "Like we did to get the gas out of the motorcycle, right?"

"Yeah, I think so. Let's pull over and look. There's no sense paddling all day if we can fix it. I remember now how my dad used to do that with his lawn mower. Bad gas would have water in it and cause it to fuck up. He also used to clean the spark plug. We need to check the spark plug and see if it's firing when you pull the cord."

They steered for the nearest sandbar and got out of the boat, both of them studying the inner workings of the old engine, trying to figure out what they were looking at. The carburetor was easy enough to find. A screw on the bottom that could be turned by hand allowed the bowl to drain when opened and Joey backed it off, then waited until the flow slowed to a drip.

"I don't know if there was water in it or not. How can you tell?"

"I don't know, but there probably was. We need to get the spark plug out and check it, too. Did you see any tools in here?"

"I wasn't looking for tools, I don't know. Check in that bag under the front seat. Grant had some shit in there."

Joey doubted he would find what they needed, but when Zach opened the bag and emptied the contents, which included extra flashlight batteries and a tube of some kind of caulk or glue with a label that said "marine sealant," there was also a small canvas roll pouch that contained something heavy. Inside it, they found three different-sized screwdriver blades and a large socket, all designed to fit a single metal handle.

"This is it!" Zach said. "This must be the tool kit that goes with the motor. This socket is bound to be the plug wrench; try it and see."

Joey took it and looked at the inside of the engine again. "Where?"

"You gotta pull the plug wire off first, dumbass! Here, I'll do it."

"How the fuck would I know? I'm not a fuckin' mechanic."

"You might have to be now, unless you want to paddle. Hey, this *is* it, look!" Zach turned the socket a half turn with the handle inserted; then the spark plug was loose enough to unscrew by hand. When he took it out and examined it, he showed Joey all the black carbon built up on the contacts. "That's what's wrong with this motherfucker. It's filthy."

"So what do we do, how do you clean it off?"

"By scraping this shit off until the metal is shiny." Joey watched as Zach pulled out his pocketknife and went to work. When he was done, the end of the spark plug did look much better.

"Let's put the wire back on and hold the end of the plug next to the metal on the motor. That's what my dad did. That's how you tell if it's firing or not. Here, I'll hold it; you pull the rope. We'll see if there's a spark."

Joey yanked the starter cord again and Zach yelled as he jerked his hand away, letting go of the plug.

"It's firing. It just shocked the shit outta me!"

Joey laughed at him. "Put it back in then, dumbass! We'll see if it'll crank now."

Zach reinstalled the plug and tightened it with the socket wrench. Then, he reconnected the fuel line from the gas tank and pulled the rope himself. Nothing happened on the first three tries, and Joey swore. But on the fourth pull, the outboard suddenly sputtered to life, running roughly at first, then smoothing out to purr almost as well as it had before the dunking.

"Son of a bitch!" Joey slapped Zach on the back. "You did it, you little shit!"

"I didn't feel like paddling anymore. Did you? Now, let's get the hell down this river!"

● ● ●

Grant approached the big camp house on the river with caution, even though it had certainly appeared deserted when he and Scully had passed it in daylight some ten hours earlier. He slipped quietly through the woods to the perimeter of the yard surrounding it, stopping to look and listen before going any closer. He was not surprised that the owners had not returned since the blackout; after all, they were probably residents of New Orleans or Baton Rouge, and likely had little hope of getting here even if they wanted to. It did surprise him that the place had apparently not yet been looted, but he was sure it was just a matter of time before it would be.

He circled around to the other side, staying in the shadows at the edge of the clearing until he reached the boathouse shed where the canoes were stored. When he had come here before with Jessica, he had dismissed the rather generic plastic kayak that was stored there along with the canoes. It was no use to him then, as he needed a boat that could take the three of them and their gear upriver, and one of the 17-foot aluminum canoes was the obvious choice. Now Grant decided the kayak merited a second look, but, like the canoes, it was chained and padlocked to its rack. He didn't have the machete that he'd used to cut through the other rack when he took the canoe weeks before. It was still in the Johnboat. But Grant didn't have to look far to find an axe next to the stacked firewood on the back porch of the cabin. Taking it back to the boat shed, he quickly demolished the two-by-four supports and pulled the chain away, allowing him to slide the kayak out onto the ground where he could examine it in the moonlight.

It was a sit-inside type of river kayak of around thirteen feet in length, the kind made for recreational day paddlers rather than serious expeditions, but Grant figured he could still make better time in it than he could paddling one of the big canoes solo. The kayak lacked watertight bulkheads or a spray skirt to keep water out of the cockpit, but that wasn't needed on the river, anyway. Once he determined that the hull was sound, he found the cheap two-piece aluminum and plastic paddle that went with it; then he dragged it down the steep bank to the river, shoving his single bag, the .22 rifle and the axe into the space under the deck behind the seat. He felt better as soon as he was afloat, and he quickly paddled the boat into the main current midstream and began a rhythmic stroke with the double-ended paddle, pushing the kayak as fast as its short waterline would allow it to go. He felt more comfortable in it on the river at night than he would have in a canoe. The plastic hull was impervious to the inevitable bumps and scrapes against logs and the gravel bottom, and the chances of tipping it and capsizing were slimmer as well. He planned to paddle until he was too exhausted to move, and as motivated as he was, he knew that would likely be until after daybreak.

A few miles downstream from where he started, he came to one of the few sections of fast water on the Bogue Chitto. Though it would hardly be considered challenging compared to rivers with serious rapids and white water, all of the river's current here was funneled over a series of clay drops that greatly increased its speed, making it a bit dicey to navigate at night. Grant back-paddled and slowed as he approached, expertly putting the kayak in the best position in the flow to maintain control. For him it was easy, even in the dark, and soon he was back in the sluggish current more typical of lazy Southern rivers.

He hadn't gone another quarter of a mile when he noticed something in the moonlight that looked familiar, caught on a submerged treetop at the edge of the channel. Grant adjusted his course, paddling directly to it until he was sure that it was what he thought it was. He reached out to grab one of the branches of the dead tree to hold his position, and then, using the paddle, lifted the object free of the tangle until he could grasp it. It was one of the two life jackets that had been in the Johnboat when he'd first met Artie and Scully, and he could not be mistaken about it because those life jackets were a type not typically used by canoeists or fishermen on the rivers around here. He checked to be sure, and verified his first impression by finding the logo of a company that made gear for offshore yachting. Grant wondered why the jacket had gone overboard, and after stuffing it under the bungee cords that crisscrossed the afterdeck of the kayak, he continued scanning the banks and snags as he resumed his downriver journey. He did not have to go far before he found something else: this time, a plastic dry bag that he recognized as one of his, from his camping gear at the cabin. Grant plucked it out of the river and opened the seal. It contained two boxes of wheat crackers and a jar of peanut butter, which were definitely from the supplies Joey and Zach had taken from the cabin. He knew they wouldn't have casually let something like that go overboard, as they might have the life jacket. Grant began to wonder what had happened. Had they encountered difficulty in the tricky stretch of water he had just traversed? Until finding this, he had assumed Joey and Zach were far ahead of him down the river, even if they had stopped somewhere for the night, but now he was not so sure. He decided it best to proceed with a bit more caution, taking care not to make any unnecessary noise with the paddle, but also to pick up the pace as much as possible. Knowing that if they did have a problem, he might come upon them at any point, Grant racked the bolt on the 10/22 to chamber a round, keeping the short carbine in his lap in the cockpit of the kayak, where he could grab it at a moment's notice.

Once he was back on the river he paddled nonstop until dawn, when he heard something ahead of him that made him pause: voices. They were far away, and it was impossible to make out what they were saying, but there was no doubt that it was human voices he was hearing. Grant let the kayak drift as he listened, not even dipping a paddle for fear of making sounds that might interfere with his ability to hear whoever it was that was talking. The current was fast enough to keep him moving downstream, ever closer, so he used a blade of the paddle as a rudder to steer him close to one bank, out of the main channel. A heavy morning mist was hanging low over the river, limiting visibility to about fifty feet, and he didn't want to suddenly run upon whomever it was without seeing them first. There was another intermittent sound between the sounds of the voices, something rhythmic and mechanical. He listened as he tried to figure it out and then it suddenly dawned on him: someone was pulling the starter rope of an outboard motor! Grant felt a rush of adrenaline as he realized the chances of it being a different boat out here were indeed slim. He began paddling again, as fast as dared, wanting to get close enough to see but careful not to hurry around a bend into full view. The voices were getting more excited and the cranking sound more frequent. There was a minute or two of silence, and then it started again, the same determined pulling on the starter rope. But this time something happened. The engine came to life, and he heard it sputter as it revved up, then smoothed out and ran normally. Cursing under his breath, Grant began paddling as hard and fast as he could, not worried at all anymore about being quiet. They were close, oh, so close, but then he heard the engine go into gear and the motor roar to nearly wide open as the boat sped away ahead of him downstream before he even got close enough to catch a glimpse of it.

Grant smashed the water with his paddle in fury. If only he'd been a few minutes faster! He could have stopped them, stopped them and freed Scully, too! Now it seemed they were as far out of reach as ever. But, he reminded himself, clearly they'd had some trouble with the outboard. He hoped it would quit again. If it did, they wouldn't have a chance of outpaddling him, even if he stopped to rest, which he didn't plan to do until he was utterly exhausted and could not go on. He surged forward, doubling his efforts with renewed energy and purpose. Maybe, just maybe, he would get his chance to make sure that Joey never saw that catamaran, and that Jessica never saw Joey.

FOURTEEN

Artie was surprised that they were actually able to tow the thirty-six-foot catamaran at a decent pace with just two people paddling a kayak. Getting it started took a some effort, but once the boat was moving, its narrow twin hulls knifed the water as easily as the kayak, frequently gliding even faster, causing the twenty-foot towline to go slack. Then, he and Jessica would catch up, and the line would jerk the stern of the kayak a bit as it went taut. With Larry at the helm steering the cat, they didn't have to worry about where it went, as long as they paddled down the center of the channel.

It was a great relief to be leaving the scene of the carnage surrounding the *Miss Lucy*, and Artie knew that even Jessica was glad to be getting away from there, despite the fact they were leaving without waiting for Grant and Scully. She paddled silently from the bow, and Artie didn't bother her with small talk, as he knew she had a lot on her mind. It was clear to him that both Jessica and his daughter thought Grant was pretty special, and Artie figured they were both right about that, considering all he had done to help them get out of a dangerous situation at such great risk to himself. He wondered what would happen when Grant did rejoin them, as he was sure he and Scully would. Would he be witness to an overt rivalry between the two girls? He wondered what Grant thought of both of them, and if he was already more enamored of one than the other. Artie knew that he had known Casey a lot longer, and she had talked about him several times, too, long before all this happened. But Grant had spent a lot of time alone with Jessica when they were searching for Casey, and from the way she was acting, he figured they must have bonded quite closely during that time together, especially considering the circumstances. If Grant weren't attracted to her at least on a physical level, Artie would be surprised. Time would tell, he figured, but it didn't really matter to him as long as all involved were happy. It was just that thinking about it gave him something other than worry to occupy his mind as they paddled.

He knew Larry felt bad about not being able to help with the towing, but there was no way he could do this work with his arm still in that condition. Artie gave him strict doctor's orders regarding that. It had been decided that he and Jessica would paddle the first hour, then Casey would take her place in the front of the kayak for the next hour. The two girls would then paddle an hour to give him a break, and they would continue to rotate off so that no one person would have to paddle more than two hours at a stretch. Once they started moving, Larry estimated they were averaging two knots, and if they could keep it up, that would put them past the Interstate 10 bridge in just under three hours, plenty of time to get safely past it before dark. They would have to anchor somewhere for the night before they reached the coast, but Larry didn't want to do so anywhere near that bridge, which was one of the few places people traveling by land might use to access this part of the river and the surrounding swamps.

There was another five-mile stretch of forested riverbanks between I-10 and the town of Pearlington at the Highway 90 bridge crossing. They would spend the night somewhere in between, and then approach the final bridge on the next leg. It was that low highway drawbridge, which had been locked down in the closed position when the pulse occurred, that had forced them to lower the mast when he and Scully and Larry had first entered this river, heading upstream under the power of the old outboard. Since that day, the mast had remained lashed in a horizontal position to the wood racks Larry had erected over the main crossbeams, and the sails and rigging stowed below in the starboard cabin. Artie knew that once they cleared that bridge, the forest along the banks would disappear and give way to an expansive horizon of salt marsh grass, as the river at that point became a tidal estuary. He knew Larry would be anxious to restep the mast just as soon as they cleared that bridge again. If the wind was favorable, they could likely sail the remaining few miles to open water.

Although the paddling was going well so far, Artie felt the same vulnerability that so bothered his brother in this winding waterway bordered by walls of trees. He knew that at every rounding of a bend they could potentially run into anything or anyone. It made him nervous, despite the fact that they were so well armed. The pump-action Remington 870 shotgun that one of the dead men from the *Miss Lucy* had carried was lying in the cockpit of the kayak between his feet, ready to grab. Jessica had the .22 rifle she had used in the ambush, and Casey carried his pistol. Larry had the AK right beside him on the helmsman's seat, too, but still, they could be ambushed in the same way they had ambushed those unsuspecting would-be pirates.

But they reached the Interstate bridge without incident or even seeing anyone along the way. If anyone *did* see them, and the strange arrangement of a man and a young woman in a kayak dwarfed by a giant catamaran in tow, then they must have been well concealed and unwilling to reveal their presence. Artie was not surprised, either, that the bridge was abandoned. It was a long, exposed span of concrete, reaching some five miles from the west to the east side of the lower Pearl River basin. Few survivors would want to risk being caught out on it now, and any that had been stranded there when their vehicles stopped that morning would either be long gone or dead. Even so, it was eerie gliding beneath it, a silent reminder of a once-busy web of connecting highways upon which millions of people had traveled at high speeds without giving a thought to the possibility that getting where they wanted to go would not always be so easy. Artie knew, because he had been guilty of it, too, that many of them bitched and complained at the slightest inconvenience—having to slow down because of a work crew, a broken-down vehicle, or even an accident. It had been so easy to take it all for granted when it was what you were surrounded with every day of your life. Larry, on the other hand, had chosen a different life. Testing himself against the ocean and willingly accepting the fickle whims of Mother Nature and all the fury of the storms she could brew, Larry was accustomed to long periods of waiting for weather to sail somewhere, or even being forced to turn back or pick an alternate destination. His lifestyle had given him a head start in adapting to this new reality, but, slowly and surely, all of them were learning to cope with it. There was simply no other choice.

Once they were under the bridge and had rounded the first bend, putting them safely out of sight of the bridge, it was once again Artie's turn to get a break from the paddling. He climbed aboard the catamaran while Jessica took his place behind Casey.

"We're doing great, Doc! I didn't expect this to go so smoothly, much less this fast."

"Well, about all Casey and Jessica have been doing for the last few weeks is riding bicycles and paddling canoes!"

"They are two tough young women, I'll tell you that! I'm a lucky captain to have a crew like this."

"I just hope the rest of that crew catches up soon."

"You and me both, Doc. I don't want to have to hang around Cat Island for long, but I'll sure feel better out there than on this river. I don't even like the idea of stopping for the night. But I know how hard all of you are working in the kayak. You've got to get some rest, but I've been thinking, we're doing so well, maybe we ought to stop somewhere in the next mile or two for a few hours, then get the anchor back up and get on down the river past that last bridge while it's still dark. The moon will be plenty bright enough to see how to navigate. What do you say, are you up for it?"

"You're the captain. Whatever you think is best, we'll do it. I'm sure we can make it if we can get at least a few hours of sleep."

"Good. Go up there and tell the girls. If they can paddle one more hour, we'll look for a place to drop anchor. It'll be almost sundown by then, anyway."

◉ ◉ ◉

Scully dozed, off and on, with his back against the tree, as he waited for dawn so he could get moving. The gash in his leg was hurting more now than it had when it had first happened, as he had known it would. It was not a clean cut, like a slash from a blade, which would have been painful enough. It was worse, because skin and muscle had been roughly torn by whatever ragged piece of metal he'd run into. The force of the current and the speed at which he was swimming underwater in an effort to escape his captors provided enough impact that the object did not have to be particularly sharp to do the nasty damage it did. Still, Scully counted himself lucky. He knew it could have been far worse. In that inky black river water, he could have hit the unseen object with his face and gouged out an eye, or, even scarier, could have been hung up and trapped there beneath the surface until he drowned. He had not stopped Joey and Zach or taken back the boat and canoe as he'd hoped to, but he was alive, and more importantly, free. It would be painful, but he could still walk, and as the darkness that cloaked the forest lightened to the gray of dawn, he pulled himself to his feet to get started.

Scully had spent the hours he was awake through the night thinking about the best course of action. He knew that attempting to travel downstream any distance on foot was futile. He could never reach the place where the catamaran was anchored that way. There was too much swamp and too many sloughs, side creeks, and dead lakes blocking the way. He thought about trying to go back to the cabin. But that was a long way, and although he was sure that he could get there on foot, it would take a lot of extra time. Of course he would have preferred to let Grant know he had escaped, and to travel with him in an effort to get to the catamaran in time. But beating Joey and Zach there would be impossible if he backtracked all that way, and it was improbable no matter what he did.

The biggest problem with going to the cabin was that he doubted Grant would be sitting there waiting around. Why would he? From what Scully had learned of him in the brief time since he'd met him, all his energies since the blackout happened had been devoted to helping Casey and Jessica get out of the city. Without them, he would have no purpose. No, Scully was sure that Grant would have left, one way or the other. Even now he was probably walking south, or perhaps he had figured out a way to get the motorcycle running. Scully couldn't believe those two had simply left Grant there free to go and do as he pleased. It showed that they really were not experienced men and still boys—naïve college boys who had been insulated from danger all their lives and didn't have sense enough to survive in this kind of reality. The kind of people Scully was used to dealing with on the islands certainly would not have left Grant alive in that situation, after robbing him and telling him they were going after the people he loved. That had been their mistake, and Scully hoped Grant would find a way to the boat on his own, but he knew it was unrealistic to think he could help him. Instead, what he had to do was get another boat and get himself down the river as fast as possible. The good thing was that he knew exactly where to find one, and not that far away. The rich person's weekend retreat they had passed shortly before they encountered the rough water was within reasonable walking distance, even in these thick woods with his injured leg. And Scully knew that two of the aluminum canoes like the one they had been towing behind the Johnboat were still there. They had all seen them in the moonlight as they passed and Joey and Zach had even commented on them. What he did not know was that the kayak he had seen there with the canoes when he and Grant went by the day before was now missing. And even as he spent the night resting against the tree to make sure the bleeding from his leg had stopped, Grant had paddled by in it less than a quarter of a mile away and was now miles ahead of him downstream.

Before he left the lightning-damaged pine tree with its supply of sticky sap that he had used to seal his wound, Scully checked his leg to be sure he had applied enough to last. The thing about the sap was that it was nearly impossible to get off skin even if you were trying. His hand was still sticky with it and even with the amount of blood running out of the gash when he'd applied it, the gooey resin on his leg was not going to come off anytime soon. Scully had seen this technique used many times while living in the bush in the Blue Mountains of Jamaica. There, at elevations far above the jungle lowlands, similar pine trees grew and the sap was an old-time remedy often used by woodcutters after an accident with a machete or axe. The sap had the double benefit of almost instantly stopping the blood flow and sealing the wound from outside infection by becoming a congealed, sticky, and airtight mess that pathogens could not penetrate. He knew that by the time the sap did dry enough to peel away, the wound would be well on its way to healing. He was just grateful to Jah this had happened in a place where he could find the gift of the resin. And if later the wound was still too slow to heal and needed stitches, then Larry's brother, Doc, could fix him up.

It took him nearly two hours to make his way to the house where the canoes were stored, and by then the sun was high enough to give plenty of light for him to check that the place was indeed empty. Scully still berated himself for foolishly walking into the sights of Zach's rifle. He wasn't about to make the same mistake twice. From the edge of the woods, he saw that there were two canoes left, and though they had been chained to the two-by-four lumber racks on which they were stored, someone had chopped through the wood to free the other boat and the short piece of chain used to secure each boat was now passing around only a thwart. Scully was relieved to see that the two remaining boats were not locked to each other either. Whoever owned them had thoughtfully purchased a separate padlock and piece of chain for each one.

The other missing boat puzzled him, though. He knew it was some kind of small kayak because Grant had made a remark about it the day before when they passed it going upriver. Someone had taken it in the short time since, and Scully couldn't say if it had been before or after he had passed by with Joey and Zach, as there had not been enough light to see anything but the silhouettes of the two canoes, which were much bigger and more visible. Could Grant have possibly made it here that fast? Scully thought that perhaps that might be the case. Who else would just happen to come along and find it now after it had sat here untouched for all this time since the blackout? If it had been Grant, then he was on the river even now and already ahead of him on the journey back to the catamaran.

The pain in his leg made him want to sit down and rest, but the prospect of catching up to Grant was too promising. He knew he could rest his leg once he was on the river in the canoe, so he decided to push on immediately. He found a paddle, and then dragged the boat down the bank to the muddy landing at the water's edge. Sure enough, there were fresh footprints and drag marks where someone had recently launched a boat. The tracks were too smeared and elongated from where whoever had made them had slipped and slid around in the soft mud for him to tell if they were even an appropriate size to be Grant's. But whoever it had been, Scully planned to do his best to catch up and find out.

Being in the canoe was much easier on his leg than walking had been, as long as he kept it angled so that the wound was in the shade, as the sun was now high enough to reach all but the edges of the river. Scully had not eaten since the afternoon before, and he was hungry. He knew he would have to stop and find a way to catch a fish or something, but for now had to make do with satisfying only his thirst. He drank his fill from a spring dripping out of a steep clay bank, and, finding an old discarded soda bottle in the debris of a log jam nearby, filled it so that he would have more of the clear, cool water for later. Then he continued on until he reached the rapids where he'd made his escape. He wondered how far the person paddling the plastic kayak could be ahead of him, and he knew that if the person was Grant, that distance was likely very far. If Grant was so determined that he took the kayak in the middle of the night, Scully was sure he was not going to stop until he was too exhausted to go on.

Catching up seemed unlikely no matter how hard he paddled, so, as he was here where the canoe had capsized and the Johnboat had been swamped, Scully decided to pull over and spend a few minutes searching the bottom to see what he could find.

It felt good to submerge his leg in the cold water, but it was painful to swim with it. Using mostly his arms, he pulled his way to the bottom from a point upstream of the accident and drifted along just above the sand, feeling with his hands and scanning the three- or four-foot radius the cloudy water allowed him to see. Scully knew that anything heavy enough to sink could not have gone far. He'd spent half his life diving wrecks, searching for lost anchors and objects dropped overboard from boats, as well as hunting fish with a spear gun underwater. He didn't find anything on the first pass, but the second time he cruised over the spot he saw something sticking out of the sand and wrapped his hand around the handle of his own favorite machete, the one that had been in the Johnboat with him since he and Artie had first made their foray upstream from the catamaran. Scully grinned and whispered a thank you to Jah as he surfaced and put it in the canoe. Now he knew he was in the right spot, so he dove again and again, determined to find everything he could. His effort was rewarded handsomely; first, in the form of food. He found several canned items ranging from chili with beans to chunky vegetable soup and tins of tuna, all from Grant's stores at the cabin. Then, the real prize: feeling with his hands in the sand, he finally found the short lever-action Winchester carbine Grant had been carrying. When he came to the surface with that, Scully was satisfied to end his search. He had not found the scoped hunting rifle Zach had pointed at him, but it didn't matter. The carbine was more useful in a canoe, anyway. He poured the water out of the barrel and worked the action to eject the cartridges. There were nine rounds in the magazine; they were all he had, but enough if used wisely. The blued-steel gun would rust without proper disassembly, cleaning, and oiling, but that would have to wait until he reached the catamaran. At least he was armed now, and he knew the lever-action would function after drying out. He opened a can of vegetable soup with his machete, and after mostly drinking it from the can, resumed his journey, so elated at his find he almost forgot the pain in his leg.

He didn't expect to find anything else, as he had watched from hiding as Joey and Zach scrambled to grab the bags and other things that were still floating. But a mile below the rapids, half-submerged and hidden in a tangle of leafy branches of a tree that had fallen in the river when the bank crumbled away in some flood, was a tan canvas knapsack.

Scully knew what it was as soon as he spotted it, and he worked the canoe in among the branches until he could lift it by one of the straps from the end of his paddle. He was sure they must have been looking for it, but unlike the plastic dry bags they had taken from Grant, this bag was barely visible above the surface. The only reason it floated at all was because of the sealed Ziploc inside it. Scully opened it to see, and sure enough, the stacks of U.S. currency he'd seen before were still there and still dry inside the plastic. It was a lot of money, but whether it was worth anything to anyone now, he didn't know. He knew it wasn't likely to do him any good out here, but it gave him satisfaction that Joey had lost something that was so important to him. He sealed the bag back up and tossed it forward into the bow of the canoe. It was worth taking it along, one way or the other. Maybe in another place or time it would come in handy.

FIFTEEN

Joey and Zach were both so wired after their unexpected swim, Scully's escape, and the hassle with the outboard, that they continued running the boat most of the following day, although at a much slower pace than before lest they encounter another tricky section of river. By late afternoon, though, they were both having trouble staying awake, so when they found a suitable sandbar on which to camp, Joey steered to it. They both felt they were safe after motoring a few hours from where they'd last seen Scully; it seemed impossible that he could be a threat to them now.

"If you hadn't dumped all our supplies and stove, we could be having a decent meal about now," Zach grumbled as they sat by a smoky fire, eating crackers, granola bars, raisins, and mixed nuts that had been packed in some of the floating dry bags.

"Just shut the fuck up already. There'll be food on the boat when we get there. What's a bunch of groceries worth anyway? Fuck, there was almost ten grand in cash in that damned bag that probably sank."

"Yeah, and what good would it do us out here if we had it? You couldn't even buy a cold beer out here with the whole freakin' wad."

"Don't even remind me of beer, asshole, when all we've got to drink is muddy river water! What I want to know is where the fuck that island man disappeared to. It was like he was a ghost or something. You'd think we would have at least caught a glimpse of him running away."

"How?" Zach asked. "There's black, but I've never seen anyone as dark as that guy. Must be a Jamaican thing. He would be invisible in the woods at night as long as he wasn't moving."

"Yeah, but he had to move to get out of the river. I just don't see how he did it so fast."

"Maybe he was hiding in the water, breathing through a reed or something like Indians used to do."

"Nah, that's just movie bullshit. But still, I'd like to know how he did it. I'm still a little freaked out by it. If he could do that, he could have taken us out if I hadn't hung on to the shotgun."

"But you did, and it probably scared the shit out of him when you started unloading it. Hell, maybe you really *did* hit him and don't even know it. It's possible."

"Maybe. I doubt it, though.

"Well, at least we got that fucking engine running. We've gone so far since then there's no way in hell he'll ever catch up, even if it never cranks again and we have to paddle the whole rest of the way."

"Shut up! Don't even say that shit."

When they woke the next morning, the sun was already above the riverside trees. They pushed the boat back into the river, and though Joey pulled and pulled, then cursed and screamed, the outboard motor sure enough refused to start. They tried checking the spark plug again, as well as the carburetor bowl, but nothing helped. They ended up spending most of the day alternating between paddling the heavy, awkward aluminum boat that was never meant to be propelled by any means other than a motor, and repeating the same futile diagnostics and attempted fixes, hoping they would get lucky. Although Zach suggested it more than once, Joey refused to even consider ditching the Johnboat and simply paddling the more efficient canoe. Instead, he decided that towing the canoe was slowing them down, so the next time they stopped he cut it loose and dragged it far enough into the woods so that anyone coming down the river would not see it.

Ironically, after this stop where once more their mechanical attempts had really done nothing, the motor just started right up on its own the next time Joey yanked the cord. This got them another twenty miles or so downriver, and then it quit again. They paddled until dark, then found another sandbar upon which to sleep, this time so plagued by mosquitos they were forced to keep a fire going all night in an attempt to smoke them away. The next day was a repeat of the second, except for a little better luck with the engine.

By early afternoon, they found themselves in a completely different environment, much lower and swampier than the land they had explored around Grant's cabin. The river was wider here, too, and the current sluggish, in many places appearing to be completely still.

"We must be getting into the big swamp where they said the boat is," Joey said.

"I think we're close, but this is still the Bogue Chitto. When we come to the end of it, we'll know when we're on the Pearl. It's a bigger river than this, especially the East Pearl."

"So there are two Pearl Rivers, an east and a west?"

"Yeah. It splits for some reason and the two run several miles apart. In between them there's nothing but woods and swamp. That's what they call Honey Island Swamp."

Joey had, of course, heard of it, growing up in Louisiana, but he'd never been there. He hardly ever gave the river a passing glance, even all those times he'd driven across it on the Interstate 10 bridge en route to the casinos of the Mississippi coast. "How are we going to find the catamaran if we have to look on two rivers?"

"We won't have to. I can almost guarantee you that it's going to be on the East Pearl. That's the one that's deep enough to be navigable from the Gulf. There are even channel markers on the part down around Highway 90, if I remember right. Besides, if that boat is a big ocean-going sailboat with a mast, the East Pearl is the only route they could have taken because it's the only one with a draw-bridge."

"I hope you're right. We don't have enough gas to run around all over a swamp that big, and it's going to get dark again soon."

The outboard continued to run, and soon they reached the confluence with the Pearl. Just as Zach had said, it was a much bigger waterway than the Bogue Chitto.

"We've got to go left here," Zach said. "This is the Pearl, but the split is upstream from the Bogue Chitto. I remember studying that on the map. We go until we get to where it forks, then turn south on the east fork. That will take us all the way to the Gulf, and we'll find that catamaran some-where along the way, I'm sure of it."

Joey suggested they switch places so Zach could steer, glad at least one of them knew something about the area, because he knew he would damned sure be lost if it were just him in this boat. He'd never seen such woods. They seemed like endless walls of green on both sides of the river, and it felt like they went on forever. In many places, the forest consisted of cypress and other swamp trees growing right in the water at the river's edge.

Joey had no way of knowing exactly how fast they were going, but the trees were whizzing by as bend after bend of the same swampy wilderness unfolded before them. It was hard to believe there was so much uninhabited land so close to New Orleans, but looking at it, he could see why no one would want to live here. There was barely any dry ground to be found, and what little there was was muddy and choked with head-high palmettos. Joey knew such places were literally crawling with snakes and alligators. Already they'd passed cottonmouths sunning on overhanging branches, and had seen two big gators on the bank. The size of the gators made him glad to be in a motorboat instead of a canoe like the one they had left behind. The only other thing that broke the green monotony of that afternoon was a huge four-lane bridge crossing that Zach said was Interstate 59. They zoomed under the gray concrete structure as fast as possible. Joey was worried that someone with a gun might be crossing over the river at the moment they went under it, so they didn't waste any time hanging around such a vulnerable spot.

"Grant said the boat was north of I-10," Zach said, once they were back in the wilderness and out of sight of the bridge. "That means it's somewhere in this next stretch, between I-59 and I-10."

"How far is it between them?"

"I don't know for sure. It's deceptive with all the twists and turns, but in a straight line it wouldn't be far at all. We need to keep an eye out; look in all the side channels and bayous so we don't miss it."

After another half hour of running the outboard at nearly wide open, just as it was nearing sunset again Joey suddenly pointed at something and waved for Zach to slow down. Joey saw that it was a boat, and a big one, but it sure wasn't a sailboat. "Well, *that's* not it," he said, as Zach throttled back to idle and they studied the anchored boat.

"No, but we should check it out. There may be gas or something we can use on board."

"You're right. Ease a little closer, slowly." Joey grabbed the shotgun that was resting on the seat between them and held it at ready, while Zach maneuvered the boat.

"That's a workboat, Joey. Some kind of commercial fisherman, probably a shrimper, but without his outriggers."

"What's it doing way up here?"

"Who knows? Somebody trying to get the fuck out of Dodge, I guess, but it looks abandoned."

"I don't know why anyone would abandon a boat like that in a time like this. It could be a trap."

"Well, if anything moves, blow it away!"

"I've got it covered. Just get a little closer so we can see what's up."

Zach steered in the direction of the anchored boat, but instead of going straight to it, he circled wide so they could look at it from every angle before getting in contact distance. Joey was ready with the shotgun, but there was no movement aboard the boat. The name painted on the stern was *Miss Lucy,* and under it the hailing port of Bay St. Louis was written in smaller letters.

"Maybe they left to go somewhere in a smaller boat. They might be back any minute."

"Maybe. But pull up closer. I want to see what that writing on the back of the cabin says."

Zach eased the Johnboat alongside until they could both read the painted words Joey had noticed. They were not neat and evenly spaced like the careful lettering on the stern. The writing was more like hastily scrawled graffiti, but when Joey read it, he knew instantly that it was not the work of vandals.

"Do you see that, Zach? That says *'Casey Nicole!'*"

"Do you think that has something to do with Jessica's friend, Casey?"

"Of course. It must be the name of the sailboat. They painted this. It's a message to fuckin' Grant and the island man!"

"What does that mean: 'De boat lock'?"

"Fuck if I know. But that's a map and it says they went to Cat Island. Do you know where that is?"

"Well, according to that map, it's near Ship Island. I've been there on the ferryboat that takes people out there to the beach. Years ago. But why would they paint their message on this boat? And where did it come from?"

"Who knows? Maybe it was already here when they got here. But it's obvious why they did it. For some reason they decided they better get the hell out of here and Grant and his Rasta friend weren't back on time."

"They wouldn't just leave them, would they? That's what the map is for, but how did they expect them to get to that island. This boat must work, that's got to be it."

"Of course it does, dumbass! That's what it means where it says 'De boat lock'. Come on, let's get on board and see if we can find a key or something. Just stay alert until we know for sure there's no one around!"

Zach shut the outboard off as soon as he had tied a line from the Johnboat to a big cleat on the deck of the fishing boat. He held the shotgun while Joey clambered aboard, then he passed it up to him and boarded himself. They walked to the back of the cabin house looking for more painted writing, but found nothing else.

"Let's go up to the bridge," Zach said. "All the engine controls and everything will be there. If they thought Grant and that Scully dude could figure it out, I'll bet we can, too."

The first thing Joey noticed as they climbed the steps to the helm station was that the wooden structure was riddled with bullet holes and most of the glass from the big windows was shattered into tiny bits that lay in piles on the deck. There were also dark stains of blood spatters on the white painted walls inside.

"Somebody shot the hell out of this tub, dude."

"Yeah, and it looks like whoever was driving when it happened didn't come out so well. Maybe it happened before Casey's dad and them got here."

"Look! There's a fuckin' key in the switch! They *didn't* lock the boat. See if it works!"

Zach studied the control panel and found the throttle lever, which he moved forward slightly from dead idle. Then he checked the shifter lever to be sure the transmission was in neutral. When he turned the key, a lot buzzer sounded.

"What's that?" Joey asked.

"It's normal; just an alarm to let you know the key's on. Hang on." He pushed another button. The alarm went silent and this time there was a slow grinding of a big engine turning in the bowels of the boat, like the sound of a truck cranking. But though the starter seemed to have plenty of power to turn the engine over, it just turned and turned without firing, kind of like the outboard had done after they got it wet. Zach tried several times and then stopped, switching off the key."

"What's wrong with it?"

"I don't know, let's go find the engine room and take a look."

All Joey could do was stare helplessly as Zach peered and poked at the big diesel in its dark compartment surrounded by heavy framing timbers below the deck. Joey could tell Zach didn't have a clue about how to get it running either, despite his success at fixing the drowned outboard.

"We're just wasting our time here, Zach. We might as well just go on in the little boat."

"To Cat Island?" Zach just laughed. "That piece of shit Johnboat isn't seaworthy enough to go all the way out to Cat Island."

"Well, at least it runs. You can't get this one running. They did something to fuck it up on purpose. That's what the message meant."

"It couldn't be anything permanent, if they thought Grant and the island man could fix it."

"How do you know? That bastard may have been a diesel mechanic down there somewhere. You're obviously not. If we can't crank it, we're just wasting time that we could be using to catch up. We might even catch them before they get to Cat Island. I mean, how fast can a fucking sailboat go?"

"Faster than you'd think. At least a catamaran can, anyway. If there's wind, that thing can probably easily outrun that old outboard, at least when they get out on open water. Besides, no matter what engine was on it, that little Johnboat couldn't handle much of a chop, much less run at speed in one."

"Well, the wind's not blowing now. Maybe it won't be when we get to the coast. I've seen it like that, just as smooth as a lake, even on the Gulf. If there's no wind they can't sail and we can go to Cat Island or anywhere else we want to go."

"If we had enough gas we could. But we don't. There's less than two gallons in the tank, really more like one and a half."

"Dammit! How much will it take to get to the island?"

"I don't know exactly how far it is from here, but it's several miles off the coast. You can barely see it from the beaches in Gulfport on a clear day. It would be stupid to head out there without several gallons, even if it *were* calm enough to go."

"Well, we just have to get some more, then, before we head out."

"Yeah, but that may be risky. It means we've got to get to a road and find some in one of the cars abandoned there, or get some from someone along the river who has it."

"There should be plenty of cars that still have gas in them. I mean, how many people have something that will run? A few, maybe, like us when we had the Harley, but still, as many cars as there are in the road everywhere, there's bound to be some."

"We should have looked at that last bridge crossing, I-59, but I know it can't be too far to the I-10 bridge. At least it's downriver. If we run out, we can paddle until we get there. But we ought to crash here a little while first. It beats sleeping on the ground. Besides, it would be safer to go up on the road in the early hours of morning, after midnight. Less chance of running into anybody that might be traveling the roads."

◉ ◉ ◉

Joey hadn't realized how exhausted they both were until they stretched out on the after deck of the fishing boat, planning to nap two or three hours or so. When he woke up, it was pitch dark, and the buzz and chirp of night insects filled the swamp with background noise, punctuated by the much louder, almost maniacal screams of an owl somewhere nearby. He listened to it for a few seconds before shaking Zach by the shoulder to wake him up.

"Get up, man! I can't believe we both passed out like that."

"What time is?"

"Fuck if I know; probably almost midnight. We need to get going, though, if we're going to go up on that Interstate looking for gas. We need to be outta there by daylight."

"Let's go, then. You're not waiting on me. I didn't even take my shoes off."

When they were both situated in the Johnboat, Joey pulled the starter rope several times, cursing by the fifth time, but then the old Johnson came to life, sputtering at first like it always did before smoothing out and running normally.

"I just hope we have enough gas to get to where we can find more."

"We probably do, don't worry. That bridge can't be more than a few miles away. I'm not worried about that as much as I'm worried about what a major pain in the ass it's going to be to get up to the road. You saw the bridge at I-59. From what I remember from driving over it, the 10's even higher, and there's nothing but swamp underneath. The only good thing is that at least we're on the East Pearl, so we're close to the edge of the river basin and the edge of the swamp. I guess we'll have to go as far as we can in the boat, and then wade or walk up the right of way until we get to higher ground."

"That's bullshit. There's got to be an easier way to get gas than that. Somebody along the riverbank in that town you were talking about is bound to have some."

"Yeah, and what are you going to offer them for it? We lost the money, even if money were something anybody would want now."

"Who said anything about offering anything? Maybe we'll just steal what we need."

"And get shot? Fuck that. I say we make our way up that bridge and find some in a car. It might not be the easy way, but it's safer."

Joey finally relented, and by staying in the middle of the river, where a broad swath of moonlight reached the water to light their way, they found their way to the bridge a half hour after leaving the old fishing boat. Just as Zach had remembered, the bridge was a massive concrete structure—two of them, actually, running parallel just a short distance apart. The pilings were smooth and impossible to climb, and the bridge deck itself was nearly as high as the treetops. They would have to follow it east until they could find dry land and an embankment to climb up to the road. Fortunately, though, there was an arrow-straight canal running parallel to the pilings on one side, and the water in it was deep enough to permit navigation in the small Johnboat. Joey steered straight down the middle of it for what seemed like half a mile and finally they reached the end, a muddy bank overgrown with cattails and other aquatic vegetation.

"I told you it would be a pain in the ass," Zach said, when Joey got out of the boat complaining about the mud, in which they both immediately sank past their ankles. "But hey, we're gonna get free gas, so it'll be worth it. How many shells have you got left for that shotgun?"

"No more, other than the eight rounds in the magazine. That's all the Rasta dude had in the boat. I put the rest of them in after I shot at him when he got away."

"Yeah, you mean after you blasted half a dozen rounds at shadows! I sure hope we don't need them now."

"Aw, fuck off! You already said I might have hit him and didn't even know it. At least I didn't lose my whole weapon! You let the rifle and that cool little carbine of Grant's go to the bottom, you dumb shit!"

"Like that was my fault! You're the asshole who couldn't handle a boat in a little fast water. You're the reason the island man got away in the first place and all our other shit, including the money, got lost."

"Well, we don't need him now or any of that other shit, do we? All the fuck we really need is gas. We know exactly where Jessica and Casey went, and I'm sure they've got everything we need on that boat. So let's just focus on getting some gas and getting our asses out to that island!"

When they finally climbed the bank and stepped into the lanes of the Interstate, they were not surprised to find it littered with abandoned vehicles of every description. The glass and paint gleamed with muted reflections on the sides facing the moonlight while long shadows spilled onto the roadway on the dark sides. Other objects, more ominous than shadows, sprawled here and there among the cars after many days rotting, too gruesome for more than a glance.

Joey and Zach gave them a wide berth as they looked for a raised pickup or SUV that would be easy to crawl beneath. Having no other means to get fuel out of a tank, they carried one of the flat-bladed screwdrivers from the outboard's tool kit, and a hatchet from the cabin that had a flat hammer surface opposite the blade. They didn't have to go far to find a jacked-up redneck Ford F-150 with mud grip tires, but when Zach crawled under it to find a place to puncture the tank, he called back to Joey that someone had already beaten them to it.

"Motherfucking gas thieves!" Joey said with a laugh.

"Probably came here by boat, like us, looking for the easiest targets closest to the water."

"Yeah, well, they couldn't have gotten them all. I guess we keep walking."

They continued east, ignoring sedans, economy cars, and diesel trucks, until they finally found a Lincoln Navigator with an untapped gas tank. Zach muttered obscenities as he looked for a good spot to place the screwdriver blade, but soon he had made a decent-sized hole. Joey slid the outboard fuel tank under the pouring gasoline until it was topped off, then they stepped away while the tank continued to drain onto the pavement.

"I wish I had a fucking match," Joey said, before they started back with the gas.

"Hey, look! We've got company, Joey," Zach whispered, pointing back to the bridge in the direction they had to go to get to the boat.

Joey felt a chill run down his spine as he turned and saw what Zach had seen first. He had expected to see one or two people, refugees like them, but instead it was a large group. Actually, he quickly realized it was a gang. They were young males and clearly urban rather than local country folk. All of them carried things in their hands that he could see in the moonlight: baseball bats, hatchets, axes, big knives... one even had what looked like a Samurai sword. He didn't see any guns, but there were so many of them, maybe twelve or fifteen, that it didn't matter. The men had spotted the two of them standing next to the Lincoln. Their ill intent was clear, even before they started running towards Zach and Joey with screams and what could only be described as battle cries. At the rate they were closing the distance, they would reach the end of the bridge before he and Zach could make it back to where they had left the boat.

"Fuck! What are we gonna do, Joey?"

Joey didn't answer. He already had the shotgun at his shoulder. He fired into the mob in a panic without even bothering to aim, hoping they would turn back at the threat of a gun. At least one ball of double-aught buckshot hit one of the thugs in the shoulder, and the long-handled axe he'd been brandishing dropped to the Interstate slab. But the rest of the gang didn't even pause or seem to notice. Joey wondered what kind of drugs they were on as he racked the slide and picked another target. He fired again, but he was shaking badly, and this time he missed completely. Then Zach howled in pain. Joey turned to look and saw him doubled over, clutching at something that had completely pierced his upper thigh. With shocked disbelief he realized it was a *fucking hunting arrow*, just before something whistled past his head so close he could feel the wind. Whoever had the bow was apparently behind one of the vehicles and out of sight. Joey let go with two more panicked rounds from the shotgun, firing wildly from the hip before dashing down the embankment for the woods as fast as he could go, leaving the gas can where he'd dropped it and ignoring Zach's pleas for help. He figured there was nothing he could do for him anyway. Zach had already fallen and was trying desperately to crawl off the road. Joey only had four rounds left and that was not enough to fight off these deranged whackos, who were coming at them like a horde of zombies. Why they were so determined he had no idea, but he wasn't about to hang around to find out. He practically dove down the embankment and plunged through the tall cattails until he reached the boat and threw himself in with enough force to set it adrift into the canal. Some of the attackers were already chasing him down the bank. Joey leveled the shotgun on them and quickly unleashed his remaining four rounds. He thought that he hit at least one squarely in the chest before he threw down the gun into the boat to exchange it for the paddle and clawed his way to deeper water as fast as possible.

Two things saved him: the rest of his pursuers were unsure how many rounds he had left in the shotgun (zero), and the deep water prevented them from charging him in the boat before he could get the outboard started. He had dropped the gas tank when he ran for his life, but there was enough fuel left in the carburetor for the motor to start and run a few minutes, and that got him far enough down the canal to be out of the sight and reach of his pursuers before the motor finally sputtered and died for the last time.

Joey unscrewed the motor mounts and lifted it off the transom, dumping it overboard in a rage. If he had to paddle, it would be easier without the extra weight. He felt bad for Zach, who he was certain must be dead by now, but what else could he have done? If he had stayed to fight, or to try to help him back to the boat, he would be dead, too. What he needed now was a place to rest and recover from the trauma of the attack. Then he would resume his journey alone. Jessica was the only hope he had left.

SIXTEEN

Casey had the last watch, from midnight to 0200, when it had been decided they would haul in the anchor and get moving again. Uncle Larry wanted to go past the small community of Pearlington and under the Highway 90 bridge in darkness, and he figured they needed to allow a minimum of four hours to do it. It was less than five miles to the bridge, so he didn't want to leave too early, either. If they timed it right, it would be getting to be daylight not long after they were south of the bridge, and they would need the light to step the mast and sort out the rigging and sails, as well as for navigating out of the river mouth.

Casey was finding it hard not to doze off, as she had not been able to get much sleep earlier while Artie and Jessica were taking their turns on watch duty. Her uncle had insisted on keeping an around-the-clock guard posted, and no one argued with the reasoning behind that. The AK-47 was lying on the cockpit seat beside her, and she had the .22 pistol close by, as well. She was just thinking it was doubtful anyone would be on the river at night, when she heard a distant sound that was at first unrecognizable, just different from any of the normal night sounds of the forest. It changed pitch frequently and grew louder, and then it was unmistakable: it was the sound of a motor! Casey felt a rush of adrenaline as she grabbed the AK and stood up in the cockpit, the flashback image playing vividly in her mind of waiting in hiding while the men on the fishing boat drew near. She tried to pinpoint the direction the sound was coming from, and after a few more seconds she had no doubt that it was somewhere to the north, in the direction from which they had come, but this sound was different from that of the big fishing boat, the motor high-pitched and buzzy. Could it be Grant and Scully returning in the Johnboat? She pushed the companionway hatch to the port hull open and called down to Larry. He had been sleep-ing soundly, but he was on deck in seconds. Jessica and Artie were not far behind. The motor sound had stopped, though, and Larry had only heard it for the last few seconds it was running before someone shut it down.

"It sounded to me like it was in the vicinity of the bridge," he said.

"You mean the Interstate we just passed under earlier, before we stopped?"

"Yeah. And it was an outboard, all right, but no telling who."

"Do you think it could be Grant and Scully?" Jessica asked. "Who else would have a motor like that?"

"It's possible, but why would they come this far down in the Johnboat? They wouldn't know where we went unless they saw the old boat and note we left. And if they did, Scully would know they couldn't take that little Johnboat out to Cat Island. They would be coming this way in the big boat. It must be someone else, probably some locals running trotlines or night hunting or something. I'm sure a lot of people that lived out here before the blackout had old outboards that would still run. But even if it is Grant and Scully, by some chance, they'll keep coming down the river if they're looking for us. What we need to do is go ahead and get moving again. We've got to get past that last bridge before daylight and get our rig up. There's no telling what kind of activity is going on around that Pearlington community in the daytime."

Since Casey had been the last person on guard duty, Jessica took the first turn with Artie in the kayak once they hauled in the anchor. Casey sat in the cockpit with her uncle as he steered by the moonlight. They had barely gotten started when once more the night was interrupted by sounds of human activity off in the distance: this time gunshots. The shots were fired sporadically, in singles and doubles in rapid succession. There was a break of silence, then four more, and nothing else. Artie and Jessica had stopped paddling to listen, but after another minute of quiet passed, Larry waved them on.

"I sure hope Grant and Scully are not somehow involved in that," Casey said.

"I really don't think it's likely. Like I said, they would have had no reason to continue in the skiff if they found that fishing boat. That could have been someone who is a really lousy shot trying to headlight a deer. It sounded like all the shots came from the same gun, and it sounded like a shotgun to me, so it most likely wasn't a fight."

"I just wish we knew for sure."

"Me too, Casey, but how? The only way would be to send someone back up to that bridge in the kayak, and there's no way you or Jessica are doing that. I don't want your dad doing it either, and I *can't* do it. So that's that. We've got to stay focused on getting this boat down the river, no matter what we hear. Just help me keep a sharp lookout for anybody coming up behind us or waiting in ambush ahead. I really hope we can slip by those houses near the bridge without attracting attention."

Though Casey listened for the outboard, more gunshots, or anything else out of place, she heard nothing as she sat there with Larry for the next hour until it was her turn to spell Jessica in the kayak. The river was much darker now—the moon was obscured by a cloudbank that had rolled in from the Gulf. Before she took the forward seat in front of her dad, Larry told her they should reach the bridge within the hour if they kept up the pace. Her dad was determined to do so, and the two of them paddled without taking a break, having figured out the afternoon before the best cadence to provide enough speed to tow the big catamaran without wearing themselves out. She was proud of the job they were doing and she knew her Uncle Larry was proud of them all, too, and happy to be moving at such a respectable pace despite the lack of an engine. She sincerely hoped no one was out there somewhere in the dark watching them pass, but the thought occurred to her that it would be quite a surreal image for anyone observing: the big seagoing catamaran gliding ghostlike in the wake of a kayak, the only sound the rhythmic dipping of their double-bladed paddles.

Casey knew they were coming up on an hour when they finally saw lights in the distance along the east bank of the river. Seeing such a sight was a surprise, and so out of place after so long, but she quickly realized the lights were only campfires or gas camping lanterns, and not a miraculous sign the electricity had suddenly come back on. From the bow of the catamaran Larry stood looking at them, too, while Jessica took the helm from the cockpit.

"Let's keep as far to the west side of the river as possible," Larry said. "Now that the moon is behind those clouds, it should be hard for anybody at any of those houses to see us if we keep enough distance. Keep it quiet, too; no more talking, and try not to splash with the paddles."

Casey did her part to follow her uncle's orders. She was nervous as she saw signs of such a large community of survivors in the place he said was called Pearlington. While they might all be good people concerned only with looking out for their needs, she knew someone with a rifle might see the big boat gliding by in the darkness and perceive it as a threat, shooting first and asking questions later. She had to consciously steady her breathing to stay calm as she paddled, wondering any minute when a hail of bullets might rip up the dark waters around her and possibly kill them all. Casey knew she was having a hard time trusting anyone now, and sadly, she didn't foresee regaining that ability anytime soon.

But despite her fear of an attack, she had to wonder who the people were and what their lives were like now in that cluster of fire-lit houses along the river. Were they the original inhabitants of that community, holding their own in hopes of a life restored to normalcy in the near future, or were they refugees or desperados who had found their way here from somewhere else? She hoped it was the former, and that if so they would be able to hang on long enough to see this through. But regardless of who they were, she breathed an audible sigh of relief as she and her dad finally towed the big catamaran beneath the bridge, and the steel grates of the closed drawbridge passed slowly overhead. And when she took a deep breath in, the air smelled of salt, sea, and freedom! They were close to the Gulf's vast expanse, where the wind would carry them far away. If only Grant and Scully had been aboard, things would be about as good as they could be for Casey, considering the circumstances.

They paddled a bit farther until they reached a wide bend in the river, bounded on either side by open expanses of salt marsh grass. The forest was behind them now. It grew all the way to the banks only upriver, where the water was fresh. Larry dropped the anchor, and Casey and her dad quickly clambered aboard the cat, hauling the kayak up onto the forward deck after them. Then, following Larry's instructions, they all set to work stepping the mast. The heavy lifting was done by the four-part mainsheet tackle and the big cockpit winch, but there was plenty for all to do: sorting the shrouds and stays, and bending on the sails and attaching them to the sheets and halyards. By the time the work was complete, dawn was giving way to sunrise, and a gentle breeze from the west was steady enough to fill the sails and breathe life once again into the *Casey Nicole*, as her builder and master steered her once again to her element.

◉ ◉ ◉

Grant's journey down the Bogue Chitto was little other than a grueling test of will and endurance. After coming so close to catching up to Joey and Zach because of their apparent troubles with the outboard, he paddled through the rest of the morning and didn't stop until the afternoon sun was so warm that he could no longer resist an hour's nap on a shady sandbar. He never heard the sound of the motor again, so he had to assume Joey and Zach had had no more trouble with it and were long gone. But regardless of where they were, he planned to push himself as hard as possible to reach the catamaran.

A normal canoe or kayak trip from the cabin to the lower reaches of the Pearl near the coast could take a week, assuming lots of stopping during the day and camping normal hours every night, setting up before dark and waiting until after sunup to leave. But Grant knew what was possible from following the exploits of serious long-distance paddlers, who could go nearly around the clock for days at a time when necessary to win a race. Though Grant didn't train for competition paddling, he was in excellent shape from going everywhere on his bicycle, and he had trained for and ridden in a few endurance cycling events and long charity rides, so he knew what it was to push well beyond his comfort zone. Thinking in those terms, he knew he might be able to compress the river trip down to two more days, or perhaps two and part of a third. After today, he and Scully would already be well overdue in their return to the catamaran. Since it had taken two days to go up the river to the cabin rather than the one he'd hoped for, they would have been a day late even if they had not run into Joey and Zach. He knew Casey and Jessica would be worried, but he hoped that Casey's uncle, who was so experienced at travel by boat, could reassure them by pointing out how hard it was to predict arrival times in any kind of boat journey due to all the variables.

It would be easier to push at a racing pace if he had proper nutrition to fuel his body, but at least he had food and he would make do with what he had rather than wish for the unattainable. When he woke from his short break he sorted out the supplies he had brought from the cabin and what he had found in the dry bag Joey and Zach lost overboard. He had learned a long time ago that raw ramen noodles could be eaten straight from the package, and that they didn't even taste all that bad. Wanting to save the wheat crackers for later, he spread peanut butter for extra protein over a brick of the ramen, and after eating that was back in the kayak within minutes. He would stop sometime later and build a small fire to cook hotcakes or bannock from the cornmeal and pancake mix. In the meantime he planned to keep an eye out for any easily gotten fish, reptile, or other animal to add to the larder.

Grant had to assume that if the motor had continued to run after he'd heard them start it, and if they had not stopped somewhere for any length of time, Joey and Zach could have reached the catamaran already. He wondered what they planned to do about Scully, but since they hadn't shot him rather than simply leaving him at the cabin, he had hopes they would likewise simply put Scully off on a sandbar or in the swamp somewhere when they no longer needed him for directions. He intended to keep a sharp eye out in any case, though if Scully *were* stranded somewhere there would be no way of fitting him into the one-person kayak and they would have to figure out alternative transportation.

He paddled through the rest of the afternoon and beyond twilight into the night. The moon was full this second night on the river, and the channel here was wider and deeper, making for slower current and fewer obstructions. Grant was tired but not to the point of exhaustion. He finally stopped when he estimated it was midnight, and craving more than crackers, ramen, and peanut butter, he built a small fire on a sandbar and let it burn down to coals.

Then he mixed up a half and half batter of cornmeal and pancake mix, adding enough water to make it the consistency of thick dough, which he twisted around the end of a green branch that he first peeled with his knife. Propping the stick up so the dough was just over the glowing coals, he waited while it baked. Though he had not seen this first hand during his time with the Wapishana in Guyana, he knew that some North American tribes baked bannock bread this way, and besides, having no skillet or oil to fry it, it was the only option he had.

The bread came out better than he expected, and Grant ate his fill as he let the fire go out and sat in the glow of moonlight on the white sand. It was a perfect night for camping on the river, and he'd enjoyed many such campsites in prior times when he was outdoors by choice rather than necessity. Even in these circumstances, Grant could appreciate the beauty of the night, and especially the utter quiet in the absence of all sounds of manmade machinery. He had known such silence in far more remote places, like the Essequibo River, but never expected to find it anywhere in the southern United States. He wondered again how far the effects of the electromagnetic pulse really reached. Did it shut down the grid in all of North America? All of the Western Hemisphere? Could it even have been a global event? Grant wondered if he would ever know. If so, it would probably be a long time from now, in the future when the infrastructure was rebuilt and order was restored in place of the anarchy that seemed to have consumed everywhere people were concentrated.

He thought about the prospect of sailing far away on the boat that Casey's uncle had built, and wondered if they would find someplace where life was normal, or at least relatively safe. Thinking of this brought a wave of anger over him as he realized that this very night, he and Scully should be aboard that boat with Casey and the others. That bastard ex-boyfriend of Jessica's had ruined everything, and Grant wondered what on Earth she had ever seen in him in the first place. He knew Casey saw right through Joey, and he was surprised she hadn't talked Jessica into dumping him a long time ago. Maybe Jessica just didn't get it. Grant thought a lot about the two girls as he sat there, and he wondered what would happen if things ever worked out and they really did sail away together. He knew they both liked him, and not just because he helped them get out of New Orleans. It had started with Casey long before, when they had met on an anthropology dig he was leading as a grad student. He'd been oblivious to it at the time, but looking back he realized there were plenty of clues he wouldn't have missed if he hadn't had such a one-track focus on his work for the department.

He hadn't even known Jessica before the blackout, though he had seen the two of them together around campus because they were roommates and close friends. Jessica was from Los Angeles and not the outdoorsy type at all, unlike Casey. When the three of them left New Orleans on bicycles, he wouldn't have bet on her coping with it if he had known all that was going to actually happen. But, as it turned out, he had actually spent a lot more time with Jessica than with Casey. While the two of them paddled the canoe together for days in their search for Casey after she was taken, they had been together twenty-four/seven. Jessica had overcome her fears of the dark and the mysteries of the deep woods and swamps that were so alien to her prior life. She had dealt with seeing snakes and alligators in the wild at close range, and the constant nighttime assaults of mosquitos they both had suffered. She had eventually caved in on her refusal to eat animal products, and had partaken of the fish he'd caught and grilled in the fire, but that was mainly driven by a lack of alternatives rather than choice. Grant had respected her preferences, only offering to share his catch rather than trying to force it on her.

And each night in the woods, Jessica had slept curled up next to him, sometimes the two of them even ending in each other's arms before waking, though it went no further than that. That it didn't certainly wasn't because he was not attracted to her, but he had been so worried about Casey that thinking of Jessica that way was not the first thing that entered his mind. Now he wondered how he would feel when he was finally reunited with them both and there was no longer the awful worry that one of them might be dead. Would he be as enamored of Casey, or would his attraction to Jessica grow stronger? Would Jessica even be interested in him in that situation, or had she simply clung to him because he was all she had at the time?

Jessica hadn't really mentioned Joey other than a few times during the first days when they were on the bicycles and all still together. Grant figured it was because she was never really in love with him, and it must have been mostly a physical attraction between them. Also they both liked the party lifestyle in the Big Easy when they had free time away from class. Now that everything had changed, he figured she was not going to be happy to see Joey when he showed up at the boat with his sidekick, Zach. Or would she? Grant had never really understood women. Compared to all of the women he'd known, the wildest rivers were far easier to read. He curled up by the dying coals of the fire with those thoughts, and fell into a deep sleep. But before doing so, he first drank as much water as he could down. He wanted to make sure he did not oversleep, and the extra water would be better than an alarm clock to guarantee he would soon need to get up.

When he slid the kayak back into the river two hours later, with dawn still at least three hours away, he felt rested enough. He would take another nap sometime in the afternoon. Steady progress until daybreak found him far down on the lower reaches of the Bogue Chitto. The forest here was almost exclusively bottomland hardwood, and numerous sloughs and dead lakes entered the river from both sides. He reached the Pearl River later in the day, slept two hours after doing so, and then made another push until well after dark. He was deep in the Honey Island Swamp along the East Pearl now, and looking for a patch of dry land so he could sleep again, when he came to the entrance to a large oxbow lake. Looking into it, Grant was startled to see anchored right in the middle a big wooden fishing boat of the type usually seen in coastal waters. There was no light or candle or any other sign the boat was occupied, so Grant cautiously approached to get a better look, paddling around it on the port side. He noticed the name *Miss Lucy* painted on the stern. He was about to turn and continue back down the river when he noticed something else. Someone had painted graffiti all over the back of the white pilothouse. Grant assumed the boat had been abandoned and some refugee had probably camped aboard, leaving their name or some other message when he or she left. He wouldn't have cared, but he was nearly delirious from lack of sleep and for some reason he was curious to see what it said. He had to come alongside the rail to get close enough to read it in the moonlight, but when he did his grogginess instantly vanished, and he was aboard the boat in a flash, after tying the kayak alongside.

He looked over the sketch map and knew exactly where Cat Island was. He had been there and to the other barrier islands in the Gulf Islands National Seashore as part of his research project on the coastal tribes that used them as hunting grounds long before the French explorer d'Iberville arrived in 1699. Cat Island was far enough offshore to be relatively safe from most people on the mainland, and he could see why Casey's uncle would choose it, but what did the other part of the note mean: "De boat lock"? Larry had intended it for Scully; that was obvious from the choice of spelling. Grant climbed the steps to the pilothouse. Even in the dark, enough moonlight shone in that he could see the bullet holes, shards of broken glass, and blood stains. He looked at the controls and found a switch with a key inserted. Turning it on resulted in a loud warning alarm. He pushed the button beside it and heard the starter turn the engine somewhere down below. It spun vigorously, with what seemed like plenty of speed to crank it, but nothing happened. He tried again and again with the same result. He went back to the main deck and found the hatch to the engine room, but it was dark as pitch down there. Reaching into the kayak, he pulled out his bag and got one of his butane lighters, then found an old marine supply catalog in the boat's main cabin, tore out some pages, and rolled them tightly into a makeshift torch. When he returned to the engine room, he could see the metal hulk bolted firmly to the wooden supports beneath it, but he had no idea what to do to get it running. He looked for loose wires and other obvious problems, but saw nothing. What he did find, though, told him that Joey and Zach had been here, too, in this exact same spot; or, if they had not, then it was a strange coincidence, indeed. Crumpled up on the floor panel to one side of the engine was the wrapper from a granola bar. He wouldn't have noticed it but for the fact that it was his favorite variety, and it was sold only by the

Whole Foods Market. Grant always picked them up at the location in New Orleans not far from his apartment, and several boxes of them had been in his store of supplies at the cabin. It was unlikely that the fishermen who owned this boat shopped there, and Grant was ninety-nine percent sure that either Joey or Zach had dropped the wrapper while sitting here staring at the same uncooperative engine that he could not figure out.

Grant pondered the implications of all this, wondering just what had happened here. What was the deal with all the bullet holes that riddled the pilothouse? When exactly did Casey's uncle or dad paint that note and map on the side of the cabin? Grant knew they would not have done that if Joey and Zach had gotten here first, because Joey would have made up some story to the effect that he and Scully were never coming. And whether they bought that story or not, he doubted they would simply leave right away. No, this had to mean they left *before* Joey and Zach arrived. That Joey and Zach had been in the engine room meant they'd read the note, too, and were trying to get the boat started. They obviously failed to do so, but they still had the John-boat and outboard, so they must have continued on, probably planning to go to Cat Island to catch up. Grant resolved to do the same. He was no diesel mechanic, so there was no point in wasting more time here. He could reach the island in the kayak, maybe even in a couple of days if he could just somehow maintain the grueling pace he'd set for himself.

Climbing back into the kayak, he paddled away in the dark, wondering what the story was behind the fishing boat, and why it was there in the first place. The large dead lake met the description of the spot where Scully had said the catamaran was anchored. But he hadn't mentioned any other boats, so the *Miss Lucy* had to have arrived after he and Casey's dad had left her uncle there and started upriver in search of the cabin. Grant couldn't figure it out, but thinking about it all gave him something to do as he paddled.

He reached another bridge in a little over an hour, and passing under the high twin spans, he knew it had to be Interstate 10. Knowing he was now only a few miles from the coast, he pushed on until daybreak found him on a long, straight stretch of river that afforded a view of more than a mile. As he continued south, the increasing light revealed the shapes of houses set back from the east bank, and the low span of yet another bridge on the horizon ahead. He knew it had to be Highway 90, the southernmost road paralleling the coast between Gulfport and New Orleans. He had taken his canoe out at the boat landing there years ago, at the end of the one trip he'd done from the cabin to the coast just to see where the river went.

Something else beyond the bridge suddenly caught his eye as he gradually closed the distance. At first, he didn't realize what it was—a large triangular object that rose up out of nowhere to be silhouetted against the sky, taller even than the top of the bridge. Then, the object started slowly moving horizontally behind the foreground of bridge, sliding from right to left, the way that the river appeared to bend. It was in that moment that he realized that what he was looking at was a sail! The boat beneath it, though, was hidden by the tall grass in the bend. The boat was quickly gaining way and moving faster, despite the light westerly breeze that barely rippled the surface of the river. Grant dug in with the paddle blades in an all-out sprint to try and make the bridge before the sail disappeared, but even as he started, he knew the effort was hopeless in this cheap, pudgy kayak that was never designed for speed. He saw the sail diminish with distance as the boat wound its way down those last reaches of river through the marsh.

By the time Grant reached the bridge, the tall grass reduced his horizon from the low vantage point of the kayak, so that he could see nothing beyond the channel immediately ahead. Was the sailboat he'd just seen the catamaran he had been so desperately trying to reach? Was he that close to catching up to his friends, only to be thwarted by a fair wind that carried them away just as he came into view? Grant didn't know, but he did know that he still had a long way to go. He carried on until he reached the mouth of the river and saw the open waters of the Sound stretching away into a blue horizon. He landed on a narrow strip of beach and stood scanning that endless vista for a sail, but saw nothing. The boat was long gone, if it had even been real. He began to doubt himself, wondering if it had merely been a mirage brought on by his fatigue.

Cat Island was way too far away to see from here. He would have to navigate parallel to the coast for many miles to the east before reaching a suitable jumping off point for the crossing. He knew he could make it out there in the kayak, but not today. He would have to sleep first, or he would collapse from exhaustion. He would leave some-time during the night, and would hope to be within sight of the island to begin the passage when daylight came again tomorrow.

SEVENTEEN

Scully reached the entrance to the oxbow lake where the *Casey Nicole* was supposed to be anchored late in the afternoon, after two days and most of two nights in the canoe. He had stopped little, the pain in his leg bearable as long as he kept it in the shade below the edge of the gunwale. The resin was still doing its job, and the gash had not opened up or bled again since he'd first applied it, but it was extremely tender and he had to be careful to remember not to bump it. All along the long journey down the Bogue Chitto and the East Pearl, he remained hopeful that he might catch up to Grant, if it were indeed he who had taken the kayak from the boat shed by the river. But though he kept his eyes peeled and stayed alert for any sign, he never found any other evidence that Casey's friend was ahead of him. Despite that, whether Grant was ahead of him or not, he still had ample reason to push hard, as he was greatly worried about the safety of his best friend, Larry, as well as Larry's brother and the two girls. He was convinced that Joey and Zach were crazy, and knew they were liable to do anything. He knew that because they had the motor, it was impossible for him to get there first, but nevertheless, the sooner he *did* get there, the better.

When Scully paddled into the lake hoping to see the sleek Polynesian-inspired catamaran he had helped Larry build, he was surprised instead to see a big wooden fishing trawler anchored in its place. Scully had half-expected to find the catamaran gone, with no way to predict what would happen when Joey and Zach showed up, but the presence of this other big boat anchored in its exact spot puzzled him. He approached it cautiously, the lever-action carbine leaning against the thwart in front of him as he eased the canoe closer. It was a working vessel; that much was obvious at a glance, as it had none of the shiny and expensive fittings of a yacht or cruiser. It was built roughly, in the old way, with traditional plank-on-frame construction like so many boats he'd spent time on while on the islands. The blue and white topsides were probably painted with ordinary house paint, and the brush marks and runs in the finish indicated it had been sloppily and hurriedly applied by a crew with better things to do than worry about appearances.

Scully wondered where the owners were, and figured the boat had been taken from them by force. A boat like this represented everything to a commercial fisherman who owned it, and it was likely a family business. Whoever had brought it here had probably killed the owners, or took it after someone else had, because other than to seek refuge from a hurricane, there was no reason for it to be this far from the coast. Whatever had happened to those who had brought it here, it didn't appear that they were on board; but he called out loudly before approaching more closely anyway. Hearing no answer, he circled around and saw the painted message on the aft side of the cabin. Scully knew immediately that Larry was the author of the message, and he also knew exactly what the phrase "De boat lock" meant, as it was clearly intended for him. *So the boat had somehow arrived here after he and Artie had left in the Johnboat, but before Larry and his brother, the girls, and possibly Joey and Zach had left on the catamaran? And what of Grant? If it had been he that took the kayak, did he find his way here, too?* It was a mystery, but Scully knew from Larry's message that the big trawler had gotten here under its own power and would run again when he did what was necessary.

Scully tied off the canoe and hopped aboard, stepping closer to the cabin bulkhead to study the map Larry had sketched in paint. He remembered their stopover at West Ship Island, as it was their first landfall after sailing directly across the Gulf from the Florida Keys en route to New Orleans. He remembered passing to the north of this Cat Island that Larry indicated and he remembered thinking it appeared richly forested. Larry had chosen the rendezvous point wisely. Cat Island was far enough off the mainland to be inaccessible to anyone without a good boat, but it was close enough to this spot on the river that he could reach it quickly, just as soon as he got the diesel running.

Scully climbed the steps to the pilothouse to try the starter, just to be sure Larry had gone through with the steps he usually took to make a boat hard to steal. When he saw the bullet-riddled and blood-splattered plywood and the shattered windows, he was sure of his earlier speculation that the owners of the boat had died at the hands of whoever took it from them. He noticed thankfully that the damage was all above the control panels, though; the instruments, gauges, and switches were still intact. He switched on the key and pushed the starter, letting it turn the engine just long enough to tell him it was not getting fuel, and then he turned it off to avoid running the batteries flat. Scully grinned as he remembered some of the runs he and Larry had made back in the day, when it was still easy and the risk still worth it. They had perfected more than a few tricks of the trade, and each of them had so much experience on so many different types of vessels that there were few things nautical they were not intimately familiar with.

Scully found his way below to the engine room and the ship's tool locker. With the hatch open, there was enough daylight streaming below to see what he was doing, but he knew he had to work fast, as he only had a couple more hours until sundown. Right away he found the misadjusted tension on the shut-off cable that made it appear from the cockpit that the kill switch was in the starting position when in reality the fuel shut-off lever was off. Scully quickly corrected this with a screwdriver and went back to the controls. This time, when he pushed the starter button, the engine rumbled to life, sending vibrations through the whole boat. He adjusted the speed down to idle and it smoothed out, ran fine for another minute, and then suddenly died. He grinned again. Larry had made an extra effort to ensure this boat would be here waiting for him whenever he arrived. Unless one of the owners or someone else with experience in maintaining marine diesels came along, it wasn't likely that a casual river traveler finding the boat would be able to motor away in it. He went back below and began the process of bleeding the fuel system, opening bleed screws at the fuel filter and injection pump and turning the engine over by hand to let the air bubbles out. Then he bled the injectors, going back and forth to the pilothouse to bump the starter and turn it over until all the air was gone and nothing but pure diesel was getting to the injectors.

When he returned to the bridge to try it again, the engine came immediately to life and ran consistently at all operating speeds. Scully left it running at idle and went back down to shut the engine room hatch and haul his canoe on deck. He did a quick walk around, looking for anything else amiss, and found no reason why the boat couldn't make a trip to Cat Island. The heavy chain anchor rode was handled by a big twelve-volt electric winch. Scully found the power button for the winch and was relieved to find that it still worked. He ran it until the boat was straight up over the anchor, then used the engine to break it out of the mud. After he hauled the anchor the rest of the way up with another push of the button, the *Miss Lucy* was now floating free. Scully put her in reverse and backed away from the cypress trees she had drifted too close to, then shifted back to forward and circled around, pointing the bow towards the river and then turning south once he was out in the main channel.

The ancient Perkins ran flawlessly, and, according to the fuel gauge, the tanks were half full. Scully kept the speed down to five or six knots in the river, but figured once he got out to open water she would probably make ten. He knew there were two bridges to pass under between him and the Gulf. The first would be the big four-lane super-highway, the likes of which he'd never seen on the islands. Then there was the smaller highway with the drawbridge that had been locked down, forcing them to unstep the mast of the *Casey Nicole* to pass beneath it when he and Larry and Artie had first entered this river. Scully wasn't sure of the vertical clearance of that bridge, but he was sure this fishing boat, with its high pilothouse, must be pushing it. Still, unless the boat had been north of the bridge before the pulse shut down the power, she must be low enough to clear. He would put aside that worry until he got there. Looking at the angle of the sun, now low enough that it was below the tops of the riverbank trees, he figured he would get there just before dark.

He reached the first bridge in just under a half hour, keeping a steady pace as he passed under the twin spans far overhead. There was nothing here other than the bridge and forest on both sides, as the roadway was inaccessible from the river. He did notice a long, straight, water-filled ditch running parallel to the bridge and leading off the river to the east. Scully figured a small boat could navigate it, but since no road came down to the river from the superhighway, the banks here were deserted. Once again, he found it strange how Americans lived. Here was all this richness of life along the natural corridor of the river: fish for the taking; deer, squirrels and more species of birds than he could count; as well as a huge diversity of plants, many of which he was sure were edible. And yet, despite all this natural bounty, the people in this country crowded in their cities and towns, and fought and killed over what little was left in the stores and in their homes. It made no sense to him, but neither did most things that most people did.

He had not gone more than another two miles below the bridge when he saw something floating far ahead of him in the middle of the channel. The river was wide here, and the bends were farther apart, so the distance was great enough that he could barely discern that it was a boat of some sort. Scully slowed the engine just a bit as he closed the gap. There was no way to avoid passing fairly close, as the boat was right in the middle of the river. As he drew nearer, he could see a lone figure sitting in the rear with a paddle. The boat was one of those square-ended aluminum Johnboats that seemed so popular here, and at first, because it had no outboard, he didn't recognize it as the very one he had recently spent so much time in, first with Artie, then Grant, and finally Joey and Zach.

Scully was close enough now to see that it was Joey who had been so awkwardly trying to keep the boat going straight as he attempted to move it downriver at a crawling pace. But now that he was upon him, Scully saw that Joey had dropped the paddle, and in its place was holding the shotgun that belonged to Larry. He looked weak and unsteady, but he brought the barrel up and was pointing it directly at him in the pilothouse. Scully realized he had made a mistake in getting this close. If he were farther away, out of shotgun range, he could grab the .357 Magnum carbine and Joey would be an easy target out there in the open in that tiny boat. But it was too late for that. Instead of reaching for the gun, he jammed the throttle forward and locked down the helm. Then he quickly ducked out the side door and practically dove to the lower deck behind the bulkhead.

The shotgun blast that he expected to hear at any moment never came. But there was a satisfying impact of the big boat hitting something hard a few seconds later, then the sound and sensation of something bumping along under the hull, the way it felt when a boat ran over a floating log. Scully glanced astern as he climbed back up the steps to grab the controls before the boat hit something else he didn't want it to, such as the riverbank. In the churning wake he saw the overturned Johnboat, barely awash, as well as a life jacket and some other items, including the wooden paddle, floating nearby. There was no sign of Joey.

He backed down on the throttle and turned the boat to starboard, making a circle around the wreckage. Joey still hadn't surfaced, but Scully remembered his own escape and knew it was possible to swim a long way underwater on a breath of air. He doubted Joey had this ability, but still, he stood waiting and watching as he drove the *Miss Lucy* in a wide arc around the scene of the collision. If Joey were still out there, he couldn't see him in the fading light. Scully knew he could have been dealt a fatal blow by the boat's big prop, but even if he did survive, Scully was confident he was no longer a threat. He wondered why the one called Zach wasn't with him in the Johnboat, and he also wondered what had happened to the outboard. And why hadn't he fired the shotgun when he had plenty of time? Was he out of ammunition? Scully shrugged his shoulders and decided it didn't matter. The fact that he had been here in the river, still in the Johnboat, at least meant that he was not on the *Casey Nicole*. He wondered, too, if there had been a confrontation, and if maybe Larry had somehow gotten his outboard back. But if so, why would he not have taken the shotgun, too? Scully couldn't figure it out, but he had a feeling he would find the answers on Cat Island. He moved the throttle forward and brought the *Miss Lucy* back up to speed, making for the last bridge that was in his way.

As he passed the community of Pearlington on the east bank of the river, Scully realized that his fears of the bridge being too low were valid. The *Casey Nicole*, being of such a sleek and low-profile sailing design, was only a few feet above the waterline at the highest part of her twin cabins. With the mast down and lashed in a horizontal position, she had cleared the locked Highway 90 bridge with feet to spare. This fishing boat with its tall pilothouse was another story altogether. Scully slowed as he approached the bridge from the north, and then put her out of gear and drifted. It was obvious now that whoever had brought her up the river had done so before the pulse event occurred, and had passed through an open drawbridge. Scully recalled from studying Larry's chart of the area that there were some other deep-water channels off of the lower Pearl River. Perhaps the *Miss Lucy* had been tied up to a private dock at some waterfront residence, or even hauled out for maintenance at some backwater boatyard. In any case, there would be no getting under this bridge without hitting the boat's superstructure, especially now, as the tide was at its highest point. Scully confirmed this by the absence of higher water marks or marine growth on the pilings. He let the boat get as close as he dared, trying to estimate just how much of the pilothouse structure was too tall. At this water level, he doubted the helm would clear, but if the water dropped even two feet at the next low cycle, then the plan he had in mind might work. It would be risky, but there was no better option he could think of. He motored a quarter mile back upriver to get plenty of swinging room, and dropped anchor in a deep area as far from the east bank of the river as he could get.

◉ ◉ ◉

After reaching the mouth of the Pearl River, Grant paddled east along the low, marshy coastline to find a place to rest for the long open-water crossing to Cat Island. The mainland shore here was uninhabited and undeveloped for several miles, as it was mostly unfit for anything other than wading birds and mosquitos. A mile to the east, Grant found a narrow strip of sand beach between the marsh grass and the shallow, murky brown waters of the Sound, and pulled the kayak ashore. It was the kind of place that would be utter hell for camping in the absence of a breeze to keep the salt marsh mosquitos and no-see-ums at bay, but since it was daytime and the wind was around ten miles per hour from seaward, he was able to sleep. The lack of shade was a problem he could do little about, other than to lie as close to the kayak as possible, waiting for the sun to angle low enough for its shadow to help a little.

He woke well after dark, when the breeze died and the sound of gently lapping waves was replaced by the hum of bugs swarming around his ears. He slapped them away as best he could, enduring dozens of bites while getting the boat back into the water to get underway. If not for the mosquitos, he would have built a driftwood fire and made some more of the bannock, but in these conditions, he decided it was hardly worth it. He paddled away from the shore and ate more of the ramen and the last of the crackers and peanut butter as he drifted. There was not a lot of food left, but as long as he had enough calories to supply him the energy to get to Cat Island, he wouldn't worry about what came after. If the catamaran was not there for some reason, he would worry then.

He had many hours of darkness to get through before setting out on the crossing, and he intended to use them by making his way east along the coast to make his jumping off point that much closer. Grant had never been in these waters, along this particular stretch of the extreme western edge of the Mississippi coast, but he knew that human habitation here began further east, at the towns of Waveland and Bay St. Louis. Who knew what conditions were like there now? But Grant didn't intend to go quite that far. He just wanted to be within sight of Cat Island before leaving the mainland, as he had no compass or charts, so a visual confirmation of his course would be the only thing to give him confidence he would find it.

The short plastic kayak was slow in open water and required more effort to keep it tracking in a straight line than a proper sea kayak would. He was grateful he wasn't fighting a crosswind as well, or it would have seemed hopeless. The still evening was a blessing, and other than the dipping of his paddle blades, the calm water was disturbed only by the occasional reentry splash of an airborne mullet. Aside from the dark background of marsh grass off to his left as he paralleled the shore, there was nothing on the horizon ahead, behind, or off to the south in the direction of open water but darkness. In normal times, Grant knew these waters would be dotted with the lights of commercial fishing boats, but if any vessels were out there, they were unlit.

Thinking about this, he wondered what was going on with the authorities by now. They had seen policemen and other law enforcement officers in the towns and cities along their route as they left New Orleans on the bikes, but nothing since. The Bogue Chitto and the Pearl River were both bounded by vast tracts of wildlife refuge land, so much of it so remote that enforcement presence was scant even in normal times. He had certainly not seen any game wardens or deputies since first arriving at the river with Casey and Jessica, and he wondered what the officers were doing now in this crisis. Had they been called to staff the roadblocks, or help at some centralized location, mobilizing in an attempt to restore order, or were they simply busy trying to protect their own families and survive like everyone else? And what about the state marine patrol and the U.S. Coast Guard? Would he encounter their vessels now that he was in coastal waters, or were they sticking to their bases and hunkering down, too? The grid going down was surely an urgent matter of national security, but if the effects of the solar flare were indeed widespread beyond the continent, or even worldwide, then every nation would be dealing with the same issues and would be concerned mainly with the situation within their borders. Grant was certain the military had safeguards and backups to prevent losing all of their capabilities simply because of an electromagnetic pulse, but where were they? Why had they seen no sign of their aircraft or other indicators they were still around and functioning?

It was interesting to consider, and thinking of all this simply gave him something to keep his mind occupied as he bent to the toil of paddling. Eventually, miles of coastline had slipped by, and the new day was dawning in the direction he was heading. He landed again to stretch his legs, relieve himself, and eat, and when the sky grew lighter while he waited, he could at last make out the thin sliver of land far to the east-southeast that he knew was his destination because it was the only one of the islands visible from this part of the coast. From this angle, Cat Island appeared almost dead ahead in the direction he'd been traveling. At this point, the mainland curved away to the northeast, and he would follow it no further. Besides being out of his way, following the shore would have put him dangerously close to the survivors in the coastal towns. The island was probably ten miles away from this point, just at the edge of visibility, but as long as he could maintain his pace and the weather didn't change, he figured he could make it there in four or five hours, even in the pathetic excuse for a kayak he was paddling.

His best chance of getting across without encountering a foul wind was in the calm of early morning, before the afternoon sea breeze kicked up, so once he had his visual bearings, Grant wasted no time in getting underway again. Pointing his stubby bow at the horizon, he settled into an easy cadence and daydreamed of his landfall on the island. He couldn't wait to see Casey and Jessica again, but what of Joey and Zach? Would they be there, too? And what about Scully? With any luck at all, he would have his answers today. He knew that Cat Island was a big island, though, and getting there was just the first step. If they were anchored on the far side, it would take hours more to paddle around the shore looking for them. And because of all the unknowns, he would have to be cautious. It would be far better to see them first and investigate the situation before making his presence on the island known.

By mid-morning, he estimated he was more than half-way across. The ragged blue blur that he had known all along was a line of distant treetops now materialized into discernible tall pines, appearing more green than blue. Separating them from the water in the foreground was a broad expanse of white beach. But he had been so focused on forward progress, on projecting himself to his destination, that he had been mostly oblivious to what was behind him, feeling little need to look over his shoulder out here on open water. After all, there were no boats visible in any other direction, so why would it be different astern? Thus he was caught by surprise when the first indication he had that he was not alone was the sound of an engine.

Grant turned to look for the source and was shocked to see a large motor vessel bearing down on him. He frantically turned the kayak to get in a better position to see it and realized that whoever was steering it had already seen him first. When he paddled hard to the south to get out of the boat's path, the helmsman adjusted course to compensate, still coming right at him. Grant knew that it was hopeless to try and outrun or outmaneuver the boat. He reached for his 10/22 and checked that there was still a round in the magazine. Whoever it was in the big boat, Grant was skeptical of their intentions.

But as he watched the boat draw closer, something about it seemed familiar, yet odd. He could now see that it was not a pleasure boat, but rather a working fishing vessel. The upswept bow was now close enough that he thought he could make out the details of wood planking rather than smooth fiberglass or steel. But something else drew his attention even more than the hull. The entire top of the pilothouse had been somehow broken away, leaving the steering station wide open and exposed like an open runabout, rather than a cabin cruiser. He stared as the distance between them decreased, and could barely believe his eyes. Could it be true? Was that really a tall black man at the wheel, a mop of long dreadlocks draping well below his shoulders? Grant stared in disbelief, recognizing Scully before the Rastaman realized just who it was he'd run upon out here in the middle of the Sound in a tiny kayak. When he did realize who he was seeing, though, he flashed a huge white grin as he throttled the boat to idle and let it drift alongside.

"Where you t'ink you goin' out in de ocean in dat little boat, mon?"

EIGHTEEN

Casey and Jessica sat on the forward deck of the big catamaran, side by side and facing out to the open sea, as the
boat swung to its anchor in Smuggler's Cove, a south wind
from the Gulf keeping the stern pointed towards the island.
Sailing out here had only taken a little over two hours once
they'd cleared the mouth of the Pearl River the morning
before. Larry had given the north shore of the island a wide
berth, as there were two larger monohull sailboats there,
their deep drafts forcing them to anchor almost a half mile
from the beaches of the semiprotected cove there. Smuggler's Cove on the south side was better in every way, except
in the event of strong weather from seaward.

Studying both boats through his binoculars as they
sailed past, Larry had determined that each contained a
family with children who were teens or younger. The boats
were anchored close together, each one with the same hailing port of Madisonville, LA, painted on its stern under the
name. It was obvious they were together. Larry didn't think
they would present a threat, but he didn't want to take a

chance or worry them about his own intentions, either, by sailing too close. The people aboard both boats returned the waves of the *Casey Nicole's* crew. They sailed on until they were around the north point of the island and out of sight. In any case, those two boats would not be able to enter Smuggler's Cove with their deep keels, but Larry said that if their crews stayed there long enough, he hoped they all could visit by dinghy as it would be interesting to learn if they had any news.

Larry spent most of their second day at the island working on repairing the damage done by the big fishing boat. He said that it was not as bad as it looked, and that out here with full sun and warm, rain-free days, the epoxy would quickly cure after each step, and he'd have her shipshape for the ocean in no time.

"Don't worry," he said, seeing the look on Casey's and Jessica's faces. "Just because the boat's ready to sail, that doesn't mean we're going anywhere. I'm not leaving these waters without Scully and Grant unless it's absolutely a matter of life or death. Unless we find out otherwise, I'm going to assume they'll be here soon."

"This island is a lot farther from the river than I'd thought it would be," Jessica said.

"I know, but Scully has already seen it, when we sailed by on the way to New Orleans. And, according to Casey, Grant has been going on field trips everywhere around New Orleans for years."

"Yeah, I'm sure he's heard of it, even if he hasn't been here, but I'm starting to wonder, too, if he could get here without Scully. What if they got separated somehow? He might be alone, and unable to get that boat running even if he finds it."

"He won't be alone. Trust me, Scully wouldn't let him out of his sight. You both just need to have a little more faith in them. They'll be here; I just know it. Meanwhile, we might as well make the best of our wait. Your dad wants to paddle over to the beach, Casey. I'm not going; I've still got work to do. Who wants to go take a walk?"

Jessica insisted that she should spend some alone time with her dad, so Casey climbed down into the kayak with him, and they paddled to the closest of the broad beaches that ringed the cove. She had wanted an opportunity talk to her dad some more, just one on one, and it was a bit of a relief to get away from Jessica's dark mood and depression over Grant's absence. Larry could deal with that for a while; she knew her uncle wouldn't mind. He had certainly enjoyed having her beautiful girlfriend aboard the charter boat on the islands the summer before, and she knew he was not unhappy that she would now be living aboard his new boat with the rest of them for an indefinite period of time. Casey didn't think of Larry as part of the same generation as her dad, anyway. He *was* a lot younger, and he acted younger still; he had no trouble relating to her and Jessica. He knew Jessica found him interesting, too. If she wasn't so damned obsessed with Grant, who knew what could happen? Casey loved Jessica dearly, but Grant was *her* crush before all this started. If she hadn't been kidnapped by that lunatic, Derek, none of this would be an issue, because Jessica and Grant would not have had so much time alone.

She didn't like the feeling, but she had to admit there was a bit of jealousy creeping into her thoughts at times, especially when Jessica made it so obvious how much she missed him and was worried about him. The last thing Casey had ever expected was to have something come between her and her closest friend, and she was determined not to let it happen. She couldn't stand Jessica's last boyfriend, Joey Broussard, and was greatly relieved when he refused to go with them and she left him behind in New Orleans. But Jessica never went long without a guy in her life, even if it wasn't a serious relationship. Without Joey in the picture, Casey wasn't surprised that Jessica was feeling lonely. But still, she didn't really believe her friend would betray her by stealing away the one guy she had clearly been attracted to since well before this happened. Jessica was a good person; it was just that she could be a little needy at times. Casey could certainly understand what she was going through. Losing her boyfriend at the same time her world had suddenly turned upside down with this blackout had been doubly traumatic. Not to mention how far away from home she was, completely and utterly cut off from any word of her parents and little sister in California.

Casey hoped that, just maybe, Larry could fill some of that void for her, and be the other friend or brotherlike figure she needed, if not something more. She didn't know what would happen when Grant showed up, but whatever it was, it would be better than this awful worrying and waiting. She just wanted him to be okay and to be with them on the boat. Whether he was more interested in her or in Jessica at this point was really up to him anyway, she knew, and only time would tell.

"Do you think Larry's right?" she asked her dad, as they hiked north along the island shore, heading to an area of tall dunes facing to the west, where they could see West Ship Island in the distance. "Do you really think Scully and Grant are going to get here?"

"Casey, you know better than any of us that anything could happen. Without phones or any other way of communicating, it's so hard not to worry. So many little things could have slowed them down. I think it's too early to really get concerned. If they're not here in a few days, well, that's another story, but we've got to try and stay positive."

"I just feel like we made the wrong decision. Maybe we should have all listened to Jessica in the first place and never split up. Anything they may have gotten in that cabin can't be worth all this."

"There's no use second-guessing what's already been done, Casey. Grant knew there was some risk, but he felt it was worth it at the time. Maybe it was the wrong thing to do, but it wasn't up to Jessica to decide. If we're going to get through this, we all have to do what's best for the group."

They reached the top of one of the dunes. From there they could see across the low-lying north point of the island. The two big sailboats were still there, their masts standing tall against the background of blue that reached to the faraway mainland, barely visible on the horizon. As they stood staring away into the distance, taking turns with Larry's binoculars, movement farther to the west caught Casey's attention.

"Dad, what is that? It's a boat of some kind!" She pointed to what she'd seen, and he saw it, too. Casey waited while he zeroed in on it through the binoculars.

"It *is* a boat, Casey! And it's not a sailboat. It's an old fishing boat, but something is missing."

Casey excitedly grabbed the binoculars from his hands as he lowered them. When she looked at the distant boat through seven-power magnification, she could see that it was mostly white with a bit of blue trim. Something *was* missing; she realized it was the top half of the pilothouse. But there was no question the boat was the fishing boat from the river: the *Miss Lucy!* "It's them, Dad! It's got to be!"

"I think you're right. And they are heading straight to the island!"

Casey and her dad stood watching as the boat passed the anchorage with the two sailboats and continued around the northernmost point, that jutted out from the island towards the city of Gulfport on the mainland. She jumped up and down, waving, even though she knew they were much too far away to be seen by anyone aboard the distant boat.

"They should be able to see our mast by now, though, Casey. Let's get back to the boat. It looks like they're heading straight to the cove!"

The two of them ran through the deep sand as fast as they could, all the way back to where they'd left the kayak. By the time they were in it and paddling out toward the catamaran, the fishing boat was rounding the last point into Smuggler's Cove, as well. Casey remembered that Larry had remarked while they were still in the river that workboats of that design drew scarcely more water than the Polynesian catamaran, so getting into the same anchorage should not be a problem. They both waved their paddles overhead in response to a blast from the *Miss Lucy's* horn. And as they drew closer they could clearly see both Grant and Scully standing at the open helm where the pilothouse had been completely torn off at about waist level.

Jessica and Larry were busy securing fenders along the rail of the *Casey Nicole* as Scully brought the *Miss Lucy* expertly alongside. The two men were already on board before Casey and her dad could climb out of the kayak. Scully and Larry immediately locked in fierce embrace, each lifting the other off the deck in turn and slapping each other's backs, while Jessica threw herself into Grant's arms. Just as Casey caught his eye, Jessica slipped a hand around the back of his head and pulled his lips to hers as she pressed her entire body against him and didn't let go. Casey just stopped and stood there, awkwardly waiting, not really knowing what to do until he finally pulled away and made his way to her.

◉ ◉ ◉

When Scully had found him midway on the crossing to Cat Island and had taken him aboard the *Miss Lucy*, Grant had been surprised to learn that he had apparently somehow passed both Joey and Zach somewhere along the way, and that Scully himself had been just a day or so behind him all that way along the river since the first night they were separated. Scully didn't know what had become of Zach, or the outboard motor that had been on the boat, but when he told Grant about running Joey down in the middle of the river, Grant was quite relieved to learn that the two of them had likely never made it to the catamaran.

Grant had said that they wouldn't know for sure unless they asked Jessica and Casey, but Scully argued that they shouldn't mention it. He said that if anyone aboard the catamaran had seen either of those two losers, they would surely bring it up, anyway, and if they didn't, it would mean they had never laid eyes on them. Grant felt that it was wrong not to tell them about their encounter with Joey, arguing that he owed it to Jessica, at least, to tell her that Joey was trying to find her. But Scully insisted that Joey's motivations were completely selfish and that telling Jessica would only hurt her more, and that learning what had happened to Joey might make her feel somehow responsible. They debated this at length but at last Grant agreed, deferring to the older man's experience. After all, as Scully said, if they *had* seen either Joey or Grant, he was sure they would hear about it immediately. They made a pact then and there to remain silent on the matter, and to make up some other excuse for the delay, which was not hard to do considering the possibilities.

As they filled each other in on their individual journeys down the Bogue Chitto and the Pearl, Grant was also surprised to learn that Scully had recovered the money that Joey had evidently lost when the Johnboat swamped. Whether or not it would be useful where they were going, it was much better to have it this way, without Joey attached and trying to use it to buy his way aboard. Scully didn't even know if Joey had survived or not after he had hit and destroyed the old Johnboat with the *Miss Lucy*. Like Scully, Grant figured it didn't much matter. Even if Joey *were* alive, he wasn't getting out here now; if he didn't drown, he would have nothing but the clothes on his back as he crawled up on a muddy bank with the snakes and alligators, likely wishing he'd never left the comfort of that secluded and well-stocked cabin on the Bogue Chitto.

Grant had been overwhelmed with relief when Scully pointed out the third mast they had seen on their approach to Cat Island and assured him that it was the wooden spar of the gaff-rigged *Casey Nicole*. He realized the distant glimpse of the sail from the morning before had indeed been real, but the vessel beneath it had been obscured behind the marsh grass that bounded the bend of the river ahead of him. Now he saw for the first time the sleek, rakish hulls of the catamaran, their finish dull primer gray, but their lines beautiful nonetheless. It was clearly a boat built for the sea, and he was eager to see more of it, but first he wanted to see his two best friends. After they tied alongside and boarded, Jessica got to him first. He had expected both her and Casey to be glad he was back and as happy to see him as he was to see them, but Jessica's passionate kiss right on the lips caught him off guard. He didn't try to stop her, but felt self-conscious and a little confused as his eyes met Casey's and then she quickly looked away, as if to give them privacy. Grant hoped she didn't get the wrong idea. *Did she think something had happened between him and her friend when they were traveling alone together, paddling and camping for over a week in a desperate search for her?*

When Jessica finally let him go, he stepped over to give Casey an equally enthusiastic hug, but he could tell from her body language and the quick peck on the cheek she gave him that they had a lot to sort out. He was sure there would be time, and he knew he would need it, too. He had a lot to figure out himself, and he was afraid his life was about to become a lot more complicated. He certainly didn't want to come between two close friends who had known each other far longer than either had known him, but it was clear to him that things would not be as casual and uncomplicated as before.

But that was all for later. The most important thing now was that they were all together again, and, finally, they were all a safe distance from the madness that had consumed the mainland, which they could just barely see in the distance to the north.

Grant liked Larry Drager immediately. He had known he would, from what Casey and Jessica had told him before, but now that they had actually met he realized how much they truly had in common. Grant understood Larry's life-style better than most people did; even though, compara-tively, his own adventures had barely begun, at least until the lights went out. Now, everyone who wished to survive was being forced into a life of challenge and risk, destined to become adventurers whether they welcomed it or not. But Grant felt fortunate that they had a captain who was already so capable in that regard. And he could sense that Larry had a mutual respect for him, too, for what he'd done in helping his niece and her friend out of a dying city. Grant was utterly amazed at the boat, and insisted on get-ting a quick tour from Larry right after the two of them were introduced. His only sailing experience had been on a friend's Hobie 16, and he was excited about the pros-pect of ocean voyaging on the Tiki 36. He wanted to soak it all in like a sponge and learn everything Larry was willing to teach him, starting in the morning with learning to use epoxy and work with fiberglass in making the repairs.

But first there was the more important matter of watch-ing the sun go down into the Gulf, and celebrating the completeness of the reunion after so many obstacles with a shot of Larry's 10 Cane, which he had retrieved from the *Miss Lucy*. Then the six of them spent the rest of the evening sitting in the cockpit under a starry sky, a gentle breeze from the Gulf keeping the mosquitos and sand fleas on the island and away from the anchorage.

"So what's the deal with the supplies you were supposed to be bringing from the cabin?" Jessica wanted to know. "After all that time away and such a long journey, all you have is some ramen noodles and an empty jar of peanut butter?"

"Yeah, what happened?" Artie asked, looking to Grant and then Scully in turn.

"Let's hear it," Larry added. "You left in that old John-boat we found with my outboard on it, and you came back in a kayak. What happened to the boat and the motor? And where is my shotgun, Scully?"

Scully gave Larry an apologetic look. "Lost dat Mossberg, Copt'n. An' de Johnson too...."

"It's my fault," Grant jumped in, before Scully could go on. "I was just being stupid. We were trying to get back faster, and it was my idea to run the river at night. I should have known better. We hit a log in the only place on that river that's a little tricky and dumped the boat *and* the canoe we were towing."

"Dat's right, mon. De river in dat place she dangerous in de dark. A mon need to wait for de day, but we wantin'

Scott B. Williams

get back to de boat soon, you know. Dat's how we got in de trouble an' lose all de cargo."

"There's an old bridge crossing there," Grant went on. "It's probably fifty years old or more, at least. Nothing much to see of it but a few old rotten pilings, but under the water there's steel cable and bracing: all kinds of dangers if you go for an accidental swim in those rapids just upstream. That's what got us in trouble. You can see how Scully got his leg torn up. It's a wonder he didn't get hung up and drowned. We couldn't really dive for the stuff we lost in that current at night with all that structure down there. The outboard broke the transom and came off and sank when we capsized, and the shotgun ended up on the bottom, too. I did manage to hang on to my 10/22 and Scully grabbed that little .357 Magnum carbine. We lost just about everything else. Most of the food from the cabin was canned goods."

"An' de can, dem don't float you know," Scully said.

"So we had the old Johnboat, but no motor and no place to mount it anyway. I knew paddling that thing a hundred miles would suck and take forever even if it wasn't damaged, and even in the canoe it would take too long to get that far downriver, at least in a slow aluminum canoe like that one. But we weren't far from the camp on the river where I first got the canoe. You remember, Jessica; you helped me get it."

Casey shuddered at the thought of that day, when Grant and Jessica had left her for what should have been an hour or so, and she had fallen into the hands of the man who had taken her to his hideaway deep in the swamp.

"Sorry, Casey. I know that's a bad memory for you."

"It's okay. So go on, what did you do?"

"Well, I got the kayak there. I remembered it from that first time. I figured, even if it wasn't the fastest kayak ever designed, it would be faster than a canoe. Besides, it was the only boat left there," he lied. "We took turns in it, towing the canoe around the clock, one of us paddling while the other took a break or slept riding in the canoe. That's all we could do, anyway, since the kayak is a solo boat. That's how we got to the dead lake where you guys were supposed to be, but it took a long time because it's a long way to paddle such a piece of crap."

"Well, the main thing is that you made it there, no matter how long it took, and Scully here knew how to 'fix' the problems my little brother left that engine with."

"Yeah, that's all that matters," Grant said, looking at Scully, who gave him a wink when no one else was looking. He had been right in insisting they keep the matter of Joey and Zach to themselves, and now Grant was glad he'd relented and listened to him.

"Absolutely," Larry agreed. "I'm just glad as hell to be out of that river and out here on the salt again. I felt like a cornered rat up in that swamp, my mast lain down and sails in the lockers. We'll finish these repairs tomorrow and start thinking about the next landfall. But I feel pretty good about this place. As long as we keep a watch, and the boat is ready, we don't have to leave immediately. The fishing looks good here, and maybe we can rig what's left of the nets on the *Miss Lucy* and use them to make a few runs to see if we can stock up and dry some fish. We'll start looking over my charts again, too, and I'll show you all the options I've been mulling over. There are lots of places that could make a suitable refuge, and we'll decide on one, but for now the best one of all is the *Casey Nicole* herself."

ALSO BY SCOTT B. WILLIAMS

The Pulse
US $14.95 | CAN $17.50

The end of an electric age. A compelling action-adventure novel that reveals what it would take to survive in a world lit only by firelight, where all the rules have changed and each person must fend for himself.

Darkness After
US $10.00 | CAN $11.95

A thrilling narrative of two teenagers fighting to survive in an America gone dark, where dangerous violence, unexpected romance, and heartbreaking betrayal await. A frightening look at how fragile our technologically dependent lifestyle really is.

Getting Out Alive: 13 Deadly Scenarios and How Others Survived
US $14.95 | CAN $17.50

Every year, ordinary people find themselves in extraordinary life-or-death situations. Delving into 13 harrowing scenarios, *Getting Out Alive* combines riveting narratives with expert advice and real-life accounts of savvy survivors.

Bug Out: The Complete Plan for Escaping a Catastrophic Disaster Before It's Too Late

US $15.95 | CAN $18.95

Warning sirens are blaring. You have 15 minutes to evacuate. What will you do? Being prepared makes the difference between survival and disaster. Guiding you step by step, *Bug Out* shows you how to be ready at a second's notice.

Bug Out Vehicles and Shelters: Build and Outfit Your Life-Saving Escape

US $15.95 | CAN $18.95

A cataclysmic disaster strikes. Do you have a vehicle you can count on to evacuate your family safely? *Bug Out Vehicles and Shelters* zeroes in on the key considerations and essential equipment for planning all your bug-out needs.

To order these books call 800-377-2542 or 510-601-8301, fax 510-601-8307, e-mail ulysses@ulyssespress.com, or write to Ulysses Press, P.O. Box 3440, Berkeley, CA 94703. All retail orders are shipped free of charge. California residents must include sales tax. Allow two to three weeks for delivery.

AUTHOR'S NOTE
ON THE GEOGRAPHY

Readers who are familiar with the swamps and wood-
lands along the Bogue Chitto and the Pearl River will
know that there are indeed some remote hideaways to be
found along these isolated waterways. I want to point out
that the descriptions detailed in the narrative have in some
cases been slightly manipulated to fit the story and that the
locations of specific houses, cabins, and other man-made
structures described are fictitious. With ever-encroaching
development in the region, there are likely more camps and
weekend retreats to be found in some areas than there were
when I last canoed from the upper Bogue Chitto to the
coastal marshes.

Even so, along these rivers and many others in the region,
it is entirely possible to experience solitude and a sense of
wilderness despite the relative proximity of cities such as
New Orleans, Slidell, and Bay St. Louis. It's also easy to get
unintentionally lost in the 250 square miles of bottomland,
hardwood forests, and labyrinthine bayous of the Lower

Pearl River Basin, where the Pearl splits into three rivers, the East Pearl, Middle Pearl, and West Pearl. These forests are so dense and junglelike that a U.S. Navy Seals special boat team conducts live-fire riverine warfare training in a restricted part of the basin in Hancock County, Mississippi.

The river enters open water at Lake Borgne, connecting to the western end of the Mississippi Sound and the undeveloped chain of barrier islands that make up the Gulf Islands National Seashore and includes Cat Island, described in this story. Like the river basin swamps, those uninhabited wilderness islands could indeed offer refuge from a breakdown on the mainland, as getting there in all but the most settled weather requires a seaworthy boat. During countless camping trips to the islands by sea kayak, I have found a world of solitude and peace on the edge of the horizon, just visible from the busy mainland to the north.